Author Note

Welcome to the Roaring Twenties! A time in America when almost every citizen broke the law and new freedoms were discovered.

When I started researching the first book in this series I was amazed by how deeply embedded Minnesota was in the illegal moonshine business. Decades before Prohibition hit, the University of Minnesota had perfected a corn hybrid that flourished in Minnesota's shorter growing season. They named this hybrid 'Minnesota 13'.

Minnesota 13 was also the name given to the whiskey moonshined from this same corn. A hub of farmers distilling, selling and transporting Minnesota 13 was formed in Central Minnesota, the whiskey became known worldwide, and it was highly sought-after for years.

The Bootlegger's Daughter is the second book in my ***Daughters of the Roaring Twenties*** mini-series. Norma Rose is the oldest Nightingale sister, and very protective of her siblings and the family business Nightingale's—a resort that caters to those with money to spend.

Bootlegging Minnesota 13 is part of the family business, and where there are bootleggers there are prohibition men ready to take them down. Norma Rose recognises Ty Bradshaw as an agent as soon as she sets eyes on him, but when he also comes to her rescue she has some hard decisions to make.

I hope you enjoy Norma Rose and Ty's story, and reading about this time period that brought more freedom and independence for women.

THE BOOTLEGGER'S DAUGHTER

Lauri Robinson

First published in Great Britain 2015
by Mills & Boon, an imprint of Harlequin (UK) Limited,
Large Print edition 2015
Harlequin (UK) Limited, Eton House, 18-24 Paradise Road,
Richmond, Surrey TW9 1SR

© 2015 Lauri Robinson

ISBN: 978-0-263-25580-5

Harlequin (UK) Limited's policy is to use papers that are natural,
renewable and recyclable products and made from wood grown in
sustainable forests. The logging and manufacturing processes conform
to the legal environmental regulations of the country of origin.

A lover of fairy tales and cowboy boots,
Lauri Robinson can't imagine a better profession
than penning happily-ever-after stories about men
(and women) who pull on a pair of boots before riding
off into the sunset—or kick them off for other reasons.
Lauri and her husband raised three sons in their rural
Minnesota home, and are now getting their just rewards
by spoiling their grandchildren.
Visit: laurirobinson.blogspot.com,
facebook.com/lauri.robinson1,
twitter.com/LauriR.

Books by Lauri Robinson

Mills & Boon Historical Romance

Daughters of the Roaring Twenties

The Runaway Daughter (Undone!)
The Bootlegger's Daughter

Stand-Alone Novels

Unclaimed Bride
Inheriting a Bride
The Cowboy Who Caught Her Eye
Christmas Cowboy Kisses
Christmas with Her Cowboy
The Major's Wife
The Wrong Cowboy
A Fortune for the Outlaw's Daughter

Mills & Boon Historical *Undone!* eBooks

Testing the Lawman's Honour
The Sheriff's Last Gamble
What a Cowboy Wants
His Wild West Wife
Dance with the Rancher
Rescued by the Ranger
Snowbound with the Sheriff
Never Tempt a Lawman

Visit the Author Profile page
at millsandboon.co.uk for more titles.

To my dear friend Jennifer Edwards.
Thanks for so graciously loaning me
your mother's name!

Chapter One

White Bear Lake, Minnesota, 1925

The steady tick of bugs hitting the metal shield protecting the streetlamp was like a clock ticking away the seconds. Patience had never been one of Ty Bradshaw's best virtues, not even when his life had depended on it during long stays in trenches overseas. A product of the Selective Service Act, he'd been one of the ten thousand soldiers shipped to France each day courtesy of the US armed forces eight years ago. Unlike many other twenty-year-olds back then, he'd come home alive.

Because he was lucky.

That's what he was counting on now. Luck. His experience using a machine gun during the days of the Great War might come in handy, too. That was up in the air. He hadn't needed to use a gun since he'd returned, and as far as he'd discovered,

Roger Nightingale didn't approve of gunfire at his resort, but the gangsters Nightingale associated with didn't care where they burned powder. They'd pump lead into people while they were sleeping. He knew that firsthand.

Maybe he did have more patience than he gave himself credit for. He'd waited five years for this chance.

Then again, maybe he was just dedicated and savoring his revenge.

Headlights turned the corner, and deep in the shadows, Ty stood stock-still. Waiting. Watching. His smile a secret, held inside where only he knew about it, along with the rush of blood flowing through his veins like an underground spring.

The car slowed and pulled up to the curb, and Ty let loose a portion of his grin as the headlights lost their glow. The long, sleek touring car put his Model T, the cheapest and most popular one Henry Ford ever made, to shame. However, his old Ford served its purpose, allowing him to maintain his cover. Ready to put the final legs of his plan into place, Ty's pulse hitched up one more notch as the touring car's engine went silent.

Roger Nightingale had arrived. A legal bootlegger—if there was such a thing—Nightingale was the man behind most of the alcohol in the upper Midwest. Yet, in Ty's eyes, "The Night" was a small fish, a means to the end. He was after the high pillow. The real McCoy. Ray Bodine. Ty had followed the trail Bodine had left of bottom-barrel boys, triggermen and torpedoes from New York to Chicago, and now to St. Paul.

With federal agents on his tail, Bodine had escaped New York by faking his own death. Using an alias, he'd made plenty of money in Chicago the past year via front men, eluding and paying off agents, and now they'd moved into St. Paul—the headwater of the whiskey trade. The vast northern woods and endless waterways made running booze—namely a local brew known as Minnesota Thirteen—a mug's dream, and Bodine wanted that more than a drunk wanted his next prescription. The mob boss would have plenty of competition here, and not just from Ty. Mobsters from all over had ties to St. Paul, and almost every loop led one way or another to Roger Nightingale. Ty had coveted that information, and now he was prepared to use it. Bringing down Bodine is what he was here to do, and he didn't care who he had to put the screws to in order for that to happen.

Palooka George's birthday was coming up in

two weeks. The one-time boxer had a long list of friends, and enemies. Gangsters far and wide would attend the birthday bash. Ty would be there, too, come hell or high water.

The Cadillac's driver's door opened—a red phaeton with four doors and a fold-down black roof. New. The red paint still had a showroom gleam that glistened brightly in the yellow-hued light cast from the bug-attracting streetlamp.

A foot appeared, and a second one, covered with black patent leather shining as brightly as the paint on the car.

With heels.

Ty was still taking note of that when what emerged next had him licking his lips to wash aside the wolf whistle itching to let loose. A fine pair of legs. Shapely, and covered in sheer silk stockings. He bit down on his bottom lip as the woman completely exited the car. The hem of her dress stopped just below her knees, giving way for plenty to be admired. He continued to admire as his gaze roamed upward, over subtle curves that had him sucking in a good amount of air just to keep that whistle contained.

Women were a lot like whiskey. He didn't need either on a regular basis, but sampling a taste every now and again was something he didn't mind doing, and Norma Rose Nightingale was one classy dame. The real cat's meow.

He'd only seen her from afar, through the lenses of his binoculars while hiding in the woods near the resort, but it had been enough for him to know he'd liked what he'd seen. He liked it now, too. The way her skirt swirled as she spun around to shut the car door. Black, or navy blue maybe, the material of her dress hugged her body just so and glistened in the glow from the streetlight outside the hoosegow.

With slow, precise movements, Ty tugged the front of his hat lower on his forehead and eased back against the building until the coolness of the bricks penetrated his suit coat—he needed the chill to douse the flames spiking in his lower belly. He could see her, but unless Norma Rose turned all the way around and peered directly into the shadows cast by the overhead awning, she couldn't see him.

Roger Nightingale, Norma Rose's father, was the person Ty had expected to visit the jail tonight. Her arrival changed his plan. He tossed around a couple of alternate options while admiring the way

Norma Rose's hips swayed as she walked around the front of the Cadillac.

A dark little hat, probably the same shade as that tailored dress, covered her short blond waves, and a small handbag with a gold-chain handle dangled from one hand. She was wearing pearls, too, a long strand tied in a knot just below rather a nice set of breasts. Dressed to catch a man's eye, that's what she'd done all right, dolled up just like the other night, when she'd been welcoming guests into her father's resort.

Nightingale's Resort was a hot vacation place for big shots with bankrolls to blow, not just those from the bustling metropolis of Minneapolis and St. Paul. Secluded deep in the woods, and just a short jaunt north of the city, the resort catered to butter-and-egg men from all over. Chicago, Milwaukee, Detroit, New York. To rent one of the dozen or more lakeside bungalows for a single evening cost more than Ty and most other folks made in a month.

Palooka George would stay in one of those bungalows. Ray Bodine would be in one, too, and Ty needed to know which one Bodine would be in, so he could get the graft on the New York mobster whose killing spree had set a ball of fire in Ty's stomach years ago.

Turning slightly, Ty watched Norma Rose step onto the sidewalk. The hoosegow was in the center of the city, surrounded by dungeons transformed into speakeasies, high-end clip joints and night-clubs pretending to serve only coffee and tea, yet she hadn't cast a single glance around. Her steps were purposeful, her back straight. Confident. He liked that.

The heels of her shoes clicked on the pavement as she strolled past the brightly lit front door of the city jail, heading straight for the unmarked chief of police's private entrance.

Ty pushed off the wall and straightened his suit coat, making sure his piece—a cheap government-issued pistol—was well-concealed beneath his arm, and waited until she'd arrived at the door before he headed across the street. Five chiefs of police had come and gone in St. Paul the past few years, and there was no reason to believe Ted Williams was any less corrupt than his predecessors. That, too, would play in Ty's favor.

Norma Rose drew a deep breath and took a moment to smooth her pleated skirt and tug at the cuffs of both gloves. The city, especially at night, was not her favorite place. Uncle Dave was going to owe her for this one. Getting arrested. He knew better. It hadn't been that long ago when food had been scarce and money nonexistent. Now her family had the finest things of anyone in White Bear Lake. Perhaps all of Minnesota. Her wardrobe was the envy of many and it certainly didn't take her high school diploma—the first in her family—to figure out she didn't want things to go back to how they used to be. One wrong move could snuff out the money flowing into her father's bank accounts. Uncle Dave was as aware of that as she.

Fueled by the ire old memories ignited, she twisted the knob on the door. Ted Williams, St. Paul's chief of police, knew better, too. Arresting Uncle Dave would not play in his favor.

The target of her indignation sat behind his desk, dressed in a blue uniform with shiny gold buttons and a flat hat spouting a badge. He jumped to his feet as she shut the door with the perfect amount of force. It didn't slam, but did cause the single lightbulb hanging by a black cord from the ceiling to sway, and certainly displayed her irritation.

"Norma Rose," Ted Williams said, rounding his desk. "I expected your father."

"He's busy." Everyone knew the resort packed people in by the dozens on the weekends, yet she reminded him, "It is Friday night."

"I'm aware of that." The police chief removed his hat and laid it on his desk. "But I figured he'd want to come get his brother-in-law right away."

She crossed the room and set her purse on the other corner of the long desk. "He's busy, so I'm here." Keeping her expression stony, Norma Rose leveled a solid stare on the man. "Why did you arrest Dave?"

"I didn't arrest him," Ted said, tugging down the hem of his uniform jacket.

Norma Rose kept her well-trained eyes from roaming. Ted Williams was a swanky-looking bird, tall and lean with sand-colored hair and periwinkle eyes. If she ever had a mind to form a crush on someone, it could very well be him. However, that would never happen. Keeping the resort running smoothly, her father satisfied, her sisters happy and, evidently, her uncle out of jail, took all her time. She was thankful for that—being busy—and liked most of it, particularly being a businesswoman. Even the big boys respected her and she was going to keep it that way. The quickest way to lose respect was to become a doxy.

"Why is he here, then?" she asked when Ted didn't elaborate.

Rubbing the back of his neck, Ted shrugged. "I got a call about an ossified egg on the street corner and sent an officer out to get him. It turned out to be Dave."

"Drunk? Dave?" Norma Rose shook her head. "That's impossible." Only the family knew Dave didn't drink. Ever.

Ted leaned against the desk. "Maybe someone slipped him a Mickey."

Norma Rose refused to let the bubble of concern that burst in her stomach show. "No one would have done that." Too many men feared repercussions to do such a thing, and others were paid too well.

Ted shrugged again, and lifted an eyebrow while his gaze wandered to where her string of pearls was tied. She lifted her chin and used an unwavering glare to challenge him to meet her gaze instead of stare at her breasts.

"Why didn't you drive him home?" she asked.

He shifted his stance and his gaze. "As you pointed out, it's Friday night. The city is hopping."

"Who called you?" she asked. The underground world Prohibition had built was vast, and undeniably corrupt, almost as fraudulent as those with their self-righteous attitudes who'd created it in the first place.

Ted shifted his stance as if uncomfortable.

New faces did pop up now and again—men and women hoping to make a fortune selling boot-legged and home-brewed spirits who might be foolish enough to challenge the monopoly her father had built. They never lasted long. "Who was it?"

"Mel Rosengren at the Blind Bull," Ted answered. "But he claimed Dave hadn't been there."

"Of course he hadn't been there," she said. "Dave doesn't patronize such establishments." The fact that her uncle didn't drink made him the perfect man for the job he held—providing samples to buyers. Actually, Dave couldn't drink. He broke out in hives and swelled up like a raccoon hit by a car and left on the side of the road to bake in the sun when he consumed so much as a teaspoon of alcohol. *Allergic* is what Gloria Kasper, the family physician, called it. Highly allergic. "Where is he?"

Before Ted spoke, the door opened—not the one to the street, but the one to the police station.

"Chief." A portly officer Norma Rose didn't recognize poked his head through the opening. "A lawyer wants to pay Dave Sutton's bail."

More than concern flared inside Norma Rose. "Bail? A lawyer?"

"Yes, ma'am."

A fresh bout of ire stung her nerves. No one would have called in a mouthpiece. She'd told her father she'd take care of this, and she would. He was busy trying to convince Brock Ness to stay and play at the resort rather than heading to Chicago to play for some radio station. She'd offered to drive into the city and get Dave because finding another musician this close to the two large parties they had coming up would be next to impossible. "I'm here to pick up Dave," Norma Rose told Ted, along with a look that said there would be no bail. A man who didn't do his job didn't deserve to be paid.

Ted's slight nod indicated he understood her silent message about the bail. Turning his attention toward the officer, he started across the room. "Where is this lawyer?"

The door opened wider and another man stepped through, one so dapper looking the air in Norma Rose's lungs wouldn't move even while a vibration rumbled through her stronger than if she'd stood on the depot platform as a freight train rolled past. His suit was black with dark gray pinstripes and his shoes were suede, black, like his shirt and tie. The hat band of his fedora was black, too, and silk. She saw decked-out men day in and day out, and not one of them had ever made her lose the ability to breathe. This man was big, taller than the police chief, and had shoulders as broad as the men who hauled barrels of whiskey into the basement of the resort. Unlike those men, his hair was cut short, trimmed neatly around his ears, and he was clean-shaven.

Strangers weren't anything new, and one rarely caught her attention. Flustered for concentrating so deeply on this one, Norma Rose forcefully emptied her lungs. Just above the pounding in her ears, she heard the man speak.

"Chief Williams," he said, holding out a hand. "Ty Bradshaw, attorney at law."

The man handed Ted a calling card, and then produced another one out of his suit pocket as he stepped closer. His eyes were dark brown, but it wasn't the color that seared something inside her. It was the way they shimmered, as if all he had to do was smile and call her doll and she'd fall onto his lap like the girls that were paid to do so back at the resort.

Well-versed on keeping her expression blank—for men gave her those types of looks all the time, which did nothing but disgust her—Norma Rose didn't so much as blink as she took the card he offered. She did curse her fingers for trembling slightly when his brushed against them.

Embossed gold writing proclaimed his name and profession just as he'd stated, and offered no additional information. Which meant little to nothing. She had embossed cards with her name on them, too.

"I wasn't aware Dave had a lawyer," Ted said.

"He does now," the newcomer stated.

His rather arrogant tone sent another rumble through her. "No, he doesn't," Norma Rose argued. Her father employed several attorneys, and if anyone in the family ever had the need, one of them would be called. This occasion didn't require a mouthpiece, just a few extra bills laid in the chief's hand. Which would not happen, either. Ted Williams was paid well to keep her entire family out of the hoosegow and the fact she was standing here, arguing with an unknown lawyer, was enough to say Ted was not earning his monthly installments.

The lawyer, Ty or Todd or Tom or whatever he'd said his name was, stepped forward, staring at her so intently she couldn't glance down to read his calling card again. Norma Rose kept her gaze locked with his, even though her stomach fluttered as if she'd swallowed a caged bird.

"Yes, he does," he said, his voice as calculating as his stare, which slipped downward.

A tremendous heat singed the skin from her toes to her nose. Everywhere his gaze touched. By the time his eyes met hers again Norma Rose was completely disturbed. And uncomfortable. This had never happened to her, and she wasn't impressed. "Since when?"

"We sat next to each other at the lunch counter in the drugstore. He had the chicken noodle soup. I had the tomato."

Norma Rose didn't care what kind of soup they'd eaten, but his explanation did give her insight she'd missed earlier. His accent was eastern. New York, if her guess was right. They couldn't pronounce *tomato* to save their souls. What was a New York lawyer doing in St. Paul? Eating tomato soup at a drugstore?

The ringing of a telephone momentarily interrupted her thoughts. She gathered them quickly
enough to say, "My uncle was mistaken. He has
no need for his own lawyer." Turning to Ted, she
said, "I'll take Dave home now."

Glancing between her and the lawyer, Ted
paused, as if not sure what to do.

"Now," she repeated, lifting her purse off the
desk, once again demonstrating Ted wouldn't be
seeing any extra cash for his efforts tonight.

"Chief." The unknown officer stuck his head
through the open doorway again. "There's a raid
downtown."

"Damn it." Ted grabbed his hat off his desk.
"Where at?"

"The Blind Bull."

The officer's answer sent a shiver up Norma
Rose's spine, as did the hint of surprise on Ty
Bradshaw's face. She'd read the calling card a second time and would not forget his name again, nor
would she forget how he smiled at her. Having
smiled like that on numerous occasions herself, she
easily recognized he was attempting to disguise,
or make her believe, that he hadn't reacted to the
news of the Blind Bull being raided, although the
news had certainly surprised him.

"Get Dave Sutton. Norma Rose will take him home," Ted told the officer.

"Yes, sir." The officer disappeared out the door.

"I'm assuming there's no paperwork for me to sign," Norma Rose said.

"Of course not. I'd have already signed it if there was," the lawyer answered.

She gave him a glare that said she wasn't talking to him, nor would she ever be. Turning to the police chief, she said, "I'll be sure to inform my father of all your assistance tonight."

"Now, Norma Rose…" Ted began cajolingly.

"Good evening, Chief Williams," she snapped before he could continue, and then marched through the doorway into the police station, where she assumed the other officer would bring her uncle.

Dave was already there, sitting in a wooden chair on the far side of the room, looking green and holding the side of his head with one hand. His sample suitcase sat between his legs. He lifted his head as she approached. "Aw, Rosie, I sure didn't mean for you to have to come down here to get me."

Norma Rose didn't say a word until after she'd looped an arm around his elbow to help him stand. Not that she was much help. His six-foot frame had a good eight inches on her and he outweighed her by a hundred pounds. He stood, though, and caught his balance when he wobbled.

Grabbing his leather suitcase in her other hand, she growled quietly, "What were you thinking, doing such a thing?"

"I didn't mean to get arrested, and I didn't drink anything, either," Dave mumbled in return, with rather slurred words. "You know I'm allergic."

"I'm talking about the lawyer," she said sharply.

"I met him—"

"I know where you met him," she said. "Come on, I have to get you home."

"Ty can give me a ride home," her uncle said, spying the lawyer.

"And have you giving out family secrets?" she hissed. "I don't think so."

"I never give out family secrets." Dave wobbled and hiccuped. "Rosie, I don't feel so good." Rubbing his stomach, he added, "I don't know if I can handle riding with you all the—"

"You'll handle it all right." She wrenched on his arm, heading toward the front door Ty Bradshaw held open. Just because she'd had a slight accident years ago when she was learning to drive, which had resulted in Dave, the one teaching her how to drive, breaking an arm, he chastised her about her driving. It wasn't her fault he'd stuck his arm out the window when she'd been forced to swerve off the road. Yet, he refused to ride anywhere with her, unless absolutely necessary. Tonight was one of those absolutely necessary times.

"I can give Mr. Sutton a ride to the resort," the lawyer said, grinning as if he knew the entire history of her driving record. "My car's right over there."

Norma Rose glanced in the general direction he pointed, just so she didn't have to look at him. A jalopy, a Model T similar to the one she'd wrecked years before. The lawyer was grinning even more broadly when she turned her glare his way. "That's quite all right, Mr. Bradshaw. Your services are no longer needed." On impulse, mainly due to how her blood had started to boil, she added, "They never were."

He lifted both eyebrows as he dipped his head slightly. However, his grin still displayed a set of white teeth, sparkling like those of a braying donkey. Norma Rose opened the Cadillac's passenger door and tossed Dave's suitcase in the backseat. The car—a gift from her father for her twenty-fifth birthday a few months ago—didn't have a scratch on it. Proof her driving skills were now stellar.

That accident had been five years ago and her first attempt to drive. She wouldn't have needed to learn how to drive back then if her younger sister by two years, Twyla, hadn't refused to give her a ride that morning. The year before, when Uncle Dave had returned from the war, he'd taught Twyla how to drive. He was also the one who'd taught Josie and Ginger when they became old enough, and he rode with any one of her sisters regularly.

"Ohhh."

The heavy groan had Norma Rose glancing at her uncle.

Sweat dripped off Dave's forehead. "I'm going to be sick." He stumbled then, all the way to the back of her car, where he unloaded his stomach.

Norma Rose's stomach revolted at the sound of her uncle's heaving. Her throat started burning and she pinched her lips together, breathing through her nose as her gag reflex kicked in. She could deal with about most everything, but not throwing up. Not the sounds, the sight, the smell. It evoked memories of death and dying. People too sick to care for one another, dying side by side in their beds.

The flu epidemic that had swept the nation had stayed for months in her home. Taking lives before it left. Her mother, her brother, her grandparents, cousins, aunts and uncles, friends. A few of them had been spared—her sisters and father— but they'd all been sick with coughs so deep and raw they'd sounded like a gaggle of geese honking, and so uncontrollable they'd coughed until they'd vomited. Once her grandmother's most cherished and prized possession, the washing machine on the back porch couldn't handle the workload. With no money to replace or repair the machine, Norma Rose had washed soiled linens and clothes in a tub with bleach so strong her hands bled.

Dave retched again and though he was downwind, she got a whiff of a smell similar to the one that had once hovered over her home. Sweat coated her hands inside her black gloves. Afraid she would lose the contents of her stomach Norma Rose slammed the car door shut and dashed around the front of her Cadillac, the slick bottoms of her new shoes slipping on the pavement in her haste.

"Fine," she told the lawyer, afraid to breathe while pulling open the driver's door. "You give him a ride home."

Chapter Two

The scent of new leather helped. Therefore, despite her desperate need to escape, Norma Rose waited until the lawyer loaded Dave in his Model T before she gunned the Cadillac and headed up the road. She drove with one eye on the mirror mounted to the spare-tire bracket near the front fender. Dim, and disappearing now and again as the mirror bounced, the reflection of the lawyer's headlights eased her remorse of not taking Uncle Dave home herself. She would not let him out of her sight, which was almost the same. If the Model T took a wrong turn, she could spin the Cadillac around and overtake the much slower car in no time.

The Model T stayed close, rumbling on the cobblestones as she weaved through traffic, turned corners and crossed numerous trolley and railroad tracks. Miles later, when the paved road heading out of the city gave way to gravel and the Cadillac stirred up a good plume of dust, headlights still reflected in her mirror. She had the windows up, to keep the dust out of her car, but knew the truck version of the Model T behind her didn't have windows and wouldn't have blamed the lawyer for putting more space between the two cars.

He didn't, and Norma Rose focused on keeping her mind on driving and off the man behind the wheel of the truck behind her as much as possible. Men, the entire lot of them, were banned from her mind, at least from that little section she kept for private thoughts. Since she ran the resort, the majority of her dealings were with men in the business realm, and that was more than enough.

Approaching headlights had her hugging the right side of the road, giving the oncoming automobile as much space as needed. Another Model T. She recognized this one, too. Brock Ness's father once used it to deliver milk to the resort. Meeting the truck this close to the city made her stomach sink.

The truck passed and she eased her Cadillac back into the middle of the road.

She'd have her work cut out in finding a replacement musician for the next few weekends.

However, that could explain why her mind was so distracted lately. Her sisters had gone berries over Brock, and their silliness must have left more of an impact on her than she'd realized. There was no other reason for her to have been so observant about Ty Bradshaw and his fancy suit. How spiffy he'd looked in pinstripes and that jaunty black hat. She could still see him in her mind and the image continued to burn a hole in her brain.

She didn't think about men in that manner. Ever. And she wasn't about to start now. There was no real reason for her to be concerned. As soon as her father set eyes on Ty, he'd be sent on his way. Very few people were brought into the family business. A lawyer from New York would never be welcomed.

Norma Rose adjusted her speed as the road grew curvy between the lakes of Gem and White Bear, and slowed more as she took the wide corner to merge onto Main Street of the city of White Bear Lake. The town was quiet, hardly a light glowing other than a few streetlights. This late, even the amusement park and the Plantation nightclub—which had recently attempted to rival the resort by bringing in various musicians—were dark and eerily silent. Forrest Reynolds at the Plantation would do better to focus on his billiard room and bowling alley. Folks of White Bear Lake liked to keep things as neat and innocent as a baby's first birthday gift, all wrapped up with a bow on top. If she and Forrest were on speaking terms, which they weren't, she might have told him that.

Located four miles north of town on the shores of Bald Eagle Lake, her family's resort didn't need to abide by the newly instated ten-o'clock curfew and noise ordinance, and catered to all those who liked things a bit more tempestuous.

A few blocks later, Norma Rose increased her speed as the town disappeared, and glanced in the mirror. Ty Bradshaw was right behind her. She couldn't help but wonder how he kept those suede shoes of his so clean. Suede loved dust. She knew. Shoes were her one love. She wore a different pair most every day. Now that she could afford to.

Her eyes had obviously spent too long looking in the mirror, because the familiar *Y* in the road appeared sooner than expected. Norma Rose had to brake quickly to make the turn, and then again as her car bounced over the railroad tracks of the nearby Bald Eagle Depot. Ty had braked, too, keeping a safe distance between their vehicles, and as she entered a stretch where tall and leafy trees hung over the road, making the already dark night denser, she found unusual comfort in the Model T headlights in her review mirror. She didn't know why, nor did she want to wonder about it.

Several curves later, she turned the final corner and drove slowly up the resort's long driveway. The lack of rain lately had made everything dry. Most people didn't understand how easily dust from the driveway entered the buildings and left a layer that had to be wiped away on a daily basis, but she did.

The parking area in front of the main resort building had cleared out considerably since she'd left. Veering around the right side of the big brick building, she wheeled her car into the garage built for family vehicles. Norma Rose parked between the two older coupes that belonged to her sisters and lifted Uncle Dave's suitcase out of the backseat before she opened the driver's door.

A groundskeeper stood ready to close the big swinging garage door as soon as she exited, just as he'd opened it moments ago. Norma Rose expressed her thanks with a nod as her gaze locked on the Model T and the men climbing out the passenger side of the car. Ty had driven beyond the main building and along the line of big pine trees that gave the row of cabins on the lakeshore seclusion. He was parked near Dave's bungalow. Her uncle's blue Chevrolet sedan was there as well, making her wonder how Dave had gotten to town in the first place.

As she crossed the lawn and headed down the lane, her thoughts faded when she noticed how heavily Uncle Dave leaned on the lawyer as they walked toward his bungalow. Not sure if he was still ill, or just tired, she walked closer with extreme caution just in case he wasn't done throwing up.

"I'll put him to bed," Ty Bradshaw said.

Dave's bungalow, a small two-room cabin, didn't hold a lot of hiding cubbies, but it did have a few, and she certainly didn't need a New York lawyer finding them. She'd already shirked her responsibility by letting the man drive Dave home, and couldn't do it again. "No," she said, "I'll do it."

Mumbling, Dave shook his head, as if saying he didn't need anyone's help.

"I believe whatever he was given hasn't worn off yet," Ty said. "Open the door."

Norma Rose hurried to comply and brushed past the men to feel for and catch the string hanging from the bulb in the center of the room. "His bed's this way," she said, entering the back room and finding the string hanging from that ceiling, as well. Light filled the room and she slid Dave's suitcase under the foot of the bed before the men entered.

As soon as Ty helped Dave onto the bed, her uncle rolled onto his side, moaning deeply.

"I'm no doctor," Ty said, "but I think he should be seen by one."

Norma Rose froze momentarily. "He's that ill?"

"I believe so."

Torn between getting her uncle aid and leaving the lawyer alone, Norma Rose spun around to give herself a moment to think without gazing at the man who seemed to have grown more handsome since she'd seen him in town. The yellow haze of the lightbulb reflected in his brown eyes, making them twinkle, and her heart skipped a beat. That was all so abnormal it took several deep breaths for her to set her thoughts in order. "You stay here and don't touch anything."

Without turning to see if he'd heard, she marched out the doorway and then scurried toward the main building. After ducking under pine boughs, she ran on her toes so her heels wouldn't sink in the plush lawn that was watered regularly to keep it green.

Spying a groundskeeper, she shouted, "Get Mrs. Kasper, and my father. Send them to Dave's cabin."

The man waved. Norma Rose turned around and ran back to her uncle's cabin, once again on her toes, which made the backs of her shoes slip off her heels. She planted her heels and skidded to a stop. The door was still open, and her uncle was being sick again. Backing up a few steps, she held her breath, twisting the chain of her purse with both hands. Anyone would think she'd get over this. She had tried, but couldn't. Just couldn't.

The lawyer appeared in the doorway. "Did you find a doctor?"

"I—" The sound of Dave's retching had her slapping a hand over her mouth.

A hand, Ty's hand, wrapped around her elbow and the heat seared her skin, yet she couldn't pull away, or protest when he led her to the end of the walkway.

"What's going on here?" her father asked, rushing through the trees along with Gloria Kasper, who was wearing her flannel robe, slippers and white floppy nightcap.

Norma Rose was able to pull her arm from Ty's grasp, and uncover her mouth.

"It's Dave," Ty said, now taking a hold of Gloria's arm and steering her toward the cabin. "He's in here."

"What's wrong with him?" her father asked, glancing at the open door.

"I'm not sure," Norma Rose answered, although her arm still stung. "Chief Williams suggested someone may have slipped him a Mickey." She swallowed. "He keeps throwing up."

Her father gave an understanding pat on her shoulder. For as big and ferocious as most people thought The Night was, Norma Rose knew differently. To her, he was as lovable as the stuffed Roosevelt bear that sat on her bed. Sweet and comforting.

When he wanted to be.

She'd admit that much, too.

"Gloria and I will handle this, honey," he said. "You go on in inside."

Norma Rose glanced toward the cabin. It was said Gloria Kasper was a much better doctor than her husband had ever been. Years ago, when they were a newly married couple, Gloria, believing her beloved Raymond was having an affair with one of his patients, started accompanying him on all of his visits, and continued to do so until his death a few years ago. Then, in the midst of the influenza outbreak, Gloria, concerned her friends would be left without medical care, had obtained her medical degree. Since then, she had saved many lives.

"Go on, now," her father repeated. "Gloria will take care of Dave. You can shoo out the last of the townies."

The townies—folks that lived all year round near the local White Bear, Gem or Goose Lakes, or in the town of White Bear Lake—were always the last to leave. Especially with the new noise ordinance in town.

The residents of Bald Eagle Lake didn't consider themselves part of the town and had formed their own community, one with a unique spirit. The resort owners, when dozens of their properties had dotted the lakes, had unified their community a long time ago. The original owners had all formed a gentleman's agreement of all for one, and one for all, and the pact still held.

"Go on," her father said, giving her a shove.

Norma Rose was at the kitchen door of the resort before she realized she hadn't told her father about Ty pretending to be Dave's lawyer. She turned around, listening. They'd have met by now.

The trees between the resort and the cabins blocked her view, otherwise she might have been able to see the lawyer walking to his car. It wouldn't take long for her father to get rid of him. Tilting her head, listening for a Model T to start, she stood for several minutes, until it was obvious Ty hadn't been asked to leave.

Yet. He was probably helping Gloria put Dave to bed or something. Then her father would send him down the road.

Norma Rose entered through the kitchen door and crossed the meticulously scrubbed room. It would have been nice to see the lawyer leave. Then she'd have no reason to continue thinking about him.

In truth, she had no reason to think about him and absolutely no time.

Exiting the kitchen, she turned right and entered the wide hallway that ran the width of the lower floor with staircases leading to the second and third floors at each end. Nightingale's took up all her time. What had been a small family resort only a few years ago was now one of the largest in the state. It had a grand ballroom—complete with a curtained stage—a dining room that could seat up to a hundred people, three smaller party rooms, several offices and a covered porch that ran the length of the building and faced the lake. All that was on the first floor. The second floor contained family and employee living quarters, as well as guest rooms like those on the third floor.

The larger the resort became, the more there was for her to do. This was the first year they weren't adding to the main building. The improvements were focused on the twenty bungalows intermittently placed around the property. Her grandfather had built most of them during the last century, when people started commuting to the lake area on the train. The vacation spot had been popular before the rail lines had been laid, but boomed when what had been a three-hour wagon ride became a twenty-minute train ride.

Many of the older resorts had closed up over the last twenty years, with people buying up the acreage to live here year round, but since Prohibition, the resorts had started to thrive again. So had the trollies coming from the cities. The streetcar company also owned the amusement park, giving people a destination as well as a way to get there.

Norma Rose turned left onto the center hallway that would pass the dining room and end at the ballroom, where Reggie, their longtime bartender, would be glad to see her. He liked things shut down by one, and considering he was back on duty by ten in the morning, she couldn't blame him.

Sometimes she wished she didn't have to report to duty until ten. But, for the most part, she didn't mind. Nightingale's was her life. She had witnessed its rise from a run-down homestead with a dancehall and few rented cabins to a glamorous showcase that rivaled hotels nationwide. Listening to her heels echoing against the wood floors, she glanced at the naturally stained wood wainscoting and grinned. If not for her, the entire resort would be painted red. That was her father's favorite color. He owned over a dozen maroon suits. His office was splattered with burgundy; she'd even specially ordered his desk to be built out of natural red mahogany.

There were plenty of red hues in all the other rooms, too, but she'd insisted on some things being left natural wood—the floors and wainscoting—and had added shades of gold and black. Black. Now that was a color. Maybe that's why she was so intrigued by the lawyer. Ty's black outfit was spectacular. Norma Rose paused before entering the ballroom to shake her head, feeling flustered that she couldn't control her thoughts when it came to the newcomer.

Most of the lights had been turned off, and she moved straight to the bar, where three locals sat. At least they were three that she liked. Smiling, she stepped up between two of their barstools. "Scooter, Dac," she greeted the men on her left before turning to her right. "Jimmy."

"Evening, Norma Rose," Scooter Wilson greeted in return. "You here to give us the bum's rush?"

Frowning, for she'd expected townies and didn't think of Bald Eagle people as such, she asked, "What are you boys still doing here?"

"Placing bets," Jimmy answered, picking his tweed driving hat off the bar beside him and placing it over his corn-colored hair. "On if we ever see Brock Ness again."

A shiver rippled her spine.

Scooter slapped a coin he'd set to spinning on the counter. "He told your father no."

Her insides slumped, confirming what she'd feared.

Neither of the three said anything else, and she knew why. Her father wasn't a gangster. He was a businessman who, at times, associated with mobsters. There was nothing illegal about that. Gangsters were very good customers. They never squabbled about the price, always paid with cash, in full, and usually in advance.

However, plenty of folks feared her father, and what might happen if they got on his bad side. He wasn't an easy man to say no to. Maybe she should have told Ty Bradshaw that.

Norma Rose hid her frustration, and nodded toward the bartender. "Reggie's ready to call it a night. You boys should drift on home."

The men gathered their hats and downed the dregs from their earthen mugs before they stood and pushed in their stools. Far more difficult to come by, yet sought after more highly than whiskey or rum, beer was readily available at the resort, for those trusted enough to remain silent.

Norma Rose walked with the men across the large ballroom, their footsteps echoing loudly. At the front door, she bid them goodbye and waited until the double doors closed behind them. Turning, she glanced at the mantel clock on the field-stone fireplace centered between the ballroom doors. One thirty in the morning.

She should go to her office and start researching musicians. A week from now would be Al and Emma Imhoff's twenty-fifth wedding anniversary and the week after that, Palooka George's birthday bash. Both parties expected top-notch music, and it was her job to provide it.

But it was late, and though she hated to admit it, she was tired. But above all, she wanted to know Ty Bradshaw was good and gone.

She'd taken no more than a single step forward when the front door opened. Walking in, her father gestured toward the registration desk. "Norma Rose, get the key to the Northlander."

All of the cabins were named, a throwback from her grandparents' Scandinavian ancestry. About to move, she froze when a second man walked through the door. The rapid increase of her heart rate had to be from anger, for she certainly wasn't happy to see *him* again.

Ignoring Ty and the grin on his face, she turned to her father. "How's Uncle Dave?"

"He was poisoned."

Norma Rose took two steps, mainly to catch her balance by grabbing hold of the wide front desk. "Poisoned?"

"Yes," her father answered, "but he's going to be fine."

Norma Rose didn't doubt that. It had been her idea to move Gloria into the resort permanently when her home in White Bear Lake had mysteriously burned to the ground last year. Someone had been upset about Gloria's belief in birth control, that's what Norma Rose had deduced. Having a physician on-site had been a good business move and Dave couldn't be in better hands.

The seriousness of her uncle being poisoned—and the threat to the entire family and community—made Norma Rose's spine quiver. "How?"

"You don't worry about that," her father said. "Get the key. Ty will be staying with us for a while."

Norma Rose bit her tongue to keep from saying several things, and kept her gaze from wandering to the lawyer. "The Northlander isn't ready for occupancy. The workmen just finished painting it today."

"I don't mind the smell of paint," Ty said, biting back a grin. Norma Rose was a classy-looking dame, that was for sure, but she was also a sassy one. As full of herself as a cat with a diamond collar.

Anger, lots of it, snapped in the blue eyes she settled upon him with more frost than a subzero night. "I haven't had a chance to have the bed made up yet."

"I know how to make a bed," Ty answered. He really hadn't made an impression on her, or he had, just a bad one. He'd have to rectify that. Becoming a welcomed guest at the resort was a necessity, and from what he'd learned, being accepted by Norma Rose was just as important as being accepted by Roger Nightingale.

She stomped around the desk, her hips swaying with each snapping clip of her heels. If an artist ever needed a model in order to draw the perfect hourglass figure, they should look up Norma Rose. The image of her backside was enough to stir the blood of a dead man.

"If *he*," she said pointedly to her father, "needs a place to stay for the night, there are a few rooms available on the third floor."

"He's staying with us for a while, not a night." Rounding the desk, Roger said, "I'll get the key, you go get some bedding."

The glare she cast at her father's back would have dropped most folks to their knees. She erased the expression before her father turned around, key in hand, and then she hooked the little chain of her purse on her elbow and marched the opposite way around the desk, so she wouldn't have to come any closer to him. Ty didn't even attempt to hide his smile. Getting on Norma Rose's good side was going to be a challenge. He liked a good challenge. He was up for it, too. Bodine had turned into a mole of late, and following his trail had grown lackluster.

"She can be a slight short now and again," Roger said while Norma Rose turned the corner. "But I couldn't run this place without her. Matter of fact, I don't run this place. She does. Has for a few years now. She does a fine job of it, too. I mostly stay out of her way."

The man handed over a single key attached to a diamond-shaped piece of leather, tooled with the resort's name. "Thank you," Ty said. "I'll remember what you said about your daughter, and try to stay out of her way while investigating what happened to your brother-in-law."

"Hell of a thing," Roger said, "Dave getting poisoned. Can't think who might have done that."

"Start writing down names," Ty said. "I'll look into every one of them."

"I will, but, it's our secret," Roger said. "Other than Norma Rose, I don't want anyone hearing about this."

"Silence is my specialty," Ty said. "I'd be out of a job if not."

"Good thing you came along when you did," Roger said.

"As I said, my last job led me here." Ty wasn't counting his eggs yet, although his instincts said Nightingale was nibbling hard on the bait.

"Those feds," Roger growled, as he nodded in the general direction his daughter had gone. "Take that hallway to the end and turn left. Norma Rose will be at the end of that hall, in the storage room. She can show you where the Northlander is located. You and I will talk in more depth in the morning."

Ty agreed, and shook the man's hand. Roger Nightingale was no fool. He hadn't got to this point in life without being thorough…very thorough. By the time they talked again tomorrow, the man would have had Ty's background checked out right up to the minute his mother had given birth to him. Ty expected as much, and would have been disappointed if things had been different.

"Good night, sir," he said, stepping back.

"'Night," Nightingale said, clearly already preoccupied by who he should call first.

Chapter Three

Norma Rose was stomping back up the hallway when Ty turned the second corner. He'd cased the joint, but was amazed by its size. It looked mammoth from the outside, but from what he'd already seen of the inside, a person could get lost and not be found for a year. Holding out his hand, he said, "I'll take that."

She clutched the wicker basket closer to her narrow waist.

"Your father said you'd show me to the cabin, but I'm sure I can find it." Ty fought the grin trying to form at the way she struggled. She had a mouthful to say, that was clear, but wasn't sure if she should say it, which was interesting. "Just point me in the right direction."

"He said to show you, and I'll show you," she said stubbornly, spinning around to lead him down the hall and through a storage area with shelves full of bedding and linens.

Noting the outside door didn't need to be unlocked before she opened it, Ty said, "If you insist, but that will just make an extra trip." Her statement had told him exactly what he'd needed to know. Norma Rose would do anything her father told her to do.

Tossing a glare over her shoulder like he was public enemy number one, she snapped, "No, it won't."

"Yes, it will," he insisted, stopping on the stoop. "I'll have to walk you back to the resort after you show me the cabin."

The moonlight flashed in her eyes as she spun around. "Why?"

"Because I'm a gentleman," he said smoothly. "And a gentleman would never let a lady walk alone in the middle of the night."

She thrust the basket at him and spun back to the door as soon as he took the handles. "Follow that pathway," she said, pointing to a well-worn dirt trail. "You'll eventually come to cabins. Five of them. The Northlander is the last one. It's marked." She pulled open the door. "There's a road leading to it, as well. If you want your automobile, you'll need to go back out to the parking lot and drive around the other side of the main building then follow the road that curves toward the lake."

"I'll get my truck in the morning," he said. "Wouldn't want to disturb the other guests." He thought about giving her a wink, but chose a smooth smile instead. "As I said, I'm a gentleman."

She was a cold one; she barely even blinked as she said, "Suit yourself."

"I usually do," he said. "As you do, too, I'm sure."

Holding the door with one hand, she leveled a stare on him. "You, Mr. Bradshaw, cannot be sure about anything concerning me, so don't pretend to be." Slowly, her gaze went from his shoes to his hat. "But I can be sure about plenty where you are concerned."

"Oh?" He shifted the basket to one hand. "Like what?"

"You'll discover that soon enough." With a haughty flick of her chin, she entered the building and closed the door with a resounding thud.

The brick structure was solid and well-built, yet Ty knew she'd be able to hear him through the open window beside the door as he let out a bellow of laughter. The echo of another door inside the building slamming filtered through the night air and Ty laughed again before he turned to follow the pathway. He started whistling, not exactly sure why, other than the fact he felt like it.

Norma Rose Nightingale had met her match in him, whether she was prepared for it or not. Mainly because no one, not even a spicy little tomato with a fine set of legs, would stand in his way of ousting Bodine. No, siree. She was just one of many good-looking women with sexy legs covering this earth. He'd tolerate her because he had to, but he wouldn't bow to her haughtiness. The sooner she discovered that, the better off they'd both be. In the meantime, getting on her good side was going to make a fine game of cat and mouse. He had time. Palooka George's party was two weeks away.

The cabin was easy to find and was a log structure much like Dave Sutton's abode. Using the key to enter, Ty set the basket down. His research had already told him this cabin didn't have a pull string hanging in the center of the room. It had been wired with light switches. Part of the renovations taking place to several of the cabins on this side of the resort.

A low whistle of appreciation escaped without him thinking about it as he flicked the little switch. The workmen camped out behind the barn in several tents had done a fine job. This place was as shiny as a freshly minted penny. He picked up the basket and walked across a thick braided rug, upon which a table and two chairs sat. There was also a small heating stove in the corner. Some serious dough had been laid down to fix up the cabin; even the bed sitting in the center of the room was new, mattress and all.

There was an old-fashioned washstand in the corner, with a pitcher and bowl, along with a new dresser, and the windows that had been left open to release the smell of paint had screens on them. A nice touch considering the number of mosquitoes he'd encountered during his walk along the trail. There'd been a water spigot on the way here, too, which the cabins would share, along with a privy and bath house.

All the comforts of home.

If he'd had a home.

Ray Bodine had seen to it that he didn't.

Ty made up the bed and stripped down to his short-legged and sleeveless muslin union suit before lying on the fresh sheets with both arms behind his head and a thick pillow beneath them. Tired, he closed his eyes.

This was nice. Far better than most of the hotels

he usually resided in. No banging of doors, noisy occupants returning to their rooms at all hours of the night, and no traffic, no sirens blaring and horns honking from dusk to dawn.

It had been a long time since he'd experienced such silence, since before the war, really, and he didn't believe he'd ever had frogs and the gentle rhythm of water washing onto the shore to serenade him to sleep.

Norma Rose's image fluttered behind his closed lids. He smiled at the idea of changing that starched little attitude of hers. He doubted she'd ever been kissed. That, too, would be fun to change.

It was all part of his plan.

Holding that thought, with a cool breeze wafting over his skin, Ty gave in to slumber.

He was up early, due to the hammering next door, but was well rested and he bade good morning to the carpenters working on the cabin beside his—named the Willow—as he collected water from the spigot in the pitcher from the washstand.

Apart from the noise of the hammers, the woods were quiet, serene with the waves of the lake still gently crashing ashore. He took his time returning to his cabin, pretending to enjoy the scenery, including the large weeping willow next to the cabin the men were working on. A large crate sat beneath the tree's long, leafy branches that hung almost to the ground.

The Duluth Building Company.

Interesting. Nightingale's resort was only twenty miles from St. Paul, yet he ordered building supplies from Duluth, a hundred and fifty miles north. Then again, Ty doubted the crate was actually used for building supplies.

After cleaning up with the water he'd fetched, Ty left his suit coat, vest and hat on the fancy brass hooks supplied for such things, and found a secure spot for his holster and gun under the new mattress before he left his cabin.

He meandered quietly, walking the full circle of cabins on this side of the main building. There were ten in total including his and all were named. Whitewater, the Cove, Double Pine and other such titles. Several had small buildings a few yards away from the main bungalow that were summer kitchens, he discovered, after sneaking peeks in a few windows.

Taking advantage of the quiet morning, he explored the layout of the other buildings on this side of the parking lot. Woodsheds, a large barn that no longer held animals and was locked tight, a laundry building, complete with the latest washing machines and surrounded by poles connecting several lines of drying wires and a set of tents that belonged to the men working on the cabins.

Crossing the parking lot, Ty paused when a curtain fluttered in one of the windows. He grinned and waved, pleased, knowing full well that Norma Rose was behind the curtain in her office, watching him.

With a chuckle, he started walking again, making his way up the road to Dave's cabin—the Eagle's Nest. He'd see Norma Rose soon, and liked the idea of letting her steam a bit as she wondered just when that would be.

Ty didn't stop at Dave's cabin. Instead he walked to the end of the road, counting a total of another ten cabins. It appeared the other side, where his cabin was, was where the renovations had started. Though not run-down, the cabins on this side were a pale green, whereas the ones on the other side were dark brown. There were signs of dry rot around the windows and along the eaves of these ones, too. A fraction of bewilderment struck Ty. Perhaps all the renovations—not just those on the cabins, but those completed on the main building over the last couple of years—weren't just a cover-up strategy.

Others might believe that, but he didn't. No resort could make the kind of money Nightingale had brought in the past few years. The workmen camped behind the barn were carpenters by day, runners by night, when their crates marked "building supplies" were full of shine, brought here and stored in the barn until they were loaded on the train via the back road that connected the Bald Eagle Depot to Nightingale's. Ty would now admit, after seeing things up close, a few of those crates had contained building supplies at one time.

His research had been thorough. The Night peddled Minnesota Thirteen whiskey. Initially a home-brew formula, it was now more sought after than the real stuff brought down from Canada, which is why Bodine wanted in. There was less overhead and more money to be made.

As Nightingale had said last night, Norma Rose ran the resort. All the renovations were probably her idea. She may not even know the base of her father's business. Except Ty didn't believe that. He suspected Norma Rose knew every last detail about her father's business.

Women were swayed by money as easily as men,

and from the looks of her wardrobe, Norma Rose liked money.

Ty was almost back to Dave's cabin when Roger Nightingale appeared on the trail leading through the pine trees.

"'Morning."

"Good morning," Ty responded.

"Sleep well?"

"Very. You?"

Ty almost laughed at the shift of Roger's eyes. Nightingale clearly knew Ty suspected he'd been up half the night checking him out. It didn't bother him. The more they understood each other right from the beginning, the better off they would both be.

"I always do," the man answered.

As they walked toward Dave's cabin together, Ty asked, "Do you have a list for me?"

Nightingale handed over a slip of paper. "You'll need to talk to Rosie, she may think of others, but that'll give you a place to start."

Norma Rose was exactly who Ty wanted to talk to, but he had a few things to investigate before then. "I'll talk with Dave first," Ty answered, pausing before opening the cabin door. "If he's up to it this morning."

Roger gestured for Ty to open the door. "If he isn't, we'll wait until he is."

Dave wasn't awake, but Gloria Kasper was. The doctor was in her mid-fifties or so, and although she didn't look her age—not last night in her night clothes, or this morning dressed in a fashionable blue dress complete with matching headband—she was formidable and stern. She probably had to be, considering she wrote out prescriptions for alcohol and birth control. Two things not easily accepted for a woman to be doing.

"It was wood poisoning, all right," Gloria said as Ty closed the door. "That government, they think we don't know what they're doing. Killing folks. But we do, and that's exactly what they're doing, still trying their hardest to make their Prohibition idea work." During her rant she'd set two mugs on the table and filled them from the coffeepot on the small stove in the corner. "They think by killing people with their tainted whiskey, people will stop drinking. The idea is as ludicrous as making alcohol illegal. They'll see sooner or later, mark my word. We ousted Andrew Volstead and we can oust the rest of them."

Ty made no comment as he took a seat indicated by Roger. Andrew Volstead, who the act had been named after, had lost his US Representative seat in 1922. From Minnesota, the man had outraged his constituency and had received numerous death threats before losing his seat. The latest rumor, which had the entire country in an uproar, was sweeping fast. Word was spreading that the government had hired teams of chemists and planted them inside specific areas known to have large still operations that fulfilled the public's need for intoxicating beverages. Ty couldn't say he believed in the conspiracy, but his supervisor had warned him to never take so much as a sip of alcohol in certain regions out east.

One more reason Minnesota Thirteen was gaining in popularity. Named after the corn variety grown in the area, the brew was considered safe and pure. Stearns County, where the vast majority was produced, was just a hundred miles northwest of White Bear Lake and known as the best moonshine region in the northwest. Every Prohibition agent knew that, and Ty had used that tidbit of information last night, while telling Nightingale he was on the tail of a snitch, someone who was trying to maneuver his way into the booze trade. It was true, that was what Bodine was doing, but Ty wasn't a private eye hired by a New York gangster to discover who the snitch was, as he'd told Nightingale. Of course, he'd had enough inside information for Nightingale to believe his story. His question was if Norma Rose would believe him. She might prove to be the hardest one to crack.

The other piece, which, in his mind, had tied everything together for Nightingale, was how he'd known about the Bald Eagle Lake area. Although it had no shipping yards, it had its own depot, with not just north and south trains like White Bear Lake, but trains traveling east and west, too. Freight trains that stopped regularly, yet not a single railroad admitted to stopping or shipping cargo out of the area.

This area was a bootlegger's dream. A hub that Ty had practically stumbled upon and hadn't told anyone about. Not even his supervisor. He'd simply said this was his chance to bring down Bodine.

"How's Dave doing?" Roger asked, ignoring Gloria's continued rant, which had gone from how if the government made alcohol legal again they could quit taxing poor folks to death to how President Coolidge, in her opinion, was little more than a teetotaler.

Ty had never met the president, but he did know

Coolidge had proposed to cut the Prohibition bureau's budget. The treasury secretary, who was also the chief Prohibition enforcement officer, wasn't fighting the idea. Andrew Mellon loathed Prohibition and put no extra efforts in its enforcement, which did make Ty's job more difficult. With a budget that barely paid for gas in his Model T, Ty needed this opportunity with the Nightingales more than ever. He'd used a good portion of his own funds—mainly reward money he'd earned from other arrests—tracking down Bodine.

As he watched Gloria Kasper top all three cups with a bump from a brandy bottle, Ty decided if he was near when either the president or Mellon met Gloria, he'd encourage them to offer her a toast—with alcohol. He'd seen the way she'd jabbed a tube down Dave's throat last night to wash his stomach with a solution of warm water and baking soda. Remembering the sight now, he had to wonder if Dave would ever be able to talk again.

"How do you think Dave is?" the woman responded to Roger. "He was poisoned and has been throwing up baking-soda water for the last eight hours."

Roger took a sip of his coffee and nodded before he asked, "You're sure it was wood alcohol?"

"Can't you smell it?" she asked.

"All I smell is vomit," Roger answered disgustedly.

Ty agreed, but made no comment. He did, however, remember how the sight and smell had disturbed Norma Rose last night. A weakness he'd file away to use if he needed it later.

"Exactly," Gloria said. "I've cleaned up everything Dave regurgitated—what you're smelling is him. That's what wood alcohol poisoning smells like. Vomit. Grain alcohol doesn't leave that stench." She leveled her big brown eyes on Ty. "Ethyl is grain alcohol, methyl is wood. Ethyl's wage is a hangover, methyl's is death."

"I've heard as much," he told her, and noted never to get on her bad side.

"It doesn't make sense," Roger said. "Dave doesn't drink."

"I didn't say the methyl was in some form of hooch," Gloria said. "When distilled properly, it's odorless and tasteless. From what came out of his stomach, my guess is they slipped it in one of those milk shakes he likes so much."

Roger's slow gaze landed on Ty with all the potency of a well-aimed tommy gun.

"Dave didn't have a milk shake at the drugstore

while I was there," Ty said. "He had soup." Picking up his cup, he added, "And coffee."

"When was that?" Gloria asked.

"Yesterday. Lunchtime. Noon or so," Ty answered.

She shook her head and said to Roger, "If Dave had drunk that at noon, he'd have been dead before they found him on the street corner last night. I don't think he drank enough to kill anyone, especially a man his size, but because he's so allergic to alcohol, its effects were ten times worse than they would have been for someone else."

"What would have happened to someone else?" Ty asked.

"Delirium, shallow breathing, racing heart, stomach cramps," Gloria answered. "But the most common is blurred vision, which often leads to complete blindness."

"Will Dave lose his sight?" Roger asked.

Ty recognized concern in the man's tone. Roger had shown he was worried about his brother-in-law, but now sincere anguish appeared on his face.

Gloria's expression softened and she reached across the table to squeeze Roger's hand. "I don't believe so. Most of his symptoms are because of his allergy, not the methyl."

"When will we know for sure?"

She shrugged. "Could be up to a week or more."

Roger nodded and drank the last of his coffee before he asked, "Do you want me to get one of the girls to come and sit with him for a while?"

"No." Gloria removed her hand from Roger's to drink her coffee. "I had one of your watchmen sit in here while I went and got dressed. I'll do that again if I need to." She glanced at the timepiece hanging around her neck on a shimmering gold chain. "I need to wake him in another twenty minutes for another dose of soda water. I'll keep doing that throughout the day, just to make sure." Sitting back in her chair she once again turned her attention to Ty. "I've seen a lot of mouthpieces, and you aren't a lawyer. Who are you and what are you doing here?"

Ty wasn't completely caught off guard. Her lack of trust was as thick in the air as the smell of vomit. He waited a moment or two, to see if Roger answered. When he didn't, Ty nodded. "You're right. I'm not a lawyer. Although I have attended law school." He didn't bother to add that it had been years ago, before he'd gone overseas. Roger Nightingale would tell her all that.

"Out east," she said. "I can tell by your accent."

He nodded again, and proceeded to tell her what he'd told Roger last night.

Even if she had been able to sleep, Norma Rose would have been in her office by sunup, digging out notes she'd made on every musician who'd played at the resort over the last couple of years. She had notes on ones that had played other places, too, even the Plantation. Years ago, the nightclub had been as big as the resort, drawing in crowds like no other. That was before Galen Reynolds had left for California and Forrest had returned.

Norma Rose's mind, though, wasn't focused on her notes, or the Plantation, or even Forrest Reynolds. None of that had been the reason she hadn't been able to sleep. The stench of a rat had done that, and the smell was still eating at her.

Ty Bradshaw.

The man who'd been roaming the resort since sunrise. She knew a varmint when she saw one, whether it had two legs or four. A grin tugged at her lips. She should feel guilty, sending the workmen over to the cabin next to his so early, but there were no other guests in the nearby cabins. They wouldn't arrive until later this week. And she did want the renovations done by then. Besides, the workmen had been up; she'd seen the lights in their tents from her bedroom window.

As her heart did a little flutter, recalling seeing Ty outside her office window a short time ago, she flipped open the cover of a writing tablet and grabbed a pen. "You are no gentleman, Ty Bradshaw," she mumbled.

Scanning the first pages of her notes, she huffed out another breath. Her mind just wouldn't focus, and it was too early to wake Ginger. Her youngest sister would pitch a fit, but Ginger knew all the local musicians. Not personally—their father did not allow the younger girls to mix with the guests or hired entertainers—but Ginger had perfect penmanship and helped Norma Rose write out contracts regularly, and was interested in such things.

Ginger would be up in a couple of hours and although her duties, along with those of Twyla and Josie, were doing laundry and cleaning cabins, Norma Rose could ask her to help find performers for the next two weekends. Ginger wouldn't mind. Twyla and Josie would.

Norma Rose just couldn't understand why her sisters weren't as dedicated to the resort as she was. They, too, remembered secondhand clothes and soup three times a day, and they loved the clothes now filling their closets, along with the cosmetics, jewelry and shoes, yet they didn't seem to make the connection that the only way to maintain all the fineries they'd come to enjoy was to keep the resort running. Making sure every minor detail was seen to. Just last week she'd had to make Twyla rewash a complete load of sheets. Brushing off bird droppings was not acceptable. Her sister was still mad at her.

Then again, Twyla was always mad at her.

Footsteps in the hall had Norma Rose lifting her head. It had been some time since her father had gone out to see Uncle Dave. She'd almost followed, but couldn't help remembering the smell. It had been strong and powerful, and she couldn't expose herself to it again. Not this early in the morning. She did want to know how Dave was, though, and kept her gaze on her door, waiting for her father to open it.

The footsteps went right past her door without slowing.

Her heart seemed to stop and start again. For the briefest of moments, she'd wondered if Ty would be with her father.

Letting out a breath, she concluded the morning cleaning had started. Part of the reason she liked coming into her office early was to get in a few hours before the chaos started. By eight, the resort would be humming with preparations for another long day and night of catering to guests.

Twirling her pen between her fingers, she gave in and let her mind focus on Ty Bradshaw. He wasn't a lawyer. He was pompous enough, and sly enough, but he just didn't look the part. He was almost too smooth. Maybe he was a runner, or a buyer, which would explain him meeting Dave, but runners or buyers never stayed at the resort. Their bosses did, but she felt sure Ty wasn't a mobster, either.

The pen tumbled onto her desk with a clatter. A Prohibition agent.

Hired to raid speakeasies, find and destroy stills, and arrest gangsters, a few had visited the resort before, but they'd never found anything. Ty didn't dress like an agent, though. Norma Rose knew clothes, and his were expensive. Prohibition agents were paid less money than factory workers, which is why they accepted money under the table so easily.

Ty could be a revenue man. When the prohis couldn't find anything, they'd send in a revenue man, looking for tax evasion. They'd find no tax evasion at the resort, either. Every dime was accounted for. She saw to that personally. The government hadn't planned very well. What they'd lost in tax dollars gained by the legal sale of alcohol, they were trying to make up with income taxes. Along with new taxes came new tax lawyers, and the resort paid several to keep abreast of every law that appeared.

Prohibition had changed the world, in some ways for the better, as with Norma Rose's new life at the resort, and in other ways for the worse. The problem she saw was that the law hadn't done what it had initially set out to do. Based on the Temperance movement, which blamed all of society's problems on the consumption of alcohol, Prohibition was to change all that. That sure hadn't happened. Crime was more rampant than ever. The law didn't say anything about the consumption of alcohol, either. It focused on the sale, transportation and manufacturing. All a person needed was a prescription and they had better access to alcohol than when saloons had lined the streets of every town.

Norma Rose didn't like the idea of breaking any laws, but Prohibition created a society where even the average person broke the law. She didn't like that, either, but, more importantly, she'd never go hungry again.

Lost in her little world of what she'd do if anyone would ever listen to her, Norma Rose didn't hear the door open. When she glanced up, the ink pen between her fingers snapped in two.

"Sorry, I didn't mean to startle you. I knocked, but—"

"You didn't startle me," she interrupted, trying to get air to settle in her lungs as she stared at Ty Bradshaw.

"I didn't?"

His gaze was on her hands, and she quickly looked down. Blue ink covered her white gloves, and the pad of paper full of her notes. A quick swipe at the pool trickling out of the pen smudged the entire sheet.

"Oh, good heavens," she growled.

"Here, let me help you."

"No." She pushed her chair noisily across the floor as he rounded her desk. "I don't need any help."

"Well, you certainly don't want to touch anything." Ty lifted the pad and carefully set it on the corner of her desk. Spinning back around, he grasped one of her wrists.

She tried to pull away, but his hold was too firm.

"I'll just take this glove off, you can do the other one," he said, already peeling the cuff over her wrist. "Do you always wear gloves this early in the morning?"

Norma Rose didn't answer. It was none of his business when she wore gloves. She managed to snatch her hand away before he pulled the glove all the way over her fingers. His nearness, and touch, had her heart beating inside her throat.

After peeling off both gloves, she held them carefully, not wanting to get any ink on her dress. Her hands were now blue, covering the red line of scars across her knuckles from her days of bleaching linens.

"We can talk later," Ty said, stepping away from her desk. "It's obvious you need to go and wash."

She definitely wanted to go, but curiosity made her ask, "Talk about what?"

"Your father wants me to go over a few things with you," he answered, on his way to the door.

"What things?"

Chapter Four

Ty held the door open and gestured for her to walk ahead of him. Norma Rose bit down hard on her frustration, struggling to keep everything concealed from his penetrating stare. She wanted to know what her father had talked with him about, was furious he'd ruined one of her best pairs of gloves and was more than a little perturbed that he had to look so stupidly handsome and at ease when he was clearly not welcome.

Staunchly, she refused to take a step.

He lifted a brow. "I'd think you'd want to get those gloves soaking. They'll soon be stained for life. Might already be."

"Don't worry about my gloves," she said, even though the blue ink was soaking into her skin and starting to itch.

"I'm not worried about your gloves," he said, stepping toward the open doorway. "I was hoping to talk to you before breakfast, but I guess it can wait."

He walked out the door and Norma Rose scrambled around her desk to catch up. "Talk about what?" she asked again, trying her best to sound only half-interested.

He glanced up and down the hall and lowered his voice. "It's a private matter. But don't worry, it can wait. I'll go see if the breakfast I ordered for Gloria is done yet and deliver it to her."

Instantly peeved, Norma Rose stated, "I'm not worried, and *I'll* go see to Gloria's breakfast and one for Dave."

The hand he laid on her arm had the sting of a hot curling iron.

"Dave's not up to eating yet," he said. "He's still throwing up every two hours."

The shiver that rippled down her spine couldn't be contained, not even when she held her breath.

"You go soak your gloves," he said condescendingly.

Her arm was on the verge of going numb, while her insides started to steam. She tugged her arm from his hold and, head up, strolled down the hallway.

He followed, which had Norma Rose holding her

breath at the commotion happening inside her. The man was an ogre. Since she'd laid eyes on him last night, he'd left her feeling like a string of pearls that had been snapped, sending beads flying in all directions. She didn't like it. Not at all.

In the kitchen, she dropped the gloves that had become twisted blue balls in her fists into a trash can and crossed the room to the sink, where she scrubbed her hands. Rather than cleaning them, she managed to spread the ink deeper into her skin, leaving both hands, up to her wrists, blue.

Norma Rose was close to boiling point by the time she dried her hands. Ty was talking with Moe, the assistant cook, as if they were long lost friends. No one—absolutely no one—was allowed in the kitchen, other than employees and family. Which Ty Bradshaw definitely was not.

"I'll take Gloria her breakfast when it's ready, Moe," Norma Rose said, interrupting their tête-à-tête.

"Oh." The cook's eyes shifted between Ty and her, as if he wasn't sure who was his boss.

That was enough to totally infuriate her. "How long will it be?"

"It's almost done," Moe said, flipping an egg. "I'll dish it up and put it on two trays. One for your father and one for Mrs. Kasper. Ty can carry one and you the other. It all won't fit on one, and would be too heavy for you."

Used to working with the temperamental Silas, Moe was well-versed on suggesting compromises and finding ways to please everyone. His skills were lost on her.

While Moe babbled on, Norma Rose settled her best menacing stare on Ty, who grinned like he'd just won a prize. The air she sucked in through her nose burned her nostrils. Never one to let employees see her distressed, Norma Rose smiled in return, a rather nasty little grin that made her feel an ounce better.

A few minutes later, with Moe still chatting, Ty answering amicably and her fuming, the trays were ready. Moe held open the back door and she and Ty, each carrying a tray, left the building.

"Careful of your step."

"I've walked this path for years, I know every stone."

"That coming from a woman with blue hands, or was today the first time you used an ink pen?"

Norma Rose kept her lips pinched together. He truly thought he was humorous. Poor man. She'd soon be the one laughing, watching him drive his old jalopy down the driveway. Her father must be worried about Dave and not have seen through Ty yet. He'd soon see everything, especially when she pointed out a few things. Like the fact Ty was most likely a revenue man looking for evidence to turn them in.

Upon arriving at the cabin, Ty shifted his tray to one hand and opened the door. Her overly sensitive nose caught the scent of vomit immediately and it turned her insides green.

"Norma Rose, you won't want to come in here," Gloria said, appearing in the open doorway. "She's highly sensitive to some things," the woman told Ty.

Norma Rose threatened herself with severe repercussions if a single part of her body reacted to the stench now threatening to overcome her.

"She insisted on carrying a tray," Ty said.

"Well, you should have stopped her," her father said, stepping around Gloria. "Take that tray inside, Ty, and Gloria, you take this one," he added, lifting the tray from Norma Rose's hand. "I'll be there in a minute."

The other two entered the cabin, and shut the door behind them. It didn't help much—the stench had already settled in Norma Rose's nostrils. Her father led her to the edge of the grass, where Ty's Model T with New York license plates sat next to Dave's Chevrolet. Ty's truck certainly didn't match his expensive outfit. Further proof he wasn't who he said he was.

"Have you come up with any suspects yet?" her father asked.

Holding a finger against the bottom of her nose, breathing in air that hinted of ink, she withheld her anger and her suspicions and asked, "Suspects for what?"

"Poisoning Dave." Her father shook his head, but replaced the grimace on his face with a slight grin. "Wood alcohol. Gloria says it wasn't too bad. That being so allergic may have saved his life. He might not even lose his sight."

"Lose his sight?" A wave of sorrow washed away some of Norma Rose's animosity. "Oh, goodness. But Dave doesn't drink," she ventured, searching for understanding.

"They slipped it in one of those milk shakes he loves so much."

"At a drugstore?"

He nodded. "Suspect so."

Understanding bobbed to the surface of her cloudy mind. "That's where he met Ty—Mr. Bradshaw."

"That was at noon. Gloria said it had to have been later than that."

"We don't know it was noon for sure," she argued.

"I do," he said sternly. "Dave rode to town with Ace Walker. I talked to Ace last night—he said he and Dave met up again around six and drove over to St. Paul to Charlie's store. I talked to Charlie, too. He said he personally made Dave a milk shake before Dave went into the back room to meet with a prospect." Her father's frown increased. "What did you do to your hands?"

There was nothing she could do to stop the heat that rushed to her cheeks. "An ink pen broke," she answered, wringing her hands together. "Who was the prospect?"

"I don't know. Charlie doesn't, either, nor Ace. Whoever it was, he was just a front man."

"What does Dave say?"

Her father glanced over his shoulder. "It may be a while before he can talk. Gloria had to put a tube into his stomach to flush it all out."

Norma Rose flinched. She honestly hadn't thought Dave was that ill last night, and regret that she'd been so callous at the police station made her stomach flip. "Goodness" was all she could say.

"Rosie, I normally don't involve you in this side of the business, but in this instance, I need your help."

It had been a long time since she had seen this kind of worry on her father's face. Although that concerned her, it didn't affect her answer. There wasn't anything she wouldn't do for him and the resort. "Of course," she said. "What do you need me to do?"

"You can start by going through the guest lists for the parties for the next two weekends," he said. "I have a gut feeling one of them has something to do with this. So does Ty."

Unable to control the flare of anger that erupted inside her, Norma Rose huffed out a breath. Her father cast an uncompromising look her way and she kept her opinion to herself. She didn't give a hoot what Ty thought. "I'll start going through the list immediately and let you know what I find."

"Not me—Ty. He'll fill me in."

She had to comment on how that grated her nerves. "I don't believe we should be involving someone else in this. Especially a stranger."

Not one to have his decisions questioned, Roger's lips tightened. "Do you think I'd have him here if I didn't trust him?"

Norma Rose squared her shoulders, prepared to explain that before last night none of them had known Ty existed, but she didn't get a chance to open her mouth.

"I spent half the night checking out his background. I can tell you what time that young man was born and what he's done every moment of every day since."

Still not impressed, Norma Rose stood by her guns. "He's not a lawyer."

"I never said he was."

"*He* did," she snapped. "He showed up at the police station like he'd—"

"And that's exactly what we're going to let others believe," her father said, interrupting her. "That he's one of our lawyers."

"Why?"

"Don't question me on this, Rosie, just do as I tell you. That's all the information you need to know." He hooked his thumbs on the straps of his suspenders and stretched, as he always did to signal the conversation at hand was over. Over in his eyes anyway.

To Norma Rose, the conversation was far from over. Though her father liked to believe she didn't know about all of the businesses he was involved in, she did, and she was also smart enough to understand that now wasn't the time to admit that, or to insist he tell her more. "Your breakfast is getting cold," she said. "I'll go through the list and let Mr. Bradshaw know if I discover anything."

Her father shook his head slowly, as if disappointed. "Ty will go through the list with you, and you, young lady, will be nice to him. I don't want anyone getting suspicious. I want them to think we've known Ty for years."

She pinched her lips together to keep from asking why. It had been years since her father had reprimanded her, but now it left her seeing red. It hurt, too, although she wouldn't admit that, not even to herself.

"And Rosie," her father said, already making his way toward Dave's cabin, "put on a pair of gloves. Your hands look terrible."

Fuming, Norma Rose marched back to the resort's main building, where she ventured upstairs to her room to retrieve a new pair of gloves, all the while trying not to become overwhelmed by the emotions bubbling inside her. The resort consumed her life, it had for years, and right now she was questioning why. If a stranger could magically appear and her father instantly let him in, pushing her and all her hard work aside, why did she let it?

Because it was her life.

With renewed determination burning, she pulled open a dresser drawer. Her dress was black with white sequins, so she chose black gloves this time and changed her white shoes to black ones.

That all completed, she headed back downstairs toward her office, still madder than she remembered being for some time. She'd go through the lists as requested, but not with Ty Bradshaw hanging over her shoulder. Many of the partygoers for Palooka George's bash had already made reservations, and she personally had set up the accommodations. Names were ticking through her head and not one raised a red flag.

Concentrating hard, she barely noticed her surroundings until she arrived at her office door, which was open. The sight inside made her nostrils flare.

Ty Bradshaw stood in front of her desk, next to the window that overlooked the parking lot, where she often watched the coming and going of guests. He turned around as she entered.

"I had Moe make us breakfast, as well," he said,

gesturing toward the table under the window. "He assured me you haven't eaten yet, either."

Norma Rose tried to tell herself her heart was beating so hard and fast because she was mad. Furious in fact. That was also the reason her palms had chosen to break out in a sweat. It truly had nothing to do with the single wild rose sticking out of the narrow vase in the center of the table, and it had absolutely nothing to do with how gallant Ty Bradshaw looked as he pulled back one of the two chairs and indicated she should take a seat. Without his suit jacket, his rolled-up shirt sleeves revealed thick and well-muscled arms, and the black suspenders clipped to his pants framed an impressively flat stomach and narrow hips.

She'd never doubted that with the right clothes, even a rat could look good. That's what he was, and she'd expose his hairy tail before the day was out. He might have pulled the wool over her father's eyes for the time being, but not hers. This man was trouble. And she'd find a way to prove it.

Then again, most rats, due to their greed, eventually exposed themselves. All she had to do was give him the opportunity.

"Moe said you like poached eggs," he said, once again nodding toward the chair he held.

He was sly, already befriending Moe and goodness knows who else. Rats could have silver tongues, too. Her father had told her to be nice to him, and she would be. In public. In private, she'd let him know just how she felt about him and his lies.

"I'm not hungry," she said, making a direct line toward her desk.

He rounded the table and sat in the other chair. "I am." Lifting the silver lid off his plate, he added, "And this smells wonderful."

Her stomach chose that moment to growl, loudly. Ignoring it and the wide grin on Ty's face as he cut his sausage into bite-size pieces, she sat and pulled open the desk drawer that held several leatherbound books.

"No one," she said pointedly, "enters my office without my permission. Remember that."

"Note taken," he said.

The glimmer in his brown eyes said he didn't take her seriously. A mistake he'd soon regret.

"Next weekend we have Al and Emma Imhoff's twenty-fifth wedding anniversary," she said. "Big Al, as all the locals know him, owns the car dealership in White Bear Lake and most of the guests, other than a few family members coming from out of town, are local folks."

"Any luck with coming up with a musician for that night?" he asked, taking a bite of toast.

Her stomach growled again, and twisted at his smugness. The fact that her father had told Ty twice as much as he'd told her burned.

"No," she said. "Therefore, the sooner we get through the guest lists, the sooner I can get back to work that needs to be done."

He touched his lips with his napkin and laid it down before saying, "You say that as if you believe going through the lists will be a waste of time."

She didn't want to notice such things—the way he used his napkin, how he'd held the chair. Manners like that couldn't be taught overnight, they were instilled from childhood, a fact that made her curious. She wasn't overly impressed by her curiosity. "It is a waste of time, Mr. Bradshaw."

He poured coffee out of the silver warming pot into his cup. "So, you've lived here, at the resort, your entire life?"

"That," she said, leaning back to cross her arms, "is none of your business. Furthermore, there is no need for small talk. I have a lot of work to do today."

"I know," he said, sipping from his cup. "Finding a replacement for Brock Ness."

Irritated she didn't have some small tidbit of information about him to toss back, she leaned forward and flipped open her registration book. "Among other things."

He set his cup down. "The Plantation pulls in some good performers, maybe they'd—"

"I don't need any help from the Plantation," she snapped. Forrest Reynolds was right next to Ty Bradshaw on her list of people she'd never ask assistance from.

"All right," he said, pushing away from the table. In less than five steps, he'd rounded her desk, where he carefully moved aside her phone and sat on the corner. His long legs, angled to the floor, completely blocked her in. "Let me see the ledger then."

His closeness disrupted her breathing, and the air that did manage to enter her nose was full of his aftershave. A woodsy, novel scent she wished was far more offensive. Norma Rose hadn't got over all that, or come up with a response, when Moe walked in the door she'd left open.

"How was breakfast?" the cook asked. "You liked it, no?"

"Yes," Ty answered. "It was very good, Moe. Just as you said it would be."

The cook, having already put Ty's empty plate on the silver tray he carried, lifted the lid off Norma Rose's plate and shook his head. "Rosie, you didn't eat your eggs."

"I—"

"She's been busy," Ty answered. He lifted the ledger off her desk. "Set it here, Moe, she can eat it now."

Moe set her plate before her and laid out silverware on a napkin while she glared at Ty for interrupting her. He, of course, was smiling.

"Eat before it gets cold," Moe said. "Can't have any wasted food."

A growl rolled around in Norma Rose's throat. She was a stickler for not wasting food, not wasting anything, and the cook knew it. Ty's grin said he knew it, too.

She grabbed her fork, and almost choked on her first bite when Ty said, "Close the door, would you please, Moe?"

The cook had already complied by the time she'd swallowed and Ty was flipping through pages. Head down, he swiftly ran a finger down the page of names she'd painstakingly written out on each line.

Glancing her way without lifting his head, he said, "Don't mind me. I'll read the lists while you eat."

She minded, all right—minded every little detail about him, but she ate, washing down the cold poached eggs and soggy toast with gulps of orange juice.

As she set down her empty glass, he asked, "How many employees do you have?"

The change of subject didn't surprise her and she suspected he already knew. He'd obviously taken the time to learn everything there was to know. "You tell me," she said, pushing her plate to the far edge of her desk.

"Counting you and your three sisters, fifty-two, and most of them live within a few miles of the resort."

Brushing crumbs off her gloves—which she normally removed while eating—she said, "You seem to have gathered a lot of information from my father in a very short time."

He flipped another page. "You forget I had lunch with Dave yesterday."

That didn't bother her nearly as much as it had

last night. Whatever Dave may have told him couldn't compare to the way her father had already taken Ty into his confidence. She took the book from his hand and laid it on her desk. "I don't forget anything. Ever." Meeting his gaze, she added, "And I know you are not a lawyer."

"You're right," he said, twisting to rest a hand on her desk so he could continue to scan the names listed in the book. "I'm not."

Norma Rose waited for him to continue, needing the time to get her nerves in order. Dang but he smelled good. Too good. And he was way too close. The hair on her arms was standing at attention. She jerked back, putting some space between them. "What are you doing here?"

"Looking over the guest lists."

"No. What are you doing *here*?"

He sat up straight, and leveled his gaze on her. He was good at that, looking her directly in the eyes, unlike most men, whose eyes often wandered. For the first time, that bothered her. There wasn't anything about him, not a single iota, she wanted to like.

"I'm a private investigator," he said.

A private eye. She'd heard of private detectives but never met one before, so she couldn't say if he looked the part or not. Waiting for more, she arched her brows.

Ty grinned, as if he found her reaction funny. "I can't say anything more than that. I will tell you that after checking out of my hotel, the Fairmont, yesterday, I happened upon your uncle at the drugstore. Later, while exploring the city, I visited the Blind Bull. I was there when I heard the police sirens and went outside to investigate. I recognized your uncle as they loaded him in the car and went to the police station to see if I could help."

Norma Rose couldn't say she was convinced he was telling the truth, but she couldn't be sure he wasn't, either. Which was strange. Her intuition usually picked up on things relatively quickly. The Fairmont was in St. Paul, but anyone driving past the four-story building could have picked up the name, and Dave had probably stopped at several drugstores yesterday. They were popping up faster than gas stations. Many of the drugstores were nothing more than fronts for speakeasies, as were grocery stores and hardware stores. There was even a telephone booth on Nicolette Avenue in Minneapolis with a hidden door that led people into a speakeasy. She hadn't seen it, and wondered how it worked.

The Blind Bull was along the riverfront, near the stockyards, which were next to the rail yard, and hosted a restaurant as its cover.

"Can we go over these lists, now?" Ty asked. "I have other work to do, and so do you."

She wanted to ask what else he had to do, but chose not to bother. The quicker he left her office, the better off she'd be. For several reasons. Number one because she'd never get to the bottom of why he was here sitting on her desk.

He flipped a few more pages, stopping on the page she'd titled Palooka George's Party, alongside the date. Using a finger, he started going down the list. "Hmm…"

"Hmm what?"

He pointed to a name. "Leonard Buckly, that's Loose Lenny, and this—" he pointed to another name a little farther down the page "—Alan Page, that's Mumbles. This here, Alvin Page, is his brother, Hammer."

Unable to deny the tick of excitement flaring inside her, Norma Rose asked, "Do you think they had something to do with Uncle Dave's poisoning?"

"I don't know, but I do know they're Chicago mobsters who'd love to get their hands on some

Minnesota action." He moved his finger a few lines down. "So would these guys. Gorgeous Gordy, Hugo the Hand, Flashy Bobby Blade, Nasty Nick Ludwig. Huh, last I heard he was still in jail." He let out a low whistle. "Shady Shelia and Nellie Ringer—those are two hard-hearted dames."

Norma Rose balled her hands into fists to keep them from trembling. She knew the list contained a few gangsters, but the names he'd rattled off were more than she expected. And they were well-known. Even she'd heard of them. Worse yet, she'd met some of them, not by the names Ty was using, but by the names she'd written in the ledger. The very names he was pointing at. A different sort of thrill shot through her.

Mobsters were followed as closely as celebrities and baseball players. To many people, they weren't outlaws. Some considered them modern-day Robin Hoods. Except, instead of stealing from the rich and giving to the poor, they were getting one over on the government for Prohibition, and people liked that.

When Forrest's father, Galen Reynolds, had run the Plantation, proclaimed gangsters had visited the place all the time. Roger Nightingale didn't believe in such tactics, but the names Ty rattled off weren't local thugs, they were big-time gangsters from Chicago and New York. They were men who had money, and spent it. People liked that, too.

"What other names do you recognize?" she asked.

"Two-shot Malone," Ty said. "One for the head and one for the heart. Knuckles Page, Roy Ruger, Fast Eddie, Smiling Jack, Point Black Luigi, Sylvester the Sly, Fire Iron Frank, Boyd the Brander."

She was memorizing the names as they leaned over the page, head-to-head. Her heart was pounding, too, beating harder with each move of his finger. Some of these people sounded dangerous, and listening to him describe them was, well, exciting.

"Cold Heart Sam, Evil Ernie, Tony the Tamer, Gunman Gunther—"

"Where is Ginger?"

Norma Rose snapped her head up at the sound of her sister's voice.

"It's her day to wash." Twyla walked into the room, but stopped when her gaze landed on Ty. Her eyes grew wide and a full-blown smile curled her bright red lips. "Hello." She stepped closer, holding out a hand. "I'm Twyla Nightingale, and you are?"

"Ty Bradshaw," he answered, straightening enough to shake Twyla's hand over the desk.

Norma Rose wanted to moan. Twyla never ignored the opportunity to meet a man. Any man. They were usually excited to meet her, too, until they learned who her father was.

Lifting a heavily painted brow at Norma Rose, Twyla indicated her interest in the rather intimate way Ty sat on the corner of the desk.

"I don't know where Ginger is," Norma Rose said coldly. She could attempt to explain who Ty was and what they were doing, but it would be a waste of breath. Her sisters were not interested in the resort, at least not the management of it. "Maybe she isn't up yet."

"Not up yet? She'd better be," Twyla said. "It's almost nine."

That was surprising. Mainly because it meant the past two hours had flown by. "Did you check her room?" Norma Rose asked.

"Of course I checked her room," Twyla said, rolling her eyes at Ty to demonstrate how silly she thought that question was. "She's not there."

"Maybe she's already cleaning cabins," Norma Rose suggested. Ginger was far more responsible than Twyla. It would have made more sense if Ginger had been the one standing in her office now. Then again, Ginger wouldn't look for Twyla, she'd just go about getting her chores done. And unlike Twyla, Ginger wouldn't wear what Twyla had on to do laundry—a bright pink, rather short dress, with a white silk scarf tied around her neck and white shoes with square heels. The very shoes Norma Rose had been wearing earlier. "I hope you don't plan on washing sheets in that outfit. You'll ruin it with a drop of bleach."

"It's not my day to wash. I just have to sweep floors and make beds," Twyla said, walking across the room to peek out the window. "It's Ginger's day to wash."

Norma Rose knew Twyla was showing off her dress, and legs, to Ty with her little strut, and it more than irritated her. "Ginger's probably already doing laundry. Now go change and start your chores."

"I can work in this," Twyla said, smoothing her hands down her side to rest on her hips. "It's Saturday and I'm going to the amusement park as soon as I've completed my chores."

"The amusement park doesn't open until noon," Norma Rose reminded her before pointing toward the door. "You have three hours of cleaning to do before then. And don't complain to me if you ruin that dress."

"What about Ginger?"

"Don't worry about Ginger," Norma Rose said.

"She'll be along shortly if she's not already there." Recalling she needed Ginger's help herself, she added, "When you do see her, tell her I want to talk to her."

"About being late?" Twyla asked hopefully.

"I told you not to worry about her," Norma Rose said. "Now go, and shut the door behind you." She waited until Twyla was almost out the door before she said, "And put my shoes back where you found them."

Twyla, in the midst of sending a very encouraging look toward Ty over her shoulder, smiled sweetly. "My white shoes got stained last weekend."

Norma Rose couldn't say why his look, that clearly said, "I'm not interested but will smile just to please you," made her as happy as it did. Smiling herself, she said, "Then find some polish and clean them. After you've put mine back in my room, and after you've completed your chores."

Twyla, looking deflated at Ty's lack of interest and being unable to get Ginger in trouble, shut the door with a thud.

Norma Rose reached past Ty. "Excuse me." She slid the phone under the arm he still had stretched across her desk and picked up the receiver.

Chapter Five

Ty had never fought this hard to keep a smile hidden. He'd discovered plenty about all four Nightingale girls, but meeting them was becoming an adventure. Twyla was a year or so younger than Norma Rose, twenty-three or -four, if he remembered rightly, which he normally did. The other girls were blonde, but Twyla had dyed her hair bright red, which looked good on her, as did the little pink dress that showed a good portion of finely shaped legs. Like her sisters, Twyla was a looker, and the devilish twinkle in her bright blue eyes could curl the hair on a man's chest. Nightingale must have his work cut out for him keeping the men all in line.

"Thelma, ring Walter's phone, please," Norma Rose said into the phone.

Every cabin and room at the resort had a phone, a highly expensive amenity. There was also a switchboard and operator just a few doors down the hall. Ty leaned back, wondering why she'd called the man who oversaw the gardeners and night watchmen. Moe, the cook, was a talker. In a conversation that lasted less than five minutes, Ty had learned who worked where and how long they'd been at the resort.

"Walter. It's Norma Rose. I want the keys removed from all the cars in the garage." She paused before answering, "Yes, even my father's. Bring them to my office."

Ty laughed, but cut it short at the little glare she cast his way. It appeared Roger didn't keep the Nightingale girls under control. Norma Rose did. In a way, that made him look forward to meeting the other two, Josie and Ginger.

His good sense kicked in, telling him he wasn't here to meet any of Roger Nightingale's daughters. Norma Rose was more than enough. He'd been careful with what he'd told her, and how he'd said it. Roger Nightingale was a smart businessman, but his daughter was intuitive. Norma Rose would be able to see through a lie with her eyes closed.

Bodine's name hadn't been on the list, at least not under any of the aliases he'd used in the past. Bodine had been known to associate with a few on the list, but Ty couldn't say if he still did. The mobster had a way of burning bridges.

"So," Norma Rose said, pushing the phone aside. "Are you a federal agent?"

The question was so unexpected, Ty was startled. The hair on the back of his neck rose. He combated the prickly sensation by shifting and sitting up straighter, and then he changed the subject. "Do your sisters steal cars on a regular basis?"

Leaning back in her chair, Norma Rose crossed her arms and eyed him pointedly with those no-nonsense blue eyes. "No, because I stay one step ahead of them."

"What about your father?"

"What about him?"

"Does he stay one step ahead of your sisters, too?"

"He doesn't have to," she said. "He has me to do that, and we're not just talking about my sisters."

Ty wanted to stand, maybe walk over and look out the window, but he knew she'd catch his unease. He glanced back to the ledger. "Is this everyone?"

She didn't sigh, or make any such sound, nor did she move, but he felt her inward shift as she tried to decipher him. He'd been up against mobsters who couldn't make him sweat and he could hold his own against her, too. It had taken him too long to get to where he was to jeopardize it all over a woman.

The sound of morning birds calling to one another filtered in through the open window, thickening the silence between him and Norma Rose. They'd come to a standoff. She wasn't going to answer any more questions from him until he answered hers. Ty wasn't impressed that he'd let it get to this point. He was usually more on top of things. Since entering her office, he'd spent more time admiring how fine she looked in that black-and-white sequined dress than keeping his focus on the prize. Which was Bodine. Not Norma Rose Nightingale.

"My position here needs to remain a secret," he said, sitting up and meeting her solid gaze with his own.

"So you are a federal agent."

"I'm a private investigator," he said quietly and glanced around for good measure. "To everyone else, I'm a lawyer. Your Uncle Dave's lawyer."

Norma Rose was rubbing her hands together and thinking. Definitely thinking. Lifting her chin slightly, she asked, "What are you investigating?"

Ty was slightly disappointed she'd given up so easily. He liked a challenging adversary. He just had to keep reminding himself that was not Norma Rose. "I believe someone may have poisoned Dave last night in order to kidnap him."

"Kidnap him? What for?"

He lifted a brow. She knew why gangsters kidnapped people.

She nodded, accepting his silent acknowledgment. "Who?"

Glancing toward the ledger again, he said, "You tell me."

Rising from her chair, she walked around her desk, her heels clicking evenly until she stopped near the window, leaned over the small table and pulled the curtain aside to peer out. Ty found himself appraising her again. Admiring her legs and the seam of her nylons that rose out of her shoes and disappeared beneath her skirt. His inspection continued upward, over her shapely derriere and subtly curved spine.

She let loose the curtain and turned, and he was glad he had his eyes on her face at that point. Norma Rose did not like to be ogled. She'd made that clear last night when the police chief couldn't keep his eyes above her shoulders. Ty also had a hell of a time keeping his eyes where they belonged, then and now.

"No one," she said with a hint of skepticism, "would attempt to kidnap my uncle. Especially not someone on that list." Gesturing toward the ledger with a gloved hand, she continued, "Whether those are their real names or not, the people on that list wouldn't risk losing my father's—" she paused as if searching for the right word "—friendship."

Why was he pussyfooting around? He wouldn't with anyone else. "Your father's a bootlegger," he pointed out.

Her gasp said more than words ever could have. She caught herself, though, and held back her glare. "He is not."

Getting a rise out of her kicked his heart into a faster speed. Yet, once again, Ty simply raised a brow.

"Prove it," she challenged.

"I don't have to." Ty slid off the desk, but only to pivot around and sit in her chair, where he leaned back. "I already know it."

Her cheeks flared red, and he'd say the reasons for that blush were spilt fifty-fifty. Fifty percent concern at her father's profession and fifty percent anger at him for relaxing in her chair. He considered resting a foot on her desk, but that might be taking things too far.

Stiffening her spine, Norma Rose planted both hands on the slight inner curve of her hips. "Not an ounce of liquor has ever been sold at this resort." Catching herself, she added, "Not since Prohibition."

He let out an exaggerated guffaw.

She paced in front of the desk, heels clicking on the wood and her breath came out in little huffs as she glared at him. "My grandfather used to make wine, lots of it, from everything. Grapes, cherries, apples, even dandelions. The basement of our house was full of it, and people came from miles around to have a glass of Nightingale wine."

This time Ty let out a real laugh, cutting it short only because she pinched her lips tight. "Do you expect me to believe the only alcohol you have at the resort is some old wine your grandfather made?"

Her eyelids fluttered shut and the deep breath she took made her shoulders rise and her ample breasts more prominent. Ty allowed himself time to examine her, knowing she was thinking hard to come up with an excuse he'd believe, but made sure his eyes were on hers when her lids lifted.

"That's not what I said." Lifting her chin, she let out a long sigh, and set a hand on her flat stomach. "The Eighteenth Amendment was passed in 1919, however, it didn't go into effect until 1920."

Although he didn't need a history lesson, and knew more about the Eighteenth Amendment and the Volstead Act than she ever would, he nodded.

"My father," she continued, "was—is—a very enterprising man. A smart one. Since he worked for the Hamm's Brewery at the time, he bought up several cases of liquor."

Ty rubbed a hand over his mouth to keep his smile hidden.

"For private consumption, of course," she added staunchly.

"Of course," he agreed. "Private consumption."

"Yes. It's perfectly legal to possess and consume alcohol."

"As long as you have a doctor's prescription," Ty added.

She bristled again. "The law clearly states it's the manufacturing, transportation and selling of intoxicating liquors that is illegal. We do none of those."

He had no doubt she knew the entire amendment inside and out, and wasn't about to hash out the intricate details, yet he couldn't help challenging her. "So, you're telling me all the alcohol consumed here is by friends and family? Private consumption?"

With her chin still hoisted, she said, "Not a single drink has ever been sold. I have receipts for every dime this place has taken in, and for what. I can show them if you'd like."

He'd bet she did. The resort did the same thing as most taverns and speakeasies. They had cover charges. Most places claimed the money was paid to see a blind pig or other such phenomenon or for the hors d'oeuvres provided, but no one went to those places just to eat, and no one really wanted to see a blind pig. But, in all the years he'd been chasing down gangsters, he'd never met a man who'd refuse a drink because it was illegal.

Roger Nightingale was an enterprising man. The resort was an upscale establishment. An evening's cover charge included a meal and entertainment. Even the lodging cost included "complimentary" drinks, and the prices Nightingale charged called to the high rollers. A man would spend whatever it takes, as long as he's getting what he wants—such as the real stuff the resort poured into their highball glasses. No branch water or rotgut. Beer was served here, too, which was highly unusual. Nightingale may have purchased several cases of liquor way back when, but he went through several cases a night, and had done so for years.

Which was why Ty was here. Bodine wanted the real stuff. The heat was on for those running it from Canada. Nightingale's gold mine had been one of the best kept secrets, and it still was in many ways. It was a place you had to know about. Ty wasn't sure how Bodine had found out, but Ty had discovered it listening to two of Bodine's front men in Chicago over a month ago.

Bodine's men had talked about their orders to find a way into Nightingale's closed group, and Ty had no doubt they would. Kidnapping Dave would have done it, but that seemed to have failed.

Ty stood. Bodine's name wasn't on that list, which meant he had a bit more investigating to do. Walking around the desk, he winked at Norma Rose. "Save your receipts for someone who cares, doll."

Her cheeks flared red once again. Getting her frustrated was so easy. Fun, too.

He pulled open the door, but she hit it with one hand, slamming it shut. Glaring, she growled, "Don't ever call me doll."

There was more than frustration on her face; this was flat-out anger, but a knock on the door prevented Ty from contemplating her reaction for too long. He lifted a brow, silently asking if he could open the door.

She stepped back and nodded.

A portly man, with wide suspenders holding up his britches and a flat felt hat covering his head, held out one hand. "Got the keys for you, Miss Nightingale."

Instantly prim and proper again—at least on the outside—Norma Rose took the keys. "Thank you, Walter." Maintaining her businesslike attitude, she marched around her desk and dropped the keys in the top drawer. "I'll need you to send a few men over to the farmhouse. We have guests who'll be arriving next week and I'd like the bushes trimmed and lawn mowed before then."

"Yes, miss, I'll see to it right away."

Ty's mind clicked like the cogs of a wheel lining up. He'd seen the farmhouse, located on the other side of a thick row of trees several yards behind the barn, but had assumed the family occupied it, even though he knew they all had rooms on the upper floors of the main building. "You rent out the house, too?" he asked, once Walter had left, and shut the door behind him.

"Yes," Norma Rose snapped. "Why shouldn't we?"

"I didn't say you shouldn't," he remarked.

"We rent it out on a weekly basis only, mainly to families," she said. "It has its own boathouse and beach."

"Who is renting it?"

Although she clearly didn't want to, she pulled another ledger down from a shelf on the wall and flipped through several pages before stopping. "Ralph Brandon and his family from Green Bay. They'll be arriving by train…"

Ty stopped listening. Ralph Brandon. That was a name he hadn't heard in a while. Ray Bodine had used it in upstate New York a few years ago, shortly before another man, positively identified as Ralph Brandon, had been found dead. Bodine wasn't on the guest list because he planned on already being at the resort when George's party took place. Spinning around, Ty headed for the door again.

"Just for the record, Mr. Bradshaw," Norma Rose said. "I don't believe anything about you. Not your tale about being a private investigator, or your story about Uncle Dave being a kidnapping target." Lifting the corners of her rose-red lips, she added, "I believe only a federal agent would know all those names you mentioned."

With one hand on the doorknob, he glanced over his shoulder. "Believe what you like."

Her stare was direct and cold. "I will, and I will see you are off this property by the end of the day."

Opening the door, he stepped into the hallway, but turned to face her. "Save a dance for me, will you?"

Her stoic expression dipped in a moment of confusion. "What—what are you talking about?"

"Find a good band for Palooka George's party," he said. "So you and I can wear a hole in the rug."

Lips tight, she brushed her skirt beneath her as she lowered herself onto her chair. "Our dance floor is made of wood, and I never dance. Not with anyone."

"One more thing I'll have to change," he said, pulling the door closed.

Norma Rose held her gloved hands tightly together, to keep the trembling at bay. That man infuriated her, and frightened her in a way she'd never been scared before. That was a hard thing to admit, even to herself.

He'd never answered her question, but inside, she knew he was a federal agent. He had to be. The Volstead Act was held up by the feds. Local boys only had to worry about state laws, which were much more lenient. She dealt with plenty of local authorities, but he'd be her first federal one. That had to be why he affected her so.

Dancing? Posh! He'd soon learn she was no doxy. She wouldn't be pursued or swayed by any man. Plenty had tried over the years. Ty couldn't frighten her, either, by naming all those gangsters like he had. For all she knew he was lying. Big-time New York and Chicago gangsters had no reason to visit Minnesota.

Unsettled, she rose and walked to the window. The barn stood directly across the parking lot. Besides the cabin that had been torn down long ago, that barn had been the first thing her great-grandfather built on the property. That was when the land had been part of the Wisconsin Territory, before becoming part of the Minnesota Territory in 1849. The rocky ground wasn't easy to work and farming hadn't paid off very well for her ancestors. Her grandfather, having lived most of his life trying to draw money from the land, had taken another approach. He'd built a dance pavilion and then cabins, when the dances became popular.

Just five years ago, the resort had been nothing more than that little pavilion and the run-down cabins. Norma Rose had been a major player in the resort's renovation since the day her father had re-opened the place, and she wasn't about to let some no-good revenue man take it all away from her.

Ty appeared in her line of vision, almost as if she'd conjured him up. He was walking toward the barn. She took a step back, just in case he turned around and saw her.

All the snooping in the world wouldn't reveal a thing. As she'd told Ty, her father was a smart man. There was no tax evasion going on here, and the other activities were so concealed a mole couldn't unearth them.

"Norma Rose."

She spun around as her door opened once again. This time it was Josie. "Have you seen Ginger or Twyla? I have a ladies meeting this afternoon and will surely be late if I have to do everything by myself."

Josie lived for the Bald Eagle Ladies Aid Society. Norma Rose didn't mind her sister's involvement, except when it interfered with things that needed to be done at the resort. "I thought your meetings were on Tuesday."

"They normally are. This is a special meeting because we're creating the decorations for Emma Imhoff's anniversary." Wearing a pair of plaid pants and a loose-fitting white shirt, which she proclaimed was the perfect outfit for cleaning cabins, Josie entered the room. Soft-spoken and generally agreeable—apart from when it came to missing one of her meetings—Josie continued, "Ruth and Frances have been coddling their roses so they'll be at their best next weekend. We plan on making lace doilies to put beneath each vase and—"

"No," Norma Rose interrupted. She was thankful Josie had an eye for decorating when it came to special events, but she didn't need the details. "I haven't seen Ginger. Twyla was looking for her earlier. Have you asked her?"

"The last time I saw Twyla, she was in our bathroom, trying to pierce her ears again." Josie shrugged. "She might have succeeded this time. There was blood in the sink when I looked in there again a few minutes ago."

Norma Rose puffed out a heavy breath. Keeping up with her sisters was exhausting. "I told her she's not allowed to have pierced ears."

"So?"

Bristling from head to toe, Norma Rose marched to the door. "I'll find them."

Josie followed, explaining that she'd finished the guest rooms upstairs, and was now on her way to the cabins. They parted in the back hall, where a whimpering sound had Norma Rose heading toward the kitchen, where she found Twyla—still wearing the pink dress and *her* white shoes—red-eyed and holding a piece of ice to one earlobe.

Moe fussed around Twyla, patting her shoulder.

Norma Rose felt little, if any, empathy. "Go and change your clothes and get to work."

"I can't," Twyla sobbed. "I'm bleeding."

One well-aimed glare had Moe stepping back. Norma Rose grabbed Twyla's hand and pulled it away from her ear. "No, you're not." Snatching the ice, she threw it in the sink. "Now go."

Claiming their father would hear about this, a red-faced Twyla climbed off the stool and ran to the door.

"I told her she should have put the ice on her ear before poking the needle through it," Moe said.

Norma Rose wasn't interested in Twyla's ear,

or worried about their father hearing about anything—Norma Rose had pretty much been in
charge of raising her sisters after their mother had
died of influenza. She made no comment as she
left the room, now in search of Ginger. Both Twyla
and Josie would be mad when Norma Rose found
their youngest sister and engaged her aid in finding suitable musicians for the next two weekends,
rather than sending her to help them with chores.

So be it. They were mad at her more often than
not. Norma Rose was always the odd one out. The
other three giggled amongst themselves, shared
clothes and jewelry and cosmetics. It was just as
well; she didn't have time to shop for new things
when they lost or damaged her loaned items and
she certainly didn't want anything to do with the
way they always mooned over some man—local
or celebrity.

Finding Ginger proved impossible. Norma Rose
checked everywhere, twice, thinking maybe they'd
crossed paths somewhere along the line. It wasn't
like Ginger to shrug off chores. No one had seen
her, not since the previous night when she'd been
crouched near the stairway leading from the ballroom, watching Brock play. Norma Rose had seen

her then, too, and had sent her to bed. That wasn't unusual. Just a nightly occurrence.

By noon, fully flustered, because she didn't have time for this, Norma Rose sought out her father. He was still at Dave's cabin, having not left all morning. After asking about her uncle, who was sleeping and doing well from what Gloria said, Norma Rose inquired, "Have either of you seen Ginger?"

"No, Twyla was here, though," her father said, grinning at Gloria. "Why?"

"I'd like her to go through a list of possible musicians."

"Maybe she went to town," Gloria suggested.

"All of the cars are accounted for," Norma Rose answered, not bothering to mention that no one went to town without her permission.

Not one to miss anything, her father lifted a brow. "Twyla?"

"It's Saturday," Norma Rose answered. "She wants to go to the amusement park this afternoon. The keys are all in my office."

Her father nodded.

"She'll be lucky if that ear doesn't end up good and infected," Gloria said. "I'll have to pierce the other one for her, so she can wear a pair of earrings instead of looking like a pirate."

Her father chuckled and nodded. Norma Rose was in no mood for the humor flashing between Gloria and her father. She'd said no pierced ears and she meant it. At times, it felt like she was the only one who understood how important it was that none of the Nightingale girls became molls. They were a respectable family, and would remain so.

Heading for the doorway, she said, "If you see Ginger, please send her to my office right away."

"Hold up there, Rosie," her father said. "You really can't find her?"

"I've looked everywhere," she answered.

"That's not like Ginger," her father said.

A tiny shiver tickled her spine. "I know. It seems no one's seen her since last night."

Saying it aloud and seeing the way her father's face grew grim increased the shiver rippling down Norma Rose's spine.

Rising to his feet, Roger pulled his maroon vest down over his thickening waist. "Where's Ty?"

"Last time I saw him, he was heading toward the barn, but that was before I started looking for Ginger," Norma Rose said half-heartedly, irked by the way her father said the name so familiarly.

"Roger, you aren't thinking—" Gloria began.

"Yes, I am," her father interrupted.

For all Norma Rose knew, Ginger hadn't even met Ty yet, so she struggled to gather what her father might be thinking. He didn't encourage any of his girls to date, so that couldn't—

"If someone tried kidnapping Dave, and failed," he said, "they could have taken Ginger."

Chapter Six

"We don't want to jump to conclusions," Ty said.

"If Ginger was kidnapped, we have to call the sheriff, and notify the police in the city," Norma Rose argued. "They can search and—"

"Hush down, Rosie," her father snapped before instantly turning his attention back to Ty. "Now, you were saying?"

"First we need to figure out the places where Ginger definitely is not," Ty said.

"Here," Norma Rose interjected. "I've checked everywhere. Don't you think it's a bit coincidental that we've never had any such happenings before, but as soon as Mr. Bradshaw appears we have not one, but two suspicious incidents? Potentially tragic ones?"

"No, I don't," her father bellowed. "I call it luck, now if—"

"Luck!" she spluttered. "If that's—"

"Roger," Ty said, interrupting her rant. "I'm glad your daughter is suspicious. The position she holds dictates she be suspicious and diligent, otherwise everything you own could be in jeopardy."

Norma Rose wasn't impressed, nor pacified by Ty's pretense, or his silver tongue. Her sister could be missing, her uncle possibly blind, and if anyone, anyone at all, cared what she thought, she had a hunch that he was behind it all. There was no other explanation.

She didn't have a chance to say any of that before a knock sounded and her father shouted for whoever it was to enter.

Walter walked in, followed by five groundsmen from her father's inner circle. These men didn't mow lawns or trim shrubs. They guarded the grounds, day and night. "I have everyone rounded up like you asked, sir," Walter said.

"Close the door," her father instructed needlessly. Walter was already doing so.

Norma Rose was forced to move slightly, making room for the big and burly men. Her father's office was large, but so was the furniture, leaving little standing room. Taking a second step backward, her heel caught and she stumbled slightly. A firm hold grasped her, and the moment she realized who held her elbow, she wrenched her arm free.

Slightly behind her, Ty smiled, and she wanted to stick out her tongue, a childish urge and something she hadn't done in years. Ty did that to her, put a notch in her suit of armor. She didn't like it. Or standing this close to him.

"I want you all to meet Ty Bradshaw," her father said. "Ty, this is Bronco Mitchell, Tuck Andrews, Duane Luck, Tad McCullough, Danny Trevino and you've already met Walter Storms."

The men stepped forward to shake Ty's hand, forcing Norma Rose back even farther, until she was standing at his side, her shoulder touching his arm. With all these men, they certainly didn't need Ty's assistance. Sheriff Withers would help, too. So would Ted Williams and several others. Kidnapping still seemed an impossibility, but Ginger was gone and needed to be found immediately.

"Ty will fill you all in," Roger said, sitting down in his chair.

The blood in Norma Rose's veins turned cold. Her father rarely turned things over to others. Especially something of this magnitude. The other odd thing was how readily her father's men-at-arms complied. There wasn't a single protest.

Ty stepped forward and nodded toward her father before starting. "Ginger, Mr. Nightingale's youngest daughter, is missing. We are not jumping to the conclusion that she was kidnapped, at least not yet, because that would mean someone had been in this house, and we all know that's highly unlikely. Right now we need to know everything you saw last night and this morning, whether or not it was out of the ordinary."

A few mumbles could be heard, and muffled curses, but for the most part, the men remained quiet, until Ty indicated who should start, and then, one by one, each described what they'd seen over the past dozen or more hours.

Both Bronco and Tuck said they'd seen Norma Rose being followed home by Ty and Dave last night, and had seen Ty go to his cabin. Others talked of the comings and goings of the workers refurbishing the cabins, and guests. Nothing out of the ordinary. Bronco then added he'd witnessed a couple from one of the cabins swimming after midnight, nude, which raised a few grins and had Norma Rose fighting to keep the heat from going all the way to her cheeks.

She failed miserably when Ty flashed a glance her way. Flustered by the heat that suddenly rushed to places other than her cheeks, she lowered her gaze, but a second later, her head snapped up as Tad McCullough explained he hadn't seen hide nor hair of the person who'd been watching the resort last week.

"What are you talking about?" she asked. "What person?"

Tad looked at her father for permission, and said, "Someone with a pair of binoculars. I saw him a couple of times, but never could get close. It might have been one of those bird-watchers that stay over at June and Harold Whitmore's place. A number of them arrived last week from out east, where the Whitmores are from."

The Whitmores had regular visitors from Maine, who knew all there was to know about birds. A couple of those men had been guests at Josie's ladies aid meeting last week, which her sister had insisted Norma Rose attend. She'd gone, and had been bored out of her wits.

"But you aren't sure," she asked Tad, "who this person was?"

"No," Tad answered. "Your father knew all about it."

"Okay, then," Ty said. "I suggest we scour every

inch of the resort. Maybe Ginger has a favorite place to read or think."

"She has her bedroom for that," Norma Rose insisted.

As if she hadn't spoken, Ty turned to Bronco. "Did you see anyone else swimming?" When the man said no, he turned to her. "Do you or your sisters go swimming at night?"

"Of course not," Norma Rose said, irritated he'd even suggest such behavior. "Ginger was in her bed, asleep, before I left the resort to go and get Uncle Dave last night."

"How do you know that?"

"Because I checked on her, like I do with all three of my sisters every night." She didn't add that this was because they weren't to be trusted. She checked every night to make sure they were alone in their beds. To be fair, Ginger rarely caused problems. Most nights when she'd check on her sisters, Ginger's nose was stuck in a glossy fashion magazine with her mind on Hollywood. Josie often sat up late planning her next ladies aid meeting. Twyla had always been a handful, but more so lately, since she'd heard that Brock Ness might be moving. Norma Rose wouldn't be surprised if all her sisters had a crush on that man. In truth she should be glad he'd left.

Working her twisting mind back to the question, Norma Rose further explained her answer. "After I took the phone call from Chief Williams, I checked on all three girls, and then I left to go get Dave."

"And they were asleep?" Ty asked.

"Ginger was asleep," she answered. "Josie and Twyla were preparing for bed."

Ty turned his attention back to the men. Rattling off cabin names and buildings on the property as if he'd lived there all of his life, he issued orders, specifying where they were to search. The men obeyed, and those who'd removed their hats upon entering the room replaced them on their heads as they left, all agreeing they'd find Ginger in no time.

"And be discreet," Ty said before the door closed.

"Yes, sir," Walter answered. "No one but us will know."

Ty nodded, and Norma Rose found herself waiting for an assignment, as well. Yet when he said, "You'll come with me," she planted her heels against the floor.

"Why?"

"I need to search Ginger's room, and will have questions."

"Be a good girl and don't argue, Rosie," her father said despondently. "We have to find your sister."

She'd never disobeyed him, ever, and wasn't about to do so now, yet a part of her protested. She didn't want to leave her father's side. She'd never seen his hands tremble before. "I know we need to find Ginger, Daddy."

He glanced up at her, and there was a sudden shift. It was as if they'd reversed roles, as if she was no longer the child and he the parent. The look in his eyes begged her to help him. To help find Ginger. She edged around Ty to give her father a hug. "We will find her, Daddy. I swear we'll find her."

"When I discover who's behind this—" He let her go and pinched his lips together, shaking his head.

Ty took her arm. "Come on."

She let him lead her out of the office, but couldn't help a glance back. The image of her father, head bowed and holding one hand against his forehead, burned in her mind as Ty pulled the door closed. Anger surged inside her, and she snapped her heels together. When she found Ginger she'd paddle her sister's behind for worrying their father so. If by some unfathomable chance, her sister had been taken... She ripped her arm out of Ty's hold. "If you're behind this, I'll see you court-martialed."

He didn't so much as glance her way. "You don't have that kind of power."

"You don't know me very well."

"Well enough," he said.

Fury burned inside her, and echoed in each clip of her heeled shoes. Without wasting another word on him, she marched forward, all the way to the kitchen, where she found a waiter and sent him out to Dave's cabin to relieve Gloria so the woman could check on her father. Then, and only then, she directed Ty toward the back staircase, and upward, toward Ginger's bedroom.

"It's at the end of the hall," she said, marching along beside him.

"I know."

"You seem to know an awful lot, Mr. Bradshaw."

"It's my job to know."

Pivoting on one heel, she snagged his arm, forcing him to stop and look at her. "You seem to have gone to a lot of trouble just to try and extort a few extra tax dollars out of the resort."

His cock-eyed grin was so arrogant she wanted to slap it right off his face.

"I couldn't care less about the taxes the resort pays."

His grin disappeared and he flipped his arm around so fast she barely saw it move, but she flinched at the grip he now held on her wrist.

"I do," he growled, "care that we find your sister." Pulling her forward, he added, "Alive."

"Of course she's alive," Norma Rose argued, not wanting to even consider otherwise. "And let go of my arm."

He let go. Her steps faltered. Whether she wanted to think it or not, the notion of her sister being taken entered her mind.

"Your father doesn't have hired watchmen for no reason," Ty was saying as he walked forward. "He knows the kind of men he does business with. Why do you think he keeps such close tabs on you girls?"

"We girls—" she began.

"Can't leave the property without being followed," he finished.

She sucked in air, but she had no comeback.

He'd stopped in front of a door—Ginger's door—and Norma Rose grabbed the knob. Ty was a federal agent all right. No one else could have discovered all he had. But, she concluded as she threw open the door, he wasn't here to find tax evasion. He must be here to shut down her father.

Over her dead body.

She gulped, thoroughly livid, and demanded, "Where is she?"

Ty didn't answer, but started roaming the room that had been painted pink for Ginger's last birthday. Norma Rose swept forward, pushing at both of his shoulders from behind.

"Where is she? What have you done with my sister?"

Ty spun around and grabbed Norma Rose by the upper arms. "I haven't done anything with your sister." He slid his hands down onto her elbows, locking her arms against her sides in order to stop her from taking another swing at him. In all his years of undercover work, he'd never come close to revealing himself, not to gangsters, lawmen, or the occasional dame who'd caught his eye. The panic in Norma Rose's blue eyes was doing something to him, chiseling away at his willpower. He wouldn't let that happen. It would take a lot more than a pretty face and a few tears, no matter how real, to break down his barriers.

"I haven't done anything to your sister," he repeated, this time quieter, calmer. "I swear. Would I be here, trying to find her, if I had? I'm not stupid, Norma Rose, neither is your father. And neither are you. Bronco watched me go to my cabin last night, and leave it this morning. Before and after then I've either been with you or your father." He eased his hands down to her gloved hands and squeezed her fingers. "Ginger may just be hiding someplace."

Ty doubted she'd been kidnapped. Bodine wouldn't want to alienate Nightingale. The gangster would want to gain Roger's confidence, which is why Ty considered Bodine to be behind Dave's poisoning. If the plan hadn't failed, Bodine could have claimed that someone switched the samples in Dave's suitcase. The only reason it had backfired was because Bodine hadn't done his research and discovered Dave was highly allergic to alcohol.

"Ginger wouldn't be hiding some place," Norma Rose said. "She'd have no need to do that."

Though she had calmed down, Norma Rose wasn't any closer to believing that Ty wasn't behind all that was going on. He pondered that as he let go of her hands to roam the room again. He refused to take her into his confidence, but gaining her trust would give him additional benefits. It was going to be tough. She had a shell as hard as an acorn.

"I need your help," he said. Knowing that wouldn't sway her, he added, "Your father needs your help. He depends on you. Greatly."

She eased a long breath out through barely parted lips. He could see she still struggled, but also that she was giving in.

"Fine."

"Good," he said. "Look for clues."

"Clues? What kind of clues?"

"Anything that looks out of the ordinary."

Standing in the center of the room, arms folded, she insisted, "There is nothing out of place. Out of the ordinary. I'd have already noticed it."

He approached her and rubbed her upper arms, noting, but ignoring outwardly, how she half attempted to twist away, while being too stubborn to move at the same time.

"I'm a private investigator, Norma Rose, so believe me when I say things are not always as they appear. Sometimes we get so used to looking at things, we overlook the obvious." Letting her go, he turned to glance around the room. "Look closer. Is anything missing?"

"No, I—"

He held up a hand. "Humor me."

Norma Rose huffed, but spun around and started looking closer. He did, too. The bed was made, but that didn't mean it hadn't been slept it. Didn't mean it had been, either. The walls were covered with a sickening pink hue. Roger Nightingale was one smart man. No male over the age of sixteen would even consider stepping foot in this room. The pink paint and white furnishings, including the four-poster bed with a big stuffed Teddy Roosevelt bear sitting on the center of it, clearly said "this is my baby girl's room." The bedspread was the same shade of pink as the walls and trimmed with layers of ruffles and lace, just like the curtains.

Wondering if Norma Rose's room was similar, Ty paused, his eyes on one particular window.

"There is nothing out of place here," Norma Rose said.

"Check the closet," he said, gesturing in that direction while he approached the window, where an edge of the sheer net panel between two pink drapes was hitched up. Spreading the drapes apart showed that the edge of the white center panel was caught in the seam between the top and bottom windows, something anyone pulling down the window from the inside would have noticed. But what if it had been closed from the outside?

The window was only open a couple of inches, leaving enough room to let in the breeze, but not for someone to climb out. A screen covered the outside, too, but that could easily be removed by twisting the little wing nuts that held the frames in place. It would be simple to remove and replace from the outside.

A gasp made him turn around. "What did you find?"

"It's what I didn't find," Norma Rose said.

He crossed the room to peer in the closet. It was neat and orderly, with dresses, too many to count, hung on hangers and more shoes than Sears and Roebuck sold in their catalog lining the floor.

"There are shoes missing, and dresses." Norma Rose hurried across the room and opened the top drawer of a tall white dresser. "And underclothes."

"How can you tell?" He bit his lip, regretting his words. A woman would notice things like that, which is why he'd wanted her to search.

"Because Ginger just purchased the missing items the other day. A purple two-piece suit and a red-and-white polka-dot dress, both with matching shoes." She crossed the room to where a standing coatrack held several purses. "Two purses—no, three—are missing, too." Moving to the closet again, she nodded. "Her red pleated dress is gone, too, and—"

Ty held up a hand. "Suffice to say clothes are missing."

She spun around, heading for the door. "We have to call the sheriff."

Reaching the door first, Ty stopped her. "Is there any chance one of your other sisters might have Ginger's missing things?"

"No. Though they try, Ginger is shorter than Josie or Twyla, and her skirts are much too shor—Never mind." She shook her head. "She wouldn't have loaned brand-new clothes to anyone."

He bit back a grin. In other words, Norma Rose wouldn't have let the other girls wear Ginger's things. "Okay," he said. "Then we have a pretty good idea that she wasn't kidnapped."

"How do we know that?"

"Do you honestly think kidnappers would have let her pack first?"

Her blush must have stung, because she spun

around so he wouldn't see it. "Then we have to call the sheriff," she repeated.

"Let's see what else we can find first," he said. "Give us a bit more to tell him."

"But she might—"

"Whether we call the sheriff now, or an hour from now, isn't going to make that much difference," he said. "Except draw attention that neither your father, nor the resort, needs right now."

He'd hit a nerve, that was evident by the way she stiffened. She sighed and turned to face him. "You're right."

Ty couldn't withhold a chuckle. She frowned. "That," he said, trying to stop another chuckle, "had to hurt."

With brows knitted together so tightly that wrinkles formed, she asked, "What?"

"You, telling me I'm right." He let out a low whistle. "That had to hurt." Leaning left and right as if examining her, he added, "Are you bleeding?"

Her face scrunched before she let out a puff of air and a full grin appeared. "No, I'm not bleeding." She patted her cheeks, as if that would remove the pink hue. "Now stop fooling around. This is serious."

"You're right," he said. "This is serious."

Ty glanced around the room one more time, making sure he hadn't missed anything. "Kidnappers would have left a note, too." Taking Norma Rose's hand, he tugged her to the doorway. "Let's go see if we can figure out how she climbed out the window."

She'd taken a step, but now stopped, looking across the room. "How do you know she climbed out the window?"

"The curtain's caught in it."

"No, it's not."

He swiveled around and pulled her in that direction. At the window, he pulled back the drapes and pointed to where the sheer panel was caught in the corner between the upper and lower glass panes. "See. If someone on the inside had pulled it closed, they'd have noticed this. But someone attempting to close it from the outside, especially while it was dark, wouldn't have."

"Ginger may have climbed out the window," she said thoughtfully, "but I can't imagine she'd have replaced the screen."

He shrugged. "If she didn't want anyone to notice, she might have. Or, she might have had an accomplice."

Norma Rose turned slowly, giving him the

once-over with a steady gaze that made his pulse quicken.

"Perhaps you are a private investigator."

"Perhaps," he repeated and lifted a brow.

She spun around. "We need to speak with Reyes."

"One of the gardeners?" he asked, following her out of the room.

"Yes."

"Why?" he questioned as they strolled down the hallway. "Were they…friendly?" He searched for the right word, not wanting to offend her when he was gaining ground.

"No," she answered, glancing his way. "Not in the way you're referring to. Ginger wasn't much into forming crushes on anyone. But Reyes would rope the moon for her if she asked."

He grinned. "You'd make a good private eye, too."

"It's called being a parent," she answered.

"You aren't a parent."

Her laugh held a hint of bitterness. "I've been more or less raising my sisters since my mother died."

"That's a lot to take on." He'd been in charge of his younger brother, Harry, while his parents ran their store, and had always watched the clock for the moment they'd arrive home and relieve him of his duties. Sometimes he wished he'd appreciated those days more, for they were long gone now.

"Not always," she said. "In many ways, taking care of the girls prepared me for running the resort." Another sigh escaped her. "And running the resort has given me insight into overseeing the girls, especially as they grow older. Besides, family is the most important thing anyone has."

His throat went thick at that, and he had to change the subject, although talking burned. "Where will we find Reyes?"

"Let's try the main beach. I asked him to rake the swimming area."

This time they took the front staircase that swept elegantly above the ballroom and then along the wall, giving guests direct access to the parties below. After crossing the large room, they went out the doors onto the long, wide balcony that overlooked the lake.

A hill covered with thick, low-cut grass, lined with various flower beds and hosting a fountain that splayed water into a circular cement pool, sloped all the way to the lake. Several boathouses and docks lined the shore on the left, whereas on the right there was a sandy spread of beach and red-and-white striped buoys floated in the water, tied together to create a safe swimming area.

"There's Reyes," Norma Rose said.

A man who was several feet out in the water pulled on a loop of rope that disappeared beneath the shimmering blue ripples.

Ty took Norma Rose's elbow as they started down the long set of steps leading from the balcony, and was a bit surprised when she didn't attempt to pull away. She waited until they reached the ground before doing that. He grinned, not insulted in the least.

Her mind clearly was on a mission. His was, too; it just took him a moment to remember it.

Upon arriving at the fine sand, she slipped off her shoes and carried them in one hand while moving closer to the water.

After sinking into the sand, which instantly filled his shoes, Ty pulled his shoes off, too.

She noticed and grinned, before turning to the man in the water. "Reyes!"

The man nodded and started walking their way, still pulling on the rope. As the water became shallower, what looked like an old bed spring appeared, covered with weeds. There was a large pile of wet slop lying on the sand, too.

"He's raking weeds out of the water?" Ty asked, a bit perplexed.

"Yes," Norma Rose answered. "They need to be maintained." She added, "Our guests expect the best, and we strive to give it to them."

In Ty's eyes, raking weeds out of the water took things a bit far. "Weeds are part of swimming, you get used to them," he said. That's what he and Harry had done.

"Not here," she said.

"No wonder you had nude swimmers here last night." He figured people had been swimming nude for years, but lately, it had become a rave. Whole groups of partygoers would jump in pools, lakes or the cold ocean back home. It seemed any available body of water would do. He assumed the amount of booze they consumed helped keep folks warm.

"That is not something we encourage."

"But you don't discourage it?"

She didn't answer as her gaze swept toward the gardener. "Reyes, have you seen Ginger?"

Ty didn't miss how the man's cheeks, though already red from the sun reflecting off the water, turned brighter.

"Was I not supposed to remove the ladder?" Reyes asked in response.

Norma Rose was good at hiding her reactions, Ty noted—almost as good as him. She barely blinked before asking, "When did you remove it?"

"This morning, just like she asked," Reyes answered.

Ty glanced at Norma Rose, but let her continue her questioning. She liked being in charge, and he needed to let that happen whenever he could. Let her think she was running the show.

"From her window?" Norma Rose asked.

Reyes nodded. "Yes. Yesterday she said she needed to wash her window and asked me to set it up and remove her screen. I offered to wash the window for her, but she said there was a long streak across it that only appeared when the sun was setting. She wanted to wait until then to wash it, and told me I could replace the screen and put the ladder back this morning, if she hadn't already done so. Since it was still there, I put it away." Reyes stomped the weeds from his bare feet. "I'll go put it back. Do you want me to wash the window, too?"

"No," Norma Rose said. "Have you seen her today?"

Reyes shook his head, but concern filled his eyes. "Walter asked me that earlier. Is something wrong?"

"No," Ty interjected, before Norma Rose could speak.

"I just need her help," Norma Rose said, tossing Ty a quick sideways glance. "I'll find her. Thank you. How bad are the weeds?"

"Not too bad," Reyes said. "A couple more sweeps and they'll all be gone until next year."

Turning her blue eyes toward Ty, she said, "We don't disturb the weed beds near the docks. The fish like them, as do the guests who come here to fish."

Ty caught on to her attempt to make this look like she was giving him a tour, and nodded. "Do the cabins come with boathouses and boats?"

She grinned and gave Reyes a nod before turning around. "They can be rented separately."

"I see," he said. "Splendid."

Chapter Seven

Greatly relieved Ginger hadn't been kidnapped, Norma Rose teetered between anger at her youngest sister and something she couldn't quite describe. It had something to do with Ty. She couldn't say she was convinced he was a private investigator. But he certainly could be. He'd clearly discovered clues to indicate Ginger had run away, but there was still more to him. She could feel it.

She could feel him, too, in their silent communication. She hadn't had to explain anything to him, he'd just started going along with her ploy to stop Reyes thinking anything was wrong.

"Yes, it is," she answered. "Quite splendid."

Ty looked at her, and it happened again, that silent communication. He started laughing. She glanced over, and after noting that Reyes was far enough away that he couldn't hear, she giggled.

"You said it first."

"I know," he answered dryly.

"I do think the resort is splendid."

"I know that, too."

He gestured toward the grass and they started walking. They weren't touching and she had gloves on, so why could she still feel the warmth of his hands when he'd squeezed her fingers upstairs? And what on earth were the flutters in her stomach?

They stopped at the edge of the grass, where Ty took her elbow, helping her hold her balance while she slid on her shoes. When he let her go to step into his shoes, she took a deep breath.

All this…this silliness going on inside her, must be nerves. She'd never had a sister run away before, and, as things stood, she needed Ty's help. Ginger still had to be found. Her father wasn't in any state to help, and there was no one else. She certainly didn't want her other sisters learning about this. Next thing she knew, both Josie and Twyla would be attempting the same thing.

"So," Ty said, nodding toward the resort. "Where would your sister run away to?"

Where moments ago warmth flowed, a chill

now shot through her veins. "Hollywood," she whispered.

"What?"

She took a deep breath in order to say it again, loud enough for him to hear. "Hollywood. Ginger is obsessed with it. She's always reading magazines, going to picture shows."

He started walking. "What time does the passenger train stop at the Bald Eagle Depot?"

Norma Rose skipped to catch up with him. "Two in the afternoon."

He cursed under his breath, but she heard it, and increased her speed, walking on her tiptoes to keep her heels from sinking.

"That only gives us about fifteen minutes," he said.

"It's only a five-minute drive." If they took the well-used shortcut through the woods, but she couldn't show him that route. "Ten at the most."

With a wave toward the trees lining the edge of the yard, he said, "My truck's at Dave's."

"I can—"

He pulled a set of keys out of one pocket.

"You can drive," she agreed, remembering the keys she'd had Walter collect. Norma Rose pulled off her shoes to run. The toes of her stockings were already full of sand. A hole would be a relief. Ty arrived at his Model T first and she shot through the door he held open.

The engine caught and puttered to life, and Norma Rose slapped one hand on the dashboard, the other on the top of the windowless door, as Ty shifted the truck into Reverse. She bit the tip of her tongue. It wouldn't take much longer to take the road and though she wanted to find Ginger, she just couldn't give away the secret trails or passageways. Rocks flew as the vehicle shot backward, and again as he shifted gear, propelling Norma Rose forward along with the truck.

A solid arm stretched in front of her, pressing her back against the seat. "Hold on."

"I am," she insisted.

He drew back his hand and maneuvered the vehicle down the lane and across the parking lot. "Keep your arms inside," he said, hitting the road like a bootlegger on the lam.

Half-expecting to see coppers chasing them if she looked behind, and excited by the inner thrill that thought caused, she said, "I know better than that."

"Uncle Dave's arm?"

"You certainly have done your research," she

said, holding on tightly as they swung around a wide curve. She had no desire to argue or worry about how he'd discovered so much about her family. The minutes were ticking by, and this was about the greatest adventure she'd ever been on.

"I don't understand how she could have snuck out," Norma Rose said, trying to keep her focus on Ginger. "Not without one of the men seeing her."

"I don't, either," he said. "The resort is well guarded. Could she have convinced one of them to lie for her?"

"You met them," she pointed out. "What do you think?"

"No," he answered. "And by now they will have learned of the ladder, considering Walter had already spoken to Reyes."

She nodded, almost feeling sorry for the night watchmen. Her father was not going to be happy to learn a ladder had been leaning against the house all night and no one had questioned it.

"What about the White Bear Lake Depot?" Ty asked. "What times do passenger trains go through it?"

"Several times a day, but they only run north and south. The only passenger trains heading east and west go through Bald Eagle, and that's once a day, at two o'clock," she answered, watching the trees whip past and holding on tighter as the rough road had her bouncing in her seat. "White Bear Lake folks didn't like it when the depot was built out here, but there were already so many trains coming out of the cities, and going back in, the railroad claimed an east-west track would be too much. Freight trains roll through several times a day, but only a few actually stop at the Bald Eagle Depot."

"Hold on," he said, gunning the truck onto the main road.

"I haven't let go," she assured him.

He grinned, and she had a hard time tugging her gaze away from his profile.

Less than a mile later, Ty pointed. "Passengers," he said excitedly. "The train hasn't arrived yet."

Norma Rose gained control of her eyes. "Park over there, by the trees, and I'll go ask Peter if he's seen Ginger."

Ty swung into a narrow spot between two other cars and cut the engine. "Be careful—"

"Of what I say," she finished, knowing what he was thinking. Throwing open the door, she added, "I was born at night, but it wasn't last night."

Norma Rose flinched, not exactly sure where that quip had come from. Always having to be the serious one didn't allow her opportunities to spout off such remarks. A moment later, another rarity took place. Her insides blossomed at how Ty chuckled. She didn't let herself laugh, but did give in to a grin.

He met her at the back of the truck, and rested a hand in the small of her back as they hurried toward the depot. Scanning the few people sitting in the afternoon sun, she nodded greetings at two familiar faces. Jane Lundstrom and Carl Vetsch both had family in central Minnesota and traveled to see them regularly. Their curious gazes went to Ty, and Norma Rose found herself standing taller, walking straighter. Folks were prone to gossip, and it wouldn't take long to get around that she'd been seen out with a man.

As odd as it was, she didn't harbor any embarrassment about being seen with Ty. He was tall and handsome, and mysterious enough that both Jane and Carl were stretching their necks to catch every movement.

Ty opened the door and she walked over the threshold, holding as much of her smugness at bay as possible. She wasn't trying to be conceited, but it did feel good to be seen out and about.

"Hello, Norma Rose," Peter Alvin said from

behind the little caged window in the center of the room.

"Hello, Peter," she responded. Despite the adventure of it all, she remembered her purpose. Walking straight to the ticket booth, each footstep echoing off the walls, she asked, "Is Ginger still here?"

"Ginger?" Peter repeated. "I haven't seen Ginger in ages. Was she supposed to be here?"

There was nothing in his stance or gaze to make her question his honesty. Stopping near the booth, she noted there wasn't even a hint of sweat on his bald head. Norma Rose knew the signs of someone trying to cover up the truth.

"Yes," she said. "I asked her to come over and inquire about ticket prices for some guests. You're sure you haven't seen her?"

"I'm sure." Peter's deep-sunk eyes were totally clear; if anything, they only held concern. "I've been here since seven this morning."

Norma Rose nodded, not sure what to say next.

Ty rested an elbow on the little shelf in front of the ticket window. "How many trains do you get through here in a day?"

"Twelve. But only four stop," Peter said. "Three freight and one passenger."

"What time are the freight trains?"

Peter glanced at Norma Rose.

Drawing up one of her many false smiles, she nodded. "He's a friend." No one in the tight-knit community of Bald Eagle gave out information freely. Especially to strangers.

"I'm looking to have some personal items shipped here," Ty added.

Peter nodded and began a lengthy explanation of train times, destinations and prices. Norma Rose pretended to be listening while scanning the long, narrow and rather sterile building, wondering about hiding places. White walls and white floor tiles, which needed a good scrubbing, gave way to two long benches and two restrooms, in addition to the ticket booth and a small office behind it.

Unless she was hiding in a bathroom, which was highly unlikely as there was no reason for Peter to lie, Ginger wasn't here. It was all so hard to believe. Ginger had talked about Hollywood, but had never given the slightest hint she would run away. What was she hoping to gain? The resort offered everything possible. Food, clothing, shelter, all the best. Though each of the sisters were expected to work each day, it was minimal, five to six hours at most, and they were paid a full wage, more than any other girls their age made. They didn't need to spend any of it, either. Father gave them money whenever they asked. He never questioned if it was for clothes or makeup or glossy magazines.

Norma Rose was the one that had to do that, in order to limit their frivolous spending. Money hadn't always come so easily, and she tried her best to make them understand that.

"Norma Rose?"

"Sorry," she said, spinning to gaze up at Ty. "I thought I heard a train whistle."

"I did, too," he said, with a grin that said he didn't quite believe her. "Peter here has given me all the information I need. Shall we go and watch the train roll in and see the passengers board?"

"Yes," she agreed. Crazy, that's what this was, the way she was enjoying herself. Pretending this was no more than a simple outing. She hadn't had an outing, especially with a male companion, for ages. Not since she'd dated Forrest. As much as she didn't want to admit it, not even to herself, Ty was fun. His secretive glances and grins kept excitement humming in her veins.

"I'll let Ginger know I already gave you all the information, if I see her," Peter said. "I'll be closing up after the train leaves."

"Thank you," Ty said. "We appreciate that."

Norma Rose agreed and fought to control her steps as they walked to the door. She was used to controlling things, yet seemed to be having a harder time doing it around Ty.

A train whistle filled the air as Ty opened the door and held it wide for her to exit first.

Ginger wasn't among the passengers, neither those arriving or departing. Norma Rose wasn't surprised, yet she couldn't quite gather if she was upset or not. It certainly was not like Ginger to run away. Twyla, yes. That wouldn't have surprised anyone, except Twyla knew that if she left, the money would stop. Ginger had to know that, too.

After the train rolled westward, she and Ty walked to his truck, where he once again held the door open for her.

Norma Rose climbed in absently. She couldn't come up with a single reason why Ginger would have run away.

"What about friends?" Ty asked as he climbed in.

"What about them?" she said, not so lost in thought she'd admit to not having any. She hadn't for years. Friendships took time, and she'd devoted all of her time solely to the resort over the past few years.

"Does Ginger have any she might have gone to see? Someone ailing or celebrating a birthday or something?"

"No," Norma Rose said. "Well, she has friends, but since graduation last month, she hasn't seen them regularly. Two got married right after they'd graduated and her best friend left last week for Duluth, where she'll go to college."

"Would she have gone to see her? The friend in Duluth?"

"Not without telling me," Norma Rose said. "She'd have asked for the money for a ticket or permission to use one of the cars. If any of her friends were sick or had birthdays, she'd have told me about that, too." Frustration building, she shook her head. "This is so unlike Ginger."

"Will Ginger attend college?"

"No," she answered. "Father won't allow that."

"College?"

"Yes, college. Not for any of his daughters." Perhaps it was due to the purpose of their mission, but she didn't mind answering his questions. He needed to know any information that might assist in finding Ginger. "I think Father's afraid that if he lets them leave, they won't come back." In some ways her father was lenient when it came to his daughters. About other things he was strict. Very strict.

"Even you?"

"Yes, even me." Norma Rose bit her lips together. She hadn't meant for that to sound so sharp, and shot a glance at Ty.

Staring straight ahead, he scratched his head. "Well, what about the amusement park? Would Ginger have gone there, like Twyla wanted?"

"Twyla's friend Mitsy Kemper works there, selling cotton candy." Norma Rose took a moment to contemplate that. "Ginger was mad at Mitsy a while back, but I don't know why. I figured it was over a borrowed scarf or something, but now that I think about it, Ginger was really angry. She didn't have a kind thing to say about Mitsy for days."

He started the engine. "Shall we go see if this Mitsy has seen Ginger? It can't hurt."

"I suppose we could." Then because she wasn't used to being away from the resort for so long, she added, "I should go tell Father where I'm at, where we're going."

"One of the men would have told him we left," Ty said, backing up. "He knows you're with me."

She couldn't deny that and the thought triggered other questions. "How could Ginger have left the resort? She wouldn't have walked."

"Can you think of anyone who was at the resort last night that she might have asked for a ride?" Ty asked in return.

Norma Rose glanced out her window to check for traffic and signaled no one was approaching. "No. It was all locals last night. No one would have given her a ride without my father's permission."

"You're sure?" Ty asked.

Her look could have spoken for itself, but Norma Rose said, "I'm positive."

"Your father keeps a close eye on all of you girls, doesn't he?"

"Yes. Is there anything wrong with that?"

"No," Ty said without glancing her way. "I'm just wondering how you, and your sisters, feel about that. Would it have made Ginger angry enough to run away?"

Skipping over the way she felt about it, for that was not something he needed to know, she said, "Twyla's the only one who complains about it. As long as Josie's allowed to go to her ladies aid meetings, she's happy, and Ginger, well, up until a month ago, she was in school every day, so it wasn't like she didn't leave the resort regularly."

He pulled onto the main highway. "So now, after a month of being home, she may have gotten frustrated?"

"Possibly, I guess, but she never said anything."

They'd only traveled a short distance along the highway before Ty started slowing again. "I need to fuel up."

"Scooter Wilson runs this place," she said as Ty pulled off the road and into the fueling station. "He was at the resort last night."

Ty had no sooner shut off the engine when Scooter appeared next to his window. "Fill 'er up?" he asked, bending down to look in.

"Yes," Ty answered.

Scooter must have heard, but he didn't move, at least not toward the gas pump. Instead he leaned down farther to look past Ty. He stared at her with an unmistakably shocked expression on his face. "Norma Rose?"

"Hey, Scooter," she answered, hoping her cheeks weren't as red as they felt.

"Hey," he repeated rather slowly, his tone questioning.

* * *

Ty rubbed a hand over his itching lips. He'd never had so much trouble keeping grins hidden. To say this man was surprised to see Norma Rose was the understatement of the year. "Go ahead and fill it up," he said. "And wash the windshield if you wouldn't mind."

"Sure," Scooter said, still staring at Norma Rose. Though he didn't speak aloud, his lips formed her name again.

Cheeks rosy red, she fluttered her gloved fingers in a little wave. Ty pinched his lips again as Scooter, still looking like he'd seen a ghost, waved back.

"The gas," Ty reminded him.

"Yeah, sure, right away," Scooter said, inching away from the window, never pulling his eyes off Norma Rose.

Ty waited until the other man started cranking on the pump. Over the noise, he said, "You don't leave the resort often, either, do you?"

She rubbed the end of her nose. "Not with someone."

"Not with *someone*, or not with a man?" He couldn't help but ask.

Her silence made him glance through the back

window, where Scooter was still staring as if Norma Rose had grown two heads.

She glanced through the window, too, and let out a heavy sigh. "Fine, not with a man, or at least not a strange one."

"You think I'm strange?"

"No, that's not—" She stopped, noticing his grin.

She smiled, too, and let out a little giggle that told him she'd embarrassed herself.

A thud at the back of the truck said Scooter had heard her giggle, too.

Ty turned to look out the driver's window, to make sure the attendant had the nozzle inside the gas tank. He seemed so fixated on Norma Rose he might be pumping gas all over the ground.

"Scooter, is it?" Ty asked when the man noticed him.

"Yeah, Scooter Wilson."

"I'm Ty Bradshaw," he offered. "I believe I saw you last night at the resort."

"Scooter, Dac Lester and Jimmy Sonny were the last to leave," Norma Rose whispered.

"Along with Dac Lester and Jimmy Sonny," Ty added. "The three of you closed down the bar."

Scooter's brows, as dark as the black slicked-back hair on his head, knitted together.

Ty was well aware that no one said such things. Joints were called speakeasies because you had to talk softly to gain entrance, and because you never mentioned being in one, or who you'd seen there. Yet, he kept his eyes on the man, waiting for an answer.

"We did." Shifting, Scooter slid his free hand into the pocket of his overalls. "I can't say I recall seeing you."

"It was dark," Ty said.

The glass bubble atop the tall pump emptied, and with barely a nod, Scooter removed the nozzle and hooked it back on the side of the pump. Picking up a bucket of water, he said, "I'll get your windshield now."

"Appreciate it," Ty said, trying to sound friendly. Instinct told him not to alienate this man, and that was enough. He never questioned his gut. "You didn't by chance see Ginger last night, did you?"

"Sure," Scooter answered.

Before Ty could respond, Norma Rose stretched across the front seat, planting herself between him and the steering wheel to stick her head out of his window. "You did?" she asked. "You saw Ginger?"

Ty tried to concentrate on the look of shock on

Scooter's face, but was rather distracted by one of Norma Rose's knees planted in his thigh.

"Yeah," Scooter said, holding a dripping rag in one hand. "She was at the top of the stairs, watching Brock play most of the night, like usual."

Norma Rose deflated so quickly Ty barely had time to catch her before she landed on his lap. He helped her back onto the seat, where, squirming, she pulled her skirt back over her knees.

Ty tugged his gaze away from the silk stockings that made her knees glisten in the sunlight and leaned out the window. Scooter was washing the exact same spot while staring through the windshield. "You didn't see Ginger after that, did you? After Brock's performance?"

"No," Scooter said. "After Brock was done performing, I helped him load up his instruments, and strapped his gas cans onto the back of his truck while he was in the resort talking with Norma Rose's father."

"Why onto the back?" Ty asked.

"Because the box was full of instruments. Every last one he owns."

"That's right," Ty said, as if remembering. "Brock's going to Chicago, to sing on the radio."

"Yep," Scooter said. "Left last night."

"How much do I owe you?" Ty asked, digging cash out of his pocket.

Scooter rattled off an amount, and as Ty paid him, asked, "Why? What's up with Ginger?"

"Nothing," Ty answered. "We're just curious about something."

Scooter glanced curiously between Ty and Norma Rose. "I didn't talk to Ginger at all last night."

"Good enough," Ty said, starting the engine.

"'Bye, Norma Rose," Scooter said, once again bending down to look in the window.

"See you, Scooter," she answered, her cheeks still rosy.

Ty bid farewell and waited until they were rolling down the highway before asking, "Would Ginger have left with Brock?"

"Brock?"

He nodded, but was more interested in the fact she was still speaking. She'd embarrassed herself completely by climbing across him and was obviously hoping he wouldn't mention it. He considered it, but he knew staying on her good side was important right now. Besides, it would be best for him to forget it, too.

"Brock would never take Ginger anywhere, let alone Chicago," she said.

"How do you know?"

"I know Brock." Shifting in her seat, she leaned against the door to look at him. "His father was shot while delivering milk in St. Paul early one morning last year. There was a raid at a nearby speakeasy and he took a bullet in the back. The doctors didn't give the family much hope, so my father sent Gloria over there, and she recommended a surgeon from Rochester. The family couldn't afford to go to the Mayo Clinic to see this special surgeon, or to pay his fees, so my father paid for it, and Brock is determined to pay him back. Every cent."

Ty had heard about Roger's generosity to local families, but hadn't heard this story, which was interesting. Someone wanted it kept secret.

"Brock doesn't like owing my father money. He barely accepted payment for performing, wanting most of it to count against his debt. What little he did take, he gave to his family for food and other bills." She shook her head. "Brock would never do anything to upset my father, and taking Ginger to Chicago would certainly upset him."

"I see," Ty answered. All he really saw was her. Keeping his eyes off her was growing more difficult. Close up, she was downright beautiful, and seeing her opening up to him, relaxed against the door like she was, had Ty's pulse thumping a bit stronger than normal. Right now, she had a fascinating little secretive grin on her face, as if—

"And I believe you're right," he said, realizing she'd been waiting for him to elaborate. Turning back to the road, and noting they were approaching White Bear Lake, he asked, "Where's this amusement park?"

She huffed out a silly guffaw. "You know all there is to know about my family, and the resort, yet you don't know where the amusement park is?"

He chuckled. She had him on that one. "I've momentarily forgotten," he said. "Must be the company." What was it about her that had his mind wandering, and not where it should be wandering?

There was that glare in her eye again, but this time it held a mocking glimmer. Norma Rose had marvelous eyes. It wasn't just the deep blue color, but also the way they spoke volumes. He grinned and lifted a brow. "It's over behind the Plantation."

"Yes, it is." Her answer was dry, bitter even. She turned about, to look straight out the windshield, and her posture stiffened.

There was more to her dislike of the Plantation nightclub than rivalry, Ty sensed. Ty couldn't ignore his instinct. He also wondered if Forrest Reynolds was the reason behind her dislike. Forrest had taken over the establishment last year from his father, Galen, who, rumor had it, had moved to California for health reasons.

Although Ty already knew the answer, he wanted to see her reaction, so he asked, "Does Forrest own the amusement park, too?"

"No," she said sternly. "The trolley company, Lowell's, own it. They have trolleys that come up here several times a day. Have done for years and years."

Another way Ginger might have gotten away. He didn't say it aloud, and he didn't need to—Norma Rose was clearly already thinking it. He hadn't completely forgotten their mission. Usually that was all that was on his mind. Then again, he usually didn't have a doll like Norma Rose sitting beside him, filling the air with a perfume he'd never forget. From this moment on, every time he got a whiff of roses, he'd think of her.

"They stop next to the park entrance. We can inquire if anyone saw Ginger," she said.

It was a split second before he grasped what she'd said. "Good plan." He might have to start reminding himself who her father was, just to keep his thoughts in order.

"Right there." She pointed toward an opening left by a car backing out. "Park right there."

After parking the truck, Ty walked around to hold open her door as she climbed out. Once again he let her do most of the talking, commenting only when the ticket man also gave him a lengthy stare. The man had already said he hadn't seen any of the Nightingale sisters, so Ty thanked him and took Norma Rose's arm, leading her toward the amusement park.

That, too, held the ticket man's attention. He almost flipped right out of his little red booth, craning to stare as they walked away.

The Plantation nightclub, a tall white building with huge pillars at the front, was barely a block away. "Ever been there?" Ty asked.

"Years ago," she said, "but I'll never step foot through the door again."

"Pretty set in your ways, aren't you?"

"Very," she said.

Out of curiosity, wondering how she'd respond, he curled his fingers around her gloved ones to guide her past a puddle in the sandy walkway. There was definitely caution in her eyes, but she didn't pull away, not even after they'd entered the amusement park.

"Where's the cotton candy?" he asked. They needed to talk to Twyla's friend and head home. His instincts were saying he was getting too curious about Norma Rose. That he was wondering about too many things that didn't have a place in his life, and had absolutely nothing to do with the whereabouts of her sister.

Once again, onlookers stared. His back teeth clenched. Norma Rose didn't have two heads, or a beard, or anything else that should have people gawking at her like she was a circus sideshow.

"The cotton candy is over by the Ferris wheel."

Her whisper made Ty glance down. She had her head bowed and her shoulders hunched, as if trying to make herself as small as possible, and red blotches covered her cheeks. Ire rippled his spine. He could shoot nasty glares at all those staring at them, but that wouldn't make her feel any better.

Rather than acknowledging her obvious discomfort, he gestured toward a row of carnival games. "I haven't seen one of those in ages."

"One of what?" she asked, barely lifting her head.

"The bell-ringing machine." Tugging on her hand, he said, "Come on, I'll win you a prize."

Chapter Eight

"We aren't here to win prizes," she whispered. "We're here to look for Ginger."

"And to act like we aren't looking for her." They weren't going to find Ginger here, he was sure. She'd run away on her own, and didn't want to be found. If she'd wanted to be found and had run away just for attention, she'd have left clues about where to look for her. She hadn't. Therefore, unless someone contacted the resort, saying they knew where she was, Ty doubted they'd find her. Instinct again.

His other instincts said Norma Rose's distress wasn't because she was out in public with him. It had something to do with the Plantation or Forrest Reynolds. That might be another mystery he'd need to solve. When the time was right—which wasn't today, or even this week. Running around looking for Ginger meant taking time out from setting up a snare to catch Bodine.

Ty led Norma Rose to the bell game and handed over the requested coin before he hoisted the rubber mallet. Hitting the base was an art he'd mastered at the amusement park in New York as a kid. It wasn't to do with strength as much as it was hitting the balanced plate in the right spot. Unless someone had added weights to rig the game, or put a lock on the lever the puck traveled on, this one had the same sweet spot as every other one made.

After assuring Norma Rose was safely at the side, Ty raised the hammer over his head and let it fall on the spot he knew so well. The red puck shot up the lever and hit the bell with a resounding clang.

The little squeal Norma Rose let out as she clapped her gloved hands together excited Ty more than the echoing bell.

"You won," she said, grinning brightly. "You won!"

Dressed like a sailor, complete with hat, the carny said, "He sure enough did." Reaching into a box near his feet, he held up a doll that looked a lot like him. "Won a sailor Kewpie doll."

Ty glanced at the miniature doll. Some might

call it cute, but in reality, it looked cheaper than a wooden nickel. He pointed toward the shelf of snow globes inside the man's little wooden shack. "How many times do I have to hit it to win one of those?" He'd brought home a snow globe of the Eiffel Tower to his mother when he'd returned from the war. She'd treasured it.

"Five times in a row," the man answered. "A clam will give you five chances."

Ty handed over a dollar bill and when the man stepped to move behind the machine, arm out, Ty shook his head. The man hunched his shoulders and stayed where he stood. The machine was rigged all right, and Ty had just stopped the carny from flipping the switch.

He hoisted the hammer over his shoulder. Five solid hits later, Ty took the snow globe the man reluctantly handed over and gave it to Norma Rose as they walked away.

"It's beautiful," she said.

"That's Niagara Falls," he told her, pointing out the waterfall scene inside the glass.

"How do you know?"

"I've seen it," he said. "Many times."

"Is it this beautiful?"

Holding the globe with both hands, she gazed

into it with a rather awestruck expression. He was momentarily thunderstruck by how young and innocent she looked. And beautiful.

She lifted those amazing blue eyes to him. "Is it?"

His mouth had gone dry, and he tried to gather enough moisture to speak. "It's far more beautiful in person," he said, suddenly realizing he wasn't just talking about Niagara Falls.

The rapture in those blue eyes once again turned to the globe, but not before the back of Ty's neck grew hot. Pulling at his collar, he said, "Let's find that cotton candy booth."

It was only a few yards away. The booth had the longest line in the park and was made up primarily of young men dressed in stylish, colorful shirts and flat, tweed driving hats. The closer he and Norma Rose got to the booth, the more he understood why those boys were lined up. The girl selling cotton candy was more dolled up than those girls visiting speakeasies on Saturday nights.

"Is that your sister's friend?" he asked.

"Yes, that's Mitsy," Norma Rose answered. "Her father owns the local drugstore."

"That explains a lot."

She glanced up at him, frowning.

He'd been thinking aloud, confirming his inner belief that Roger Nightingale would not encourage or allow his daughters to be friends with a girl who dressed like that. The low-cut neckline of her pink dress exposed as much skin as in the painting of the mermaid on the building behind her booth. The glitter in her eyes also hinted that Mitsy enjoyed male companionship. Searching for an answer to explain his statement to Norma Rose, he whispered, "She has on enough makeup for three women."

"They sell cosmetics at the drugstore," she answered.

The drugstores also needed alcohol to fill prescriptions. Ty didn't say that aloud but it made sense. Mitsy's father and Roger were business associates. That was why Roger allowed his daughters to associate with the man's daughter, but Ty doubted Nightingale liked it.

"Norma Rose?" a screechy voice all but yelled. "Glory be!"

The long line of men dispersed, staring at them. Ty felt Norma Rose's distress and placed a hand in the small of her back, ushering her past the young men.

"Imagine seeing you here," Mitsy continued, "with a man, no less."

Ty had to forcefully pull his back teeth apart.

"Hello, Mitsy," Norma Rose said.

Though she sounded causal and more in control than he felt, he sensed how hard Norma Rose fought to maintain her composure.

"Oh, look, you have a snow globe," Mitsy squealed. "No one ever wins one of those."

Misty's hair was dyed the same shade of red as Twyla's. Some might think it made her look cute. To Ty, it made her look like trouble. "I won the snow globe for Norma Rose," he said, laying a coin on the ledge. "And now I want to buy her some cotton candy. You do sell that, don't you?"

"Of course," she answered, all giggly. "I was just so surprised to see Norma Rose." Mitsy plunked a stick wrapped with spun sugar off the holder and handed it through the waist-high opening of her booth. "Did you give Twyla a ride to town?" Frowning, she added, "She called and said there was something wrong with her car."

"No, Twyla's not with us," Norma Rose said. "She can't make it to town today."

Groans echoed from the men around them, and one by one, they started walking away.

"What?" Mitsy asked. "Can't make it?"

Ty's nerves twitched at the men's mumbling, which had nothing to do with cotton candy.

"Because Ginger's still mad at me, you won't let Twyla come to town?" Mitsy continued snootily. "Is that what this is all about?"

"Why is Ginger mad at you?" Norma Rose asked.

"I don't know," Misty sniffed. "She acts like I stole her boyfriend or something. Like she's ever had one. Everyone knows the Nightingale girls don't date, ever since—"

"What are you and Twyla up to this time?" Norma Rose interrupted.

Ty wanted to hear the answer, but more than that he wanted to know what Misty had been about to refer to. That had put a pinch in Norma Rose's lips.

"Nothing," Mitsy said, obviously lying.

Looking for Ginger here was a waste of time, and this young girl—several years younger than Twyla—was trouble with a capital *T*. Ty took Norma Rose's arm. "Let's go."

Norma Rose agreed with a nod, after shooting Mitsy one final glower.

Ty guided her around the booth, in the direction that several of the young men had gone. "Wait right here for a minute," he said, handing her the cotton candy. This had nothing to do with Ginger, but his curiosity was too great.

She took the candy in her free hand. "Why?"

"I'll tell you in a minute." Ty hurried to catch up with two of the men. A moment later he had the information he needed and as he walked back to Norma Rose, he contained a chuckle. She had her hands full with her sisters, that was for sure.

"What are you shaking your head about?" she asked.

He took her elbow and gestured toward the parking lot with his chin.

"What did they say?"

"Aren't you going to eat that?" he asked, instead of answering, pointing at the cotton candy. There were too many people still watching, and he wasn't sure what her reaction might be. "Or don't you like it?"

She tore her eyes away from the men he'd spoken to and sighed. "I like cotton candy, but…" She held up both hands, showing they were both occupied.

He took the snow globe. She just sighed again.

"What?"

"I can't eat cotton candy with gloves on. They'll get all sticky."

"Take them off."

"I can't. My hands are blue, remember?"

He laughed. "That's right. The ink pen."

"The ink pen," she repeated.

He tore a chunk of sugar fluff off the paper tube and plopped it in her mouth before she could protest. Before he thought about the repercussions.

Her eyes were round as coins, and rather bedazzled-looking.

To cover up the way his fingers tingled from having touched her lips, he plucked up another chunk of fluff and popped it into his mouth. "It's good," he said. "Fresh."

She nodded. "Cotton candy doesn't last long. It gets watery and tough."

"Yes, it does," he agreed. "Want some more?"

"No, thank you."

He wondered if him feeding her that candy had affected her as much as it had him. He'd felt something deep down, where things normally didn't go, places he kept locked up for good reasons…and always would.

They walked in silence past the various booths, with people still watching their every step. He'd worked hard last week to gain the information he had about the resort, Roger and all four of his daughters, and the curious stares confirmed exactly what he'd assumed. Lips were tight, very tight, when it came to the resort and the Nightingale family.

As they once again maneuvered around the mud puddle in the center of the trail near the entrance, she asked, "What did those men tell you?"

She'd learn about it sooner or later, so he said, "It seems your sister Twyla and Mitsy have a little side business going on."

"A side business? What are you talking about?"

"They run a booth here on Saturday afternoons."

"Twyla sells cotton candy with Mitsy?"

"No," he answered.

"Then what?"

They'd arrived at his truck and he opened her door. Once she was seated, he handed her the snow globe. She was still waiting for him to answer, but he just shut the door and walked around to the driver's side. There was hope on her face, hope that cotton candy was all those two girls were selling.

After he'd climbed in and started the engine, she asked, "What are they up to now?"

"Now? Have they done things in the past?"

"Too many things to even talk about," she said. "I'm sure you noticed their red hair." When he nodded, she added, "That was last month."

"How old is Twyla?"

"Twenty-three," Norma Rose answered with a heavy sigh. "But she says as long as father treats her like a child, she's going to act like one."

"She has a point," Ty said.

Norma Rose's gaze turned thoughtful for a moment. Then, leaning her head against the back window, she tilted it his way. "What are they doing now?"

Withholding the desire to take her hand, just to give her a touch of comfort, he started the truck. "They're running a kissing booth."

"A what?"

"A kissing booth. You know—"

"I know," she snapped.

"Only charging a dime."

He could have sworn she cursed beneath her breath, while he was ready to laugh out loud. For as hard as Roger Nightingale tried, he was creating delinquents rather than daughters. Other than Norma Rose, of course. The man should recognize that she was so responsible because he allowed her to be, and that her sisters weren't because he didn't give them any responsibility.

It really was none of his business. Not the way Nightingale raised his daughters, or how unfair he felt it was for Norma Rose to be responsible for those girls. Having backed out of the parking spot, Ty shifted gears and headed toward the main road.

Norma Rose leaned her head against the window again. "Good heavens."

Taking one hand off the wheel, he took the cotton candy from her hand. "Take your gloves off. I've already seen your blue hands, and you're going to need this sugar to keep up with your sisters."

"What do you mean by that?"

He laughed. "I wasn't implying you aren't sweet enough. Sugar gives you energy."

She set the snow globe between them and pulled off both gloves before taking the cotton candy. After eating a few mouthfuls, she reached over and fed him one. "You're going to need the energy, too. We still haven't found Ginger."

By the time they'd arrived at the resort there was nothing left of the cotton candy. He'd eaten several more mouthfuls, pulling them off himself, half-afraid she'd feed him more if he didn't. There was something too intimate about the gesture. He didn't do intimacy. Didn't have time for anything that might put warmth in his heart. It had been cold too long, and needed to stay that way.

He wouldn't know who he was without the bitter chill inside him.

"Do me a favor," Norma Rose said as he pulled into the parking lot.

Having laid the empty paper cone on the floorboard, she was pulling on her gloves, covering up her blue hands. Once again, Ty fought a smile. "What's that?"

"Don't tell my father about the kissing booth. He has enough on his mind."

Shutting off the engine, he asked, "You do that a lot?"

"What?"

"Cover up for your sisters? For your father?"

A hint of sadness clouded the bright blue of her eyes. "Yes," she said. "That's what I'm here for."

Ty no longer wanted to smile, nor could he deny the pang he felt in the center of his chest.

Norma Rose turned her gaze to the resort building sitting before the truck as her answer repeated itself in her head. That's what she was here for. To cover everything up, the things she couldn't make go away. It had never seemed that way, yet today, right now, she knew that was her real purpose. The heaviness that admission created was almost painful.

She pushed out a sigh, but it didn't help. She grabbed the door handle. "Let's go and see if they discovered anything in our absence."

Ty was at her door before she opened it, and held it wide as she picked up the snow globe with one hand and reached down for the now empty cotton candy tube with the other. It had been years since she'd eaten cotton candy, and she'd forgotten how it melted as soon as it touched her tongue.

"Leave that," he said. "I'll throw it away later."

Considering people were already going to question her whereabouts, she left the paper on the floor and then returned the snow globe to the seat before climbing out.

"Not this," Ty said, retrieving the globe.

"That's yours," she said.

"I won it for you," he said.

The feeling inside her was impossible to explain, or to identify. Not willing to focus on what it was, she took the globe and thanked Ty. Inside, she stopped in her office to put the snow globe on her desk. "I need to go wash my hands."

"I'll talk with your father," Ty said. "Tell him what we discovered. Or do you want me to wait for you?"

If Ginger had been found, when they'd pulled

up Bronco would have said something rather than just waving from his post. She shook her head. "Go ahead."

He lingered in the doorway for a moment, as if he wanted to say something else, but then stepped aside and gestured for her to go ahead of him.

Norma Rose didn't look back as she walked down the hall to the powder room, but she knew Ty watched her. She had a feeling that if she did turn around she'd never be able to make sense out of anything. Especially not what was happening inside her. None of it had anything to do with Ginger, either.

What was happening to her? It was barely four o'clock and yet she was exhausted, as if she'd worked days without rest. She couldn't blame that on Ginger, either. With her sister missing, she should have been in panic mode, but she wasn't. Ever since Ty had assured her that Ginger had run away, there was a tiny part of her that was happy. Glad her sister had escaped. That was not something she'd ever have imagined feeling.

Entering the room, Norma Rose removed her gloves and turned on the water, washing away the stickiness of the cotton candy. Her hands were still blue and despite everything, she smiled at that.

Smiled.

She must be exhausted. There was nothing funny about blue hands. There was nothing to be relieved about when it came to Ginger running away, either, and she knew she shouldn't be standing there thinking about cotton candy and snow globes. But no matter how hard she tried, her mind kept going back to the afternoon. A chill rippled her spine, recalling the stares burning holes in her as she'd walked beside Ty. Unlike Bald Eagle folks, the people of White Bear Lake gossiped. About some things. About her. They had way back when and they would again now.

Norma Rose turned off the water, but let her hands rest on the taps. She was no longer sixteen and poor, carrying water from an outside well to wash remade clothes and darning her socks each night to get one more day out of them.

She'd come a long way since those days, and was never going back. Let them talk. Let them wonder who Ty was. She had far more important things to do, and as her mother once told her, gossips were often narrow-minded people, and narrowed-minded people were often gossips because they were jealous.

Feeling better, but still thinking about cotton

candy and snow globes—she'd need more time than washing her hands had given her to work herself out of that barrel—Norma Rose opened the door. The hall was empty. Ty would tell her father all they'd learned, and— Her mind paused right there. When had she started to trust him? He would tell her father all he needed to know. Meaning he wouldn't say a thing about Twyla's little adventure. She trusted him to keep that quiet.

Her blue fingers trembled slightly. She'd never trusted anyone, not like this, not with such secrets. One more thing she'd have to add to her list of notions to ponder. Right now, she would grab a new pair of gloves and find Twyla. There wasn't much more she could do about Ginger, until they found her, but she could put a stop to Twyla's shenanigans.

Wearing a fresh pair of black gloves, Norma Rose walked down the hall to Twyla's closed bedroom door. Filling her lungs with fresh air, and holding it in until she couldn't any longer, she let out the air and knocked on her sister's door.

"Go away, I'm busy."

Twisting the knob proved the door was locked. Norma Rose walked back to her room, where she retrieved a master key from the hidden drawer in her jewelry box. Returning to Twyla's room, she unlocked the door and threw it open.

Her sister, sitting at her vanity table, crying, wasn't what she'd expected to find.

"What's wrong now?" Norma Rose asked, sighing.

Twyla's mascara had streaked black lines down both cheeks. Without a word, her sister simply turned her head around.

"Oh, good heavens," Norma Rose groaned, at the sight of the darning needle sticking out of Twyla's earlobe.

"It's stuck," Twyla said.

There was no whine or cry in Twyla's tone, and that's what struck Norma Rose. Her sister was as disgusted as she was. She closed the door and crossed the room, sitting down on the bed.

"When are you going to grow up, Twyla?"

Twyla turned around to face her. "When are you going to let me?"

"Twyla—"

"Don't," her sister interrupted. "Don't start, Norma Rose. And don't give me that condescending look, either. You have no idea what it's like. Yes, you were seventeen when Mother died and you took over her role without an ounce of complaint, but I was fifteen. I could have done more then, and I could do more now if anyone would ever give me the chance."

Norma Rose had been ready to react, but as Twyla had continued, Ty's words came to mind, when he'd said that Twyla had a point. She let the point settle. "How can you expect to be given a chance when you act so immaturely?"

"I haven't always acted like this. For years I've tried to show you and father that I'm responsible and mature, but you never acknowledged any of it. I did everything I could and neither of you saw anything but a child. That's why I decided to act like a child, until one of you was ready to see I was serious."

"It's a little difficult to take someone seriously when they have a darning needle sticking out of one ear."

"See?" Twyla threw her hands in the air.

Norma Rose sighed.

"Father wouldn't even let any of us go to college," Twyla said. "What kind of parent does that? We could afford it."

Understanding Twyla was deadly serious, Norma Rose agreed. "Yes, we could afford it, but you hated school."

"So? I still would have liked the decision to be mine."

Ty's comment wouldn't leave her mind, and Norma Rose nodded. "I can understand that." She understood more than anyone might know. There'd been a time when she'd dreamed of going to college herself. There hadn't been any money then, but she'd dreamed of what else might be out there. "I'm sorry," she said, for several reasons. "Honestly, I am."

"I'm sorry, too," Twyla said. "And I'm tired of it. So tired of it." She stood and walked to the bed, where she sat down by Norma Rose. "Do you remember how close we were before mother died?"

"Of course I do. All four of us shared a bedroom," Norma Rose reminded her.

"And it wasn't so bad," Twyla said. "Because we shared more than a room, we shared lives. We shared secrets and clothes and laughs."

A shiver rippled over Norma Rose. "We shared soup, too," she said. "One kettle full, for all of us, to last the whole day."

"I remember that, too," Twyla said. "We all do. I'm not saying I want to live like that again, I don't want to share a room with any of you, but I do want—oh, never mind, I shouldn't have said anything."

"But you did," Norma Rose said, "so finish it. What is it you do want?" Maybe it was time she was honest about a few things, too. "Because I have to tell you, I'm tired, too."

She wasn't exactly sure how she'd expected Twyla to respond, but it certainly wasn't with empathy.

"As you should be," Twyla said, laying a hand on Norma Rose's knee. "You work sixteen hours a day, every day, and there's no reason you should. You used to let us all help, but since business took off, all you let any of us do is wash sheets and sweep floors."

Norma Rose opened her mouth, but Twyla lifted her hand. "Let me finish. Yes, the laundry and cleaning has to be done, but there is more all of us could do. Granted, you let Josie help with special party decorations, but why can't she decorate the dining room every day? Or the ballroom, or even just the entranceway? Have you seen how she folds the towels for guests? They're practically works of art. And Ginger—"

Norma Rose held her breath. Had Ginger been found while she'd been gone?

"You're worried about replacing Brock, well, Ginger could do that in a flash. She knows more about music and performing than half the musicians in the area, and I know she'd rather do that than make beds."

"She's told you that? When?" Norma Rose asked, hoping Twyla's answer would tell her that Ginger was home safe and sound.

"She didn't have to tell me that," Twyla said. "It's obvious, just as it's obvious that she's as tired of being treated like a child as I am."

"You've talked to her about this today?"

"No, I haven't seen her today, but that's not the point," Twyla said. "Ginger, Josie and I are tired of just being Roger Nightingale's daughters."

Norma Rose couldn't fathom how to respond to that.

Twyla laughed. "Don't look so shocked. We love Daddy, and we love you, but we are grown women and it's time both you and Father started treating us as such."

Still not sure what to say, Norma Rose pointed out the obvious. "This coming from a *woman* with a darning needle stuck in one ear."

"Oh, for Christ's sake," Twyla stormed.

"Watch your mouth," Norma Rose scolded.

Twyla pressed both hands to her forehead and groaned. Leaning closer, she hissed, "It's the 1920s, women can curse, they can drink, too, and have sex without worrying about getting pregnant."

Norma Rose was utterly speechless. She couldn't put any of her thoughts into words.

Twisting her head, Twyla said, "Pull the damn thing out. I won't feel a thing. My ear's been numb for an hour."

"Then why were you crying when I walked in?"

"Because I'm so frustrated with my life," Twyla said.

"Because you weren't allowed to go to the amusement park and sell kisses with Mitsy?"

"Exactly! I'm twenty-three years old and my only friend, the only *girl* I'm *allowed* to visit, is an eighteen-year-old brat. Even though I live at the largest speakeasy in the country, the only excitement I get is going to the amusement park to sell kisses out the back side of the cotton candy booth for a dime." She leaned closer. "Now pull the damn needle out."

Knowing she couldn't grasp it with her gloves on, Norma Rose took them off and pinched the needle with one hand and held Twyla's ear with the other. "Hold still."

"I am."

At first it was slow going, but then the needle began to move. With gentle but steady force, Norma Rose pulled it all the way out and, not knowing what to do with it, handed it to Twyla.

"Thanks." After taking the needle, Twyla asked, "Why are your hands blue?"

"An ink pen broke."

"There's bleach in the laundry room." Twyla walked across the room and dropped the needle on her vanity table.

Norma Rose pulled her gloves back on, and was reminded of all that had already happened today. "Why today?" She hadn't meant to say it aloud, but when Twyla spun around, she repeated it. "Why today? Why are you telling me all this today?"

"I don't know," Twyla said, walking back to the bed. "Maybe because of Brock."

"Brock?"

"Yes. He knows what he wants and he even went against our father to make it happen. Josie and Ginger and I talked about that. How brave Brock had to be to do that, to go to Chicago."

Norma Rose had thought the same thing. Originally she'd thought that her father would be able to convince Brock to stay and play at the resort for the rest of the summer, considering the debt Brock's family owed. That's why she'd only suggested to Wayne Sears that he might be needed to perform at the resort tonight.

"I don't like acting like this, Norma Rose," Twyla said. "Like a spoiled child, but every time I've gone to you or Father with an idea of how I could help out, you've shooed me away like I was thirteen. I'm not, and I've got to tell you, if it wasn't for the watchmen guarding this place twenty-four hours a day, I'd have run away a long time ago."

Norma Rose's heart did a complete somersault. She'd assumed as much, and had told Twyla more than once that if she didn't work at the resort, there would be no money for clothes, or cosmetics, or even food. "You would have?"

Twyla nodded. "Yes, I would have. And if something doesn't change soon, I still might. Money or no money."

Norma Rose swallowed the lump in her throat. "That's why you couldn't find Ginger this morning. She ran away last night."

"No!"

"Yes."

Chapter Nine

Norma Rose was in the front lobby, showing Twyla how to write out receipts, explaining why it was so important that every person entering the ballroom purchased a meal, whether they ate it or not, when they noticed the sheriff's car pull in.

"What's going to happen?" Twyla asked.

"I don't know. Father just had me call him to tell him he wanted to talk about something. No one has said anything about Ginger being missing."

"He's not going to find her," Twyla said.

Norma Rose didn't answer and turned to meet Sheriff Ned Withers, a tall man without a single strand of hair on his head, at the front door.

"Thank you for coming so quickly, Sheriff," she said. "My father is in his office. This way."

"Norma Rose," he said, and then nodded toward her sister. "Twyla."

"Hello, Sheriff," Twyla answered, before bowing her head, grinning.

Norma Rose grinned, too. The sheriff was a man of few words until he got a few glasses of something under his belt, then you couldn't shut him up. The entire county stayed clear of him after he'd been drinking, but no one made mention of it during the day. Knocking before pulling open her father's office door, Norma Rose said, "The sheriff is here."

"Ned, come in," her father said. "I want you to meet Ty Bradshaw."

Ty rose from the chair. "Hello," he said, extending a hand.

Once he'd shaken the sheriff's hand, Ty's gaze shot to Norma Rose. She knew he was curious about Twyla and why she'd been told about Ginger's disappearance, but Norma Rose hadn't had a chance to explain it yet. She wasn't exactly sure why she wanted to, or what had really happened upstairs between her and her sister. It was a nice change, though, and she planned on talking to Josie as soon as she arrived home from her ladies aid meeting. It was time they all started working together instead of against one another.

"Rosie?"

She turned to her father.

"The door," he said.

With a nod, she closed the door, with the men inside and her outside. That didn't bother her quite as much as it would have this morning. The phone on the front desk jingled and she quickly crossed the room to pick it up. She'd called Wayne Sears and he said he'd be there by eight. If he was canceling, she didn't have a backup plan.

"Nightingale's," she said into the receiver.

"Is Roger Nightingale there?"

Thankful it wasn't Wayne, she replied, "Yes, he is, but he can't talk right now."

"Norma Rose, this is Brock Ness."

"Oh, Brock," she said, now recognizing his voice. "I'm sorry, but Daddy is talking with the sheriff." Wondering if he might have seen something, she revealed, "Ginger ran away last night and we can't find her anywhere."

"I know," he answered. "She stowed away in the back of my truck."

Her heart leaped into her throat. "What?" That was unbelievable in too many ways to count. "She's with you? In Chicago? Is she all right?"

"She's fine," he answered. "I'll—"

"Where are you? I'll have Daddy call you right away."

He told her and she instantly recognized the name of the radio station that had offered Brock the contract and hung up without even saying goodbye. Hopefully her father hadn't said anything to the sheriff yet. No one wanted Ginger's name rolling through the police stations.

"She's with Brock?" Twyla asked.

"Yes," Norma Rose answered, as she turned and hurried to their father's office. Without knocking, she rushed straight to her father's side. Kneeling down, she whispered in his ear. "Ginger's with Brock in Chicago."

He jerked his head back. "What?"

She nodded.

"Excuse me, Sheriff, something has come up that I need to deal with immediately," her father said, standing up. "I just wanted you to meet Ty here. He's one of my newest men. One I know you'll treat as well as the others."

Sheriff Withers didn't look at all surprised and replaced his hat on his head as he stood. "You know I will, Roger." He shook Ty's hand. "Nice meeting you, Mr. Bradshaw."

"Call me Ty, Sheriff, and it was nice meeting you, too," Ty said.

"Twyla will see you out," Norma Rose said, nodding to Twyla, who was now standing in the doorway. Both her father and Ty looked at her quizzically, but she simply smiled.

Twyla closed the door behind the sheriff and her father instantly asked, "Ginger's with Brock?"

"Yes, he said she'd stowed away in the back of his truck."

Her father cursed, several times, before he grabbed the phone. "What's the name of that station?"

She told him and walked around the desk to where Ty stood. She'd sworn Ginger wouldn't be with Brock and now would have to accept being told she'd been wrong.

"Well, that explains how she got away from the resort," he whispered, while her father shouted to be connected to the station in Chicago. "Bronco said he'd checked under the tarp after Scooter had tied it down, but then he'd helped a guest to their cabin. She must have used that time to climb under the tarp because moments later your father talked to Brock, at his truck, and confirmed Brock was alone in the front seat."

"How do you know all that?"

"Your father and I talked to both of them after you and I got back this afternoon. He wasn't impressed to learn about the ladder Reyes had left at her window."

"Why didn't Scooter or Bronco put the ladder away?"

"Because Ginger told them the same thing she'd told Reyes. That she wanted to wash her window. They both claimed no one planning to run away would have drawn attention to the ladder."

"She really thought this through, didn't she?" Norma Rose said.

"Yes, she did," Ty answered.

"Is it true?" Her father's voice echoed in the room. "My Ginger's with you?"

Norma Rose held her breath, considering what a tight spot Ginger had put Brock in. He certainly didn't deserve that.

"Damn it," her father growled. "That girl is so like her mother, God rest her soul." He let out a string of curses that had the windows rattling.

After a pause, he shouted, "Like hell you will! You put her on a train by herself and she'll end up in California."

Ginger had never been shy when it came to talking about moving to Hollywood. Her father, like Norma Rose, thought it had just been talk, but after all Twyla had just admitted, Norma Rose was surprised Ginger hadn't headed for California. If she'd figured out a way to climb in Brock's truck, she could have figured out a way to board a train without being seen. Homeless folk rode the rails every day.

"You don't let her out of your sight," her father said. "I need time to figure out what to do. This couldn't have happened at a worse time." After another curse, he said, "Any harm comes to that girl, boy, and you'll take a fall. A big one."

Her father didn't make false threats, and Norma Rose's empathy for Brock increased tenfold. Her gaze went to Ty, and she quivered inwardly, for that moment hoping he was the private investigator he claimed to be.

"Don't tell her we've talked, either," her father said. "She may bolt. I'll call you at this number tomorrow."

As her father slammed the phone down, he settled his gaze on Norma Rose. "You should have seen this coming."

Although her insides exploded, Norma Rose froze. She should have known this is how it would play out. Anything her sisters did wrong came back to her.

"Norma Rose couldn't have seen this coming any more than you could have," Ty said. "And you certainly can't blame her sisters' behavior on her. She's not their mother."

The redness seeped out of her father's face, and he sighed. "You're right," he said rather helplessly. "You're right."

Norma Rose wasn't sure what affected her more, the way Ty had stood up for her, or the way her father had so meekly agreed. Both tossed her somewhere between yesteryear and never land. She was clueless as to how to react.

"The important thing is that Ginger has been found, and that's she's safe," Ty said. "Do you trust Brock?"

"Brock is very trustworthy," Norma Rose said, gathering her wits enough to speak. Ty's hand was on the small of her back, patting her gently, and the action stole sensible thoughts faster than she could form them. "Very trustworthy."

Her father looked at her, and then at Ty, before he nodded. "Yes," he said. "Brock is. I guess if I have to put my trust in someone—for one of my daughters—he'd be one I know I could count on."

Shaking his head, he continued, "The apple doesn't fall far from the tree and in this case, I'm glad. Brock's father is as honest as the day is long. That's why I had to step in when the doctors didn't give him much hope." He shook his head. "Brock didn't want his family indebted to anyone, and swore to pay back every dime. He nearly has, too."

"All right, then," Ty said. "The next step is, what are you going to tell people?"

"About what?" Norma Rose asked, pulling her mind away from the warmth seeping up her back and trickling down her legs.

"People are going to notice Ginger isn't here," Ty said.

The warmth disappeared as a shiver shot down her spine, taking with it her relief of knowing Ginger was safe. People would notice. And talk.

"Yes, they are," her father said.

The chill remained as Norma Rose glanced between Ty and her father. They both expected her to know the answer to that one.

The air burning her lungs refused to move. It was as if she'd jumped off the deep end of the dock, into a never-ending hole. She'd been here once before, years ago. She'd been the one people were talking about. No one would believe her side of the story then and there was no reason to believe they would this time, either.

"Don't fret, Norma Rose," Ty said. "Give me a few minutes to think this through and we'll come up with a viable excuse that no one will question."

The blood was still pounding in her ears, even though the air rushed out of her mouth, giving way for fresh.

"And you'd better make damn sure your sisters don't get any harebrained ideas to follow suit," her father said.

The air caught again. She didn't have control over her sisters, and she never had. That had been an illusion Norma Rose would never believe again.

Her father sighed and leaned back in his chair, looking as if he'd aged in the few hours since they'd learned of Ginger's absence. "Why couldn't they all be like you, Rosie?"

Why indeed? A better question would be why she couldn't be more like her sisters. Brave enough to make waves, or to learn how to ride those waves despite everything.

Ty wasn't exactly sure what he saw behind Norma Rose's eyes, but it struck him to the core, and sent him reeling. He might as well have been that red puck shooting up the lever to strike the bell at the amusement park. Except there was no resounding ringing of the bell, no little sailor doll to win.

He'd been shot, though, catapulted right into a place he'd never wanted to go. It was as foreign as it had been traveling across the ocean, in a strange and hostile country. He'd survived that journey, and in the years since, he'd used what he'd learned. How to pinpoint his focus, to never take his eye off the target, to never let what flew past his peripheral vision interfere with his aim, his goal.

For years, ever since returning home to a world that had changed, taking away everything he'd held close and dear, he'd honed in his vision on one target, searching only for ways to get a clear shot.

Bodine had become that target. Nothing had changed that in five years. Not a single person, place, or thing had altered his aim or his goal. Yet, somehow, somewhere, between last night and this evening, he'd lost sight of the bull's-eye that had haunted, teased and twisted him inside out.

Ty knew the dangers of these mixed-up thoughts and, needing a way to clear his vision, he nodded toward Roger. "I'll be back."

"Where are you going?" Roger asked.

"I do my best thinking alone." He didn't glance

toward Norma Rose; the heartrending glimmer he'd seen a moment ago would play with his better judgment, just as she'd done all day.

Ty strode out the door and past Twyla, who was sitting behind the desk. Her gaze was curious, but there wasn't any of the probing she'd blistered him with this morning, and that, too, gave him reason to be wary. The rapport between Twyla and Norma Rose had changed this afternoon, leaving more questions unanswered, but he'd be damned if he was going to let them gain his interest. He didn't need to solve any more problems for the Nightingales. Hadn't needed to solve any in the beginning. He was here to take down Bodine.

The evening air, still warm from the day's sunlight, met him as he stepped outside, and he took a deep breath, needing to cleanse and refresh his soul, and the purpose he was committed to.

He crossed the parking lot and followed the path behind the barn that led through the woods, to the farmhouse Bodine had rented. He'd never before lost his focus of the gangster, of the carnage he'd left back in New York, and standing there, staring at the two-story farmhouse, painted white with green trim, Ty searched his innermost being for that purpose, willing it to return.

Memories came first, visions of his parents, shot

dead in their beds, along with Harry, massacred in the hallway. One man with an old rifle against front men with machine guns.

His captain hadn't wanted him to enter the house, the home he'd grown up in, where he'd watched his younger brother while his parents worked from sunup to sundown in the bakery just two doors down, baking bread that had sustained not only their family, but also several others living in the lower east side. His hadn't been the only family lost that night. Bodine had taken out the entire block, to make a statement.

The gangster had claimed Lincoln Street as his own, and he'd chosen the center block to prove it, where innocent families had resided, those who hadn't participated in his lotteries yet had paid his extortion fines all the same.

Bile rose in Ty's throat, burning and bitter. He'd been prepared to take down a bootlegger or two with Bodine. Casualties, just as there'd been in the war.

He blew out a heavy, burning gust of air. Nothing had changed.

Nothing.

Bodine still needed to be taken down, and he was still the man to do it. He'd left being a cop on the beat to become a detective, and then, by special invitation, had joined the elite team the federal government had formed, private eyes focused solely on big-name mobsters. New York gangsters, the families who'd started out running lotteries decades ago and had grown into intricate organized crime syndicates that used extortion and murder to rule entire cities.

Four top members of Bodine's family, including Ray's brother and uncle, were in Leavenworth Penitentiary right now, where they belonged, because of Ty and his due diligence, and Ray Bodine would soon be rotting right alongside them. Only a handful of people knew Ray hadn't died in the shootout that had gutted his cartel. Ty was one of those people and so was his boss, who rarely left Washington, DC; the rest were Bodine's family—his wife and kids.

They'd gone so far as to have a funeral, had paraded the coffin down the street and into the cemetery, as if that was solid proof of his death.

Ty had known it was fake, but couldn't convince his boss until Bodine resurfaced. Not the man himself, but torpedoes and hit men who left Bodine's footprints. They led to Chicago, and then to St. Paul, and Ty had followed.

Alone.

Other agents followed, too, but they were after the front men, drug dealers, rum runners, bootleggers and other two-bit players that Ty didn't give the time of day to. His focus was the big man himself.

"Ty?"

He closed his eyes, trying to shut out everything about Norma Rose and her family. It didn't work. Not only did she repeat his name, but she also stepped closer. To where he could feel her even though they weren't touching.

"Go back to the resort, Norma Rose."

"Are you all right?"

He moved forward, away from her, stepping onto the small porch framing the front door. "I'm fine."

"Why don't I believe you?"

"You'll soon have guests arriving," he told her.

"Yes, I will."

She'd stepped onto the porch, and her closeness twisted things he'd yet to unravel tighter yet. He didn't care about her, or her family. All he cared about was Bodine.

"Ty—"

"Tell them Ginger went to visit the college her friend will be attending," he said, pulling the suggestion out of thin air since he hadn't given it another thought.

"They won't believe that," she said. "Father—"

"They will if you're convincing enough." He turned to face her, but set his gaze over her left shoulder, not prepared to look her in the eye. Those magnificent eyes were too clear, too easy to read. He didn't need any more of that. She'd already knocked a kink in his armor, one he had to repair. "You and Twyla have made up after years of bickering. Folks are going to find that hard to believe, too."

"I wanted to explain that to you. We—"

"Don't bother," he snapped. "It's none of my business."

"What happened?" she asked. "Why are you—"

"Your sister has been found." Not looking at her was growing impossible. Brushing past her, he stomped down the steps. "Now I have to focus on your uncle's case, and I can't do that with you following my every footstep."

"Maybe I can help. Like you did with finding Ginger."

Hearing the clip of her heels on the steps, he kept walking. "You have more than enough to do managing your family and the resort."

"I can manage more—"

She was more persistent than a swarm of mos-quitoes, and he spun around. Damn if a part of him didn't want to grin at the way her lips snapped shut. "I don't want your help, Norma Rose. Nor do I need it. Now run back to your resort and make your customers happy with your complimentary booze."

Her eyes turned ice blue and her glare became as frosty as a December windshield. Her chin rose into that determined lift she'd carried into the po-lice station last night. Without another word, she marched past him, like a soldier going to war. He knew the feeling, how her insides were a mixture of fear and hatred—emotions put there on purpose.

He watched her walk away, battling his own twisted emotions. It was just as well that she went back to hating him now. When he took down Bodine, her father's operation would go down with it.

Ty flinched at the knot that coiled deep inside. She'd hate him like she'd never hated before. Like the way he hated Bodine. After all it was similar. The way he'd take away what she loved. Her re-sort. Her livelihood. Her family.

Chapter Ten

Over the years, Ty had seen everything from seedy whiskey joints that never washed their glasses to high-end car clubs where the men didn't drive, but were *driven* to the club by chauffeurs and had women hanging on their necks with fingers laden with more jewels than the Queen of England had inherited over the centuries. Tonight, standing in the shadows of the old, big barn, he watched people enter the resort, and had to admit, from what he saw, that Nightingale's was an elite club. More upscale than he'd surmised from his earlier observations.

There were no chauffeurs, but the men had on fine suits, and the women, well, he guessed he understood why Norma Rose wore gloves to breakfast. Even when she didn't have blue hands.

In spite of all he'd hashed out in the last hour, he smiled. Yeah, she'd hate him when all this was over, but he'd never forget her. Years from now, after all the gangsters were behind bars and the cities had turned into peaceful havens, he'd still remember how that ink pen had snapped and how her startled look had brought about one of the first genuine smiles he'd experienced in years.

The smile on his face slipped, almost painfully. He knew the gangsters would never all be behind bars—others would just rise up in the holes left by those arrested. But, Norma Rose would hate him when this was all over, forever. He might hate himself, too.

Such was life. He'd long ago committed his existence to retribution, and had given up everything else to have it. Revenge, the longing that had burned inside him for years, didn't leave room for anyone. Not family, not friends and most certainly not a woman. Those were vices he couldn't afford. They not only tied a man down, they left a trail, and a man with a secret life couldn't have that. People connected to him could get hurt, too. They were bound to, and Ty didn't ever want to experience that kind of pain again.

Not feeling was a much better existence.

Accepting that resolution, Ty stepped out of the shadows and waited for a car—a big fancy one that had more lights on it than the string marquees on Broadway—to find a place to park before he maneuvered through the lot to his truck.

He backed out of the parking spot and slowly made his way to the tree-lined path that led to his cabin. There was a lot of work to do before Bodine showed up, and it included being inside the resort, even though he'd rather not be there.

Traveling light was the way of a federal agent. The suitcase under the seat of his truck held one additional suit, two shirts and a few sets of Munsingwear union suits and pairs of socks. He'd pull out a clean set—recently washed and dried in a hotel room—visit the bath house and then attend the party.

Dusk lasted for hours this far north in the summer, and as he parked his truck, the gray light was more than enough for him to notice the white paper cone rolling to a stop on the floor of the passenger seat.

Ty let it be.

"This is pretty. Where'd you get it?"

Norma Rose turned from her office window, where she'd watched Ty drive away. She should be wishing he'd gone in the opposite direction—

and left the resort—but she couldn't dredge that thought up. She was mad at him, and loathed the very thought of him, but even more so, she wanted to know what had filled his eyes with sorrow.

"From the amusement park," she said, referring to the snow globe Twyla held. The bits of glitter were catching light as they swirled around the waterfall, sparkling like real snow.

"The strongman game?" Twyla asked, setting the globe on the desk. "No one ever wins one of these. The game's rigged."

Still dressed in the pink outfit, along with the borrowed white shoes, Twyla had a folded pink scarf around her head, leaving her red waves showing above the band that was tied fashionably below one ear. Her earlobes, which still had to be red and swollen, were covered, yet a pair of dangling earrings hung below the scarf.

Wanting to discuss anything expect Ty, the snow globe—which she moved closer to the center of her desk so it wouldn't accidently get knocked off—or the amusement park, Norma Rose asked, "Why'd you pierce the second ear after the first one hurt so much?"

Twyla shrugged. "Well, I couldn't walk around wearing just one earring, could I?" Without waiting for an answer, she continued, "It was one of those things in life that once you start, you have to finish it. Besides, it gave me a good excuse."

"Excuse for what?"

"For not going to the amusement park," Twyla answered, before hugging herself as she let loose an exaggerated shiver. "Have you ever worked a kissing booth?"

"Of course not."

"Well, don't." Twyla laughed. "I will admit some of it was fun, and a few kisses were rather amazing, but for the most part, I'd rather vomit in my mouth than kiss some of those men again."

Norma Rose stopped the direction her mind wanted to sail down. "Why'd you do it?"

"Do we really have to go down this street again?" Twyla asked, frowning. "I already told you why I did it and apologized." Her eyes turned pleading, but her voice was serious. "Just give me a chance, Norma Rose, and I'll prove to you how much help I can be around here."

Twyla had already been a big help. She'd taken over seating the guests in the dining room as they arrived and making sure their first round of drinks was promptly delivered. The assistance had been needed. With their father still in his office, or perhaps with Uncle Dave, who was now recovering nicely, Norma Rose had her hands full. Wayne had arrived and she'd had to go through his music, assuring he could provide the music that their guests expected. An amateur compared to Brock, Wayne was not up to the standards the resort was known for providing.

Her sister was putting her best foot forward, too. Though Twyla greeted each guest enthusiastically, she'd dowsed the overzealous flirting she'd poured over most men the past few months.

Serious herself, Norma Rose said, "I'm counting on that, and you. Between all that's going on with Ginger and Uncle Dave, I have a feeling Father isn't going to be as involved with the resort as usual for the next few days."

The door had opened while she'd been speaking.

"You can count on me, too," Josie said, entering the room and closing the door behind her.

Twyla had told Josie about Ginger, and Uncle Dave, while Norma Rose had been fuming over Ty's change in attitude, and now, looking at her sisters, a hint of a chill rippled her spine, making her question if her sisters had some sort of conspiracy going on.

"You're going to need all the help you can get

with Wayne Sears beating on the piano keys," Josie added.

Norma Rose sighed. "He's not quite up to our standards."

Josie walked to the window. "No one's arrived for the past few minutes, but I'll keep a look out and station myself at the front desk, while you two take care of business."

Dressed in a white fringe-covered dress, with matching pantyhose and shoes, Josie had a gold headband spouting a single white feather. Not used to seeing this sister dressed so fashionably, Norma Rose was still contemplating how stunning the outfit was when Josie spoke again.

"Few musicians can match Brock's skills. That's why he was offered a radio contract."

"And Ginger is with him," Twyla added. "In Chicago. I can hardly believe that."

"I can," Josie said.

"Why do you say that?" Norma Rose asked, bracing herself.

"Because Ginger is in love with Brock," Josie said, glancing out the window again.

"No," Twyla said.

Norma Rose sucked in a breath, knowing she'd need it.

"Yes." Josie looked at them both squarely as she settled her backside against the table Ty had so causally eaten at this morning. "I can't believe you both hadn't seen that. Why do you think she was so furious with Mitsy Kemper? Mitsy went out with Brock one time."

"Mitsy's gone out with every man from here to St. Paul," Twyla answered with more than a hint of disgust.

"And beyond," Josie said. "Good thing her father owns a drugstore."

"Why?" Norma Rose asked, puzzled.

"For birth control. Rubbers," Josie said, as if it was a subject she spoke about daily.

Norma Rose almost choked on her own tongue. Yet she wanted to bypass that subject, for now anyway, and managed to say, "But you had a crush on Brock." Turning to include Twyla, she said, "Both of you."

"Who didn't have a crush on Brock?" Twyla asked. "He's a flame."

Josie nodded in agreement. "He is—everyone carried a torch for Brock, but Ginger was beyond that, she was all soppy over him, and got mad when Mitsy boasted about kissing him." Grinning broadly, Josie added, "Wouldn't it be the bee's knees if they actually got married?"

Twyla squealed excitedly. "Yes, that would be berries, just berries."

"If I'd known she planned on running away with him," Josie said, "I'd have given her some sisterly advice. And a rubber or two."

Norma Rose lost her voice completely, and hadn't yet found it when Josie clapped her hands.

"I see headlights. I'll go write them a receipt," Josie said to Twyla, "while you check the dining room. I had to seat the last people at the bar until a table opened."

Josie crossed the room, and Norma Rose, head still spinning, had barely turned around before her sister had already opened the door.

Twyla was close on Josie's heels, but she paused. "Don't look so shocked, Rosie. You didn't honestly believe they only plan birthday parties at those ladies aid meetings, did you?"

Norma Rose felt for the corner of her desk as the door closed, and found it before her knees gave out.

Rubbers? Marriage? Oh, goodness.

Ginger was in Chicago, with a man she believed she was in love with, and Twyla and Josie had been given free rein to mingle with the guests. What was happening around here? What had she been thinking?

The door opened again before she had a chance to answer her own questions.

Josie poked her head in. "The sheriff's here."

"Well, sell him a meal ticket," Norma Rose said, glad this at least was an easy problem.

Josie shook her head. "He doesn't want a ticket. He needs to talk to Father. Says it's urgent."

Norma Rose pushed off her desk and smoothed her black skirt over her still rather wobbly knees before preparing to leave her office, but had yet to take a step when Sheriff Withers walked in and closed the door behind him.

Instead of his regular uniform, the sheriff had on a dark suit and hat. Furthermore, sweat dripped off his jowls. "I drove my wife's car," he said, "to not attract attention."

His wife's yellow breezer was as well-known as his state-issued sedan with the gold star on the doors. "Oh?" Norma Rose said, not letting anything show. It was good to know she hadn't lost all of her acting abilities. A poker face was hard to master, but she had become an expert over the years and the fact the skill had eluded her for most

of the day was bothersome. Ty was the reason behind that.

"There's a snitch among us, Norma Rose," the
sheriff said quietly. "Worse than that, actually."
He twisted his hands and glanced over both shoulders, even though they were clearly alone. "It's a
fed. An agent working undercover."

A bath and clean clothes hadn't done anything
for Ty's mood. For the first time in a very long
time, he wanted to be alone with his thoughts,
but he still left his cabin. He usually spent a lot of
time alone, and that could be part of the problem.
Since arriving he'd been rather preoccupied by the
happenings at the resort. Now that Ginger was no
longer a concern, at least not to him, he could concentrate on more important things. Like how and
when Bodine had poisoned Dave.

People sat on the terrace facing the lake, eating
meals delivered by waiters through open doors
that also let out music—if it could be called that.
He'd heard a lot of musicians over the years, and
couldn't remember hearing one tear apart a song
quite that badly. The piano wasn't out of tune, so
only the fingers hitting the ivory could be blamed.

He made his way around the building and headed

toward the other row of cabins to check in on Dave before going to get a meal himself. However, upon entering the trees, he paused. Norma Rose and a man were heading up the walkway to Dave's cabin. It only took a moment to recall the man was the sheriff, though now wearing a suit.

Ty waited until they entered, then he weaved a path through the trees, staying hidden until he was three cabins down before he dashed across the dirt roadway. Then he made his way around the back of the cabins, working his way toward Dave's.

The window in Dave's bedroom was open, but between the waves rushing onto the shore only a few feet away and the hushed voices, he could barely make out a word. Ty weighed his options, and listened to his gut, which said to lay low.

It wasn't long before the door opened. Ty carefully peered around the corner. Norma Rose, alone, stomped across the dirt road. Her strut, with arms swinging and back stiff, shouted loud and clear. She was mad. Extremely.

After a full five minutes, making sure Norma Rose wasn't waiting in the trees, Ty snuck around the cabin next door and then casually walked around it and up the road to Dave's.

His single knock was responded to immediately

by Roger Nightingale. Stepping through the doorway, Ty feigned surprise and nodded toward Withers, who was sitting at the table along with Roger, Dave and Gloria. "Evening, Sheriff."

Withers responded, "Mr. Bradshaw."

The tension was thick and heavy, and glances bounced between all four of the table's occupants. "Am I interrupting something?" Ty asked. "I can come back."

"No," Roger said. "Come in. The sheriff was just leaving."

Reading men, especially the things they tried to hide, was one of Ty's specialties, and Withers hadn't expected to leave so soon. The sheriff rose.

"Yes, I was." Nodding toward Roger, Withers added, "You'll let me know if you need me."

"I always do," Roger said.

Ty stayed where he stood, waiting to open the door for Withers, once the man was done saying goodbye to Dave and Gloria. As he closed the door behind the sheriff, Roger instructed him to take a seat.

There'd definitely been a new development, and not acknowledging that was Ty's best choice. In a situation like this, waiting to be told always provided more information. "I was on my way to supper," he said, moving across the room and taking the now vacant chair. "But thought I'd stop in to see how you're doing." He nodded toward Dave. "Looks like you're a lot better."

"Lots," Dave said. "Thanks."

"I haven't done anything yet," Ty answered, leaning back in his chair. "But I am here to find out what happened to you. Who slipped you the Mickey. And I will."

Gloria had risen and set a cup of coffee that held a splash of the labeled brandy bottle in front of him as she took her seat again. After taking a sip, Ty asked, "You remember anything you can share?"

His eyes were bloodshot and his pallor was still the color of a sailor on his first trip across the ocean, but otherwise Dave seemed no worse for wear.

"There's nothing to share," Dave said. "I bought a milk shake at Charlie's drugstore in St. Paul and went into his back room to wait for a prospect who never showed up." After taking a drink of water from his glass, Dave added, "I felt an edge coming on and the next thing I remember was the police station and you telling me it was time to go."

"There's something else we need to talk about," Roger said gruffly.

Life was full of the unexpected, and Ty was always prepared for it. "The news Withers brought?"

"You heard?" Roger asked.

Ty shook his head. "Assumed. Why else would he be here in street clothes." He phrased it as a statement, not a question. The assumptions he had could lead in several directions. He just needed a bit of conversation to tell him which path to take.

His line of business made Roger Nightingale a hard man, and tonight he looked the part. Formidable in his three-piece maroon suit, with his graying bushy brows knitted together and his blue eyes glittering with antagonism. But in the short time Ty had been at the resort, he'd seen the man in other roles. A worried brother-in-law, a savvy resort owner and, most telling of all, a parent who'd thought—if even just for a moment—the worst had happened to one of his children.

"Minneapolis is full of snitches," Roger said. "So is St. Cloud. But money talks in St. Paul, and it talks in these parts, too. Informants know that, and stay clear, knowing they'll only be sent on wild-goose chases at best. And end up in a pine box at worst."

Ty refrained from answering. He kept his breathing smooth, even as his pulse started knocking hard beneath his skin. It was impossible for anyone to have learned his identity, but not impossible for them to wonder about it. Especially Norma Rose, which might explain her stomping away from the cabin.

That stuck. She'd have been skipping like a school girl if she'd convinced her father he was a snitch. The smile that thought created, although well concealed, gave him more reassurance than anything Roger could say. Ty lassoed his thoughts to hear what the man was saying.

"Times around here were tough. During the war, the government begged farmers to grow more crops. Shiploads went overseas every day, but as soon as the fighting stopped, so did the demand. Folks in this area had more land than they could afford. They'd mortgaged everything they owned to acquire more land and buy new equipment. The bills started choking them, and they had no way to pay them."

Ty picked up his coffee cup, but never took his eyes off Roger, letting him know he was listening, and interested.

"Minnesotans are a hearty lot," Roger continued. "We are strong-willed and determined, and find ways. When all others moan and beg for help, we put on our boots and start kicking. Minnesota Thirteen didn't come by accident."

Ty was completely interested. The homemade whiskey coming out of central Minnesota was exactly what Bodine was after, the money and conglomerate behind it. Few other mobsters had tried, but the farmers didn't let strangers in. The extortion that worked in the big cities hadn't worked here, and as far as he'd learned, Nightingale was the only man exporting large quantities. Not personally, of course, but he brokered the deals.

"Those Germans have always taken their still-making seriously, and making whiskey that is often better than the stuff the Canadians export has provided them with a way to feed their families again. It's allowing entire communities to thrive. Hardware stores, grocery stores—hell, the entire automobile industry would be nothing but empty lots if not for bootleggers."

"Amen," Gloria agreed.

"My business is no different," Roger said. "The resort employs more people than some factories. If not for Nightingales, Dol's grocery store would only be half its size, Lester would only need a portion of the cows he milks every morning and Scooter wouldn't sell enough gas to keep his doors open."

"As well as most every other business around here," Gloria said. "Money makes money, there's no mistaking that."

Roger's chair creaked as he leaned back and crossed thick arms over his barrel chest. "And I won't let some sniveling snitch stick his nose where it doesn't belong."

Ty withheld the urge to swallow. Maybe Norma Rose had convinced her father. It was impossible, though. His file was sealed in cement and dropped in the river. So to speak. In truth, someone digging hard enough might uncover something. But only if there was a snitch in his department, which consisted of two people. Him and his boss.

"Who do you think it is?" Ty asked.

"An outsider," Roger said. "Everyone around here wants things to stay just as they are. They remember what it was like, just a few years ago, eating nothing but potato soup on good days. It's outsiders that wanted drinking to end. Not Minnesotans."

"People all across the nation were against Prohibition," Ty said, though he wondered why. More of the nation had voted wet than dry, but the drys down south, added to the big cities of New York and Washington DC, had been enough to calculate a win.

"Yes, they were, and are," Roger agreed. "And Minnesota Thirteen is keeping them wet." He intertwined his fingers and popped his knuckles. "Withers thinks the snitch is a fed. A federal agent sent up here to infiltrate the community."

"Why here?" Ty asked. "Minnesota Thirteen is brewed west of here, more north of St. Cloud."

"A man can be at any one of those stills—Avon, Holdingford, Albany, Melrose—within a few hours from here," Roger answered. "Running shine is risky, and men do it in many ways—hay wagons, extra gas tanks, crates and barrels marked bibles or produce, even piano boxes or under the floorboards of a truck hauling a bull." With a guffaw he added, "A calf sells for five bucks, so does a bottle of shine. But those are little runners. Local deliveries to speakeasies and blind pigs. The big shipments, the ones that make it to Chicago, New York, California and beyond, take real transportation."

Ty's pulse was knocking again. He'd known Nightingale was in deep, and the amount of money already invested in the resort proved this man was making money left and right. The latest figures estimated over two million a week was made on illegal alcohol sales in Chicago alone. A man making that kind of money wouldn't think twice about putting a bullet in someone trying to stop him.

"The same trains that haul in sugar and yeast and bottles and kegs, haul out sugar and yeast and bottles and kegs, just in a different combination." Roger was rubbing his chin now, rather thoughtfully.

Ty took another sip of his coffee. Nightingale wasn't giving out any specific details, but was leaving a lot of room for assumptions.

"So, where does Withers think this snitch is?" Ty asked.

"His informant doesn't know. Right now it's hearsay from someone who'd heard, from someone who'd heard. It's happened before, someone needing a little cash claims to know something, and so the story goes, but this time my gut tells me there's more to it than just a hungry homeless person or a drunk flyboy. I'm also thinking whoever is behind Dave's poisoning could be connected to the snitch, if not the man himself."

The ounce of relief that oozed over his stomach

wasn't as strong as Ty would have liked. "Then my work is cut out for me," he said. "Catching two birds with one stone."

"Your work is cut out for you," Roger agreed with a nod. "I want that snitch. I want him in my office by the end of the week."

Unwilling to set himself up for failure, Ty shook his head. "I told you I've got some suspicions and inklings, but I'm going to need more than a week."

"I've got my suspicions, too," Roger said. "And I won't give you more than a week."

He should have seen this coming. Staring into his empty coffee cup, he let the others—Roger, Dave and Gloria—watch him intently and form a few more suspicions and doubts. When the air was as thick as morning fog, he pushed the cup away and stood. "Then I'm not your man."

Chapter Eleven

Normally the music had people dancing, but Wayne, despite how hard he tried, just didn't pull people off their seats. In fact, when they did stand up, they walked toward the door, not the dance floor.

Norma Rose had watched that happening, but her searing mind wouldn't let her try to resolve the issue. "This isn't any of your concern, Rosie," her father had said when she'd taken the sheriff to Dave's cabin. "Your concern is seeing that everyone at the resort is happy—now go to it."

He'd been stern, too, more so than usual, and that grated on her nerves. It *was* her concern. She knew who the snitch was, and that burned. Ty Bradshaw had left his mark on her, with all his gallantry. Pretending to be a gentleman. Taking her out in public. Winning her a snow globe. Buying her cotton candy. All the while he was a fed set on taking her very livelihood away.

"We have to do something, Norma Rose."

She blinked several times, bringing her fury-filled vision into focus. Twyla and Josie stood beside her, in the doorway leading from the dining room into the ballroom, where tables and bar stools on either side were emptying out. She wasn't sure which sister had spoken—they both looked at her gravely.

"People need to start dancing," Josie said.

"And drinking," Twyla said. "They need to be full of giggle water to dance to this." Shaking her head, she added, "I never knew Wayne was this bad."

"He wasn't the last time he played here," Norma Rose said. At least he sure hadn't seemed this bad. He had the notes right, but the tempo was so slow the notes didn't connect, instead they dragged into one another painfully.

"I've got an idea," Twyla said, "but I don't want you turning into a fire extinguisher on me."

Norma Rose had played the role of chaperone so long, not doing so would most likely be impossible, yet the way she was feeling right now, she didn't care what Twyla did. Or if people started dancing or not. If her father didn't care, why should she? One slow night wasn't going to close them down.

But a snitch would.

"What is it?" she asked, holding in a sigh, mainly because she knew she did care. About the resort, and about a snitch. No federal agent would pull the wool over her eyes.

"Just give me permission, and you'll see," Twyla said.

Her father had told her to make sure people were having a good time. "Go ahead," Norma Rose said. "I'll probably regret it, but what's one more amongst many."

Twyla frowned. So did Josie. Norma Rose pulled up one of her false smiles, which just made her feel worse than ever.

"Are you all right?" Josie asked.

"I'm fine," Norma Rose answered. "Fine and dandy."

Twyla tugged on her pink scarf, settling it in place while a slightly sinister, yet demure smile curled the corners of her red lips. Before Norma Rose could voice her doubts, Twyla grabbed Josie's hand.

"Come on, sis," Twyla said. "Fetch Scooter and meet me on the dance floor."

Norma Rose willed her feet to stay planted as her sisters scurried away. The urge to call them back bubbled up her throat. It was hard, and painful, but she swallowed the urge and watched. What harm could they *really* do? The crowd was not having a good time, and Nightingale's resort hadn't gained the reputation it had by unhappy customers. Granted, some were here just to have a few drinks and relax, but others weren't.

Twyla was behind the bar, talking with Reggie, and Josie was leaning on Scooter's shoulder, being a bit more friendly than Norma Rose had ever seen, and that caused another stabbing sensation in her stomach. Josie wouldn't tell Scooter about Ginger. Her sisters had been sworn to secrecy, but she might share information about Ty. Her suspicions—that he was a snitch—Norma Rose hadn't divulged. To them, he was an attorney. And a welcome guest.

Some guest. He wasn't even here in the ballroom or the dining room. That didn't make her happy, either. He was probably out snooping around, trying to find something—anything—to report back to his cronies. How could she keep an eye on him, expose him for what he was, if she didn't know where he was?

Carrying a tray with half-full glasses, Twyla made her way over to Wayne and sat down on the piano bench beside him. When the song ended, to the relief of many, Twyla handed him a glass and picked up one herself. She stood and held the glass high in the air.

The crowd had already been quiet, but now turned ghostly silent. One could almost hear the cigarettes sizzling as people took long draws while staring at the stage.

"Don't know how many of you have heard," Twyla shouted, "but Brock Ness headed to Chicago last night to perform on the radio. We're gonna miss him around here."

The crowd responded with murmurs and a couple of louder comments, agreeing with her. Someone yelled, "Already do!"

"He's probably already playing on the radio down there in Chicago, and right now, we're going to tip one for him." Twyla waved her glass. "Reggie's pouring glasses for everyone, so if you've got a dead soldier at your table, wave your hand, so we can get a glass to you."

Hands went up across the room, and four girls carried trays around, passing out glasses to people growing more eager by the minute.

"How we doing?" Twyla asked a couple minutes later. "Everyone got a glass? Hold 'em up!"

A few shouts indicated others still needed a drink, and Norma Rose somehow ended up holding one as well.

"Now how we doing?" Twyla asked. "Show me your glasses, folks, get 'em up! Everyone's going to toast Brock!"

The crowd was coming around, shouting and cheering. Even those in the dining room. Norma Rose almost cracked a smile. Toasting Brock was a good idea, but would it last? One toast wouldn't make for a night of fun.

The girls kept passing out glasses, setting them on tables even though everyone had a drink in their hand and were waving them about. People clambered to their feet, then shouted Brock's name.

"Swell!" Twyla yelled above the ruckus. "Brock, wherever you are, this one's for you!" She knocked back the drink like she'd been doing so for years.

The crowd roared and followed suit. Norma Rose took a sip and had a hard time swallowing. Her throat felt on fire, but in honor of Brock, she held her breath and finished her glass.

Twyla set her empty glass on top of the piano with a resounding thud, and then picked up a second glass. "Grab another soldier, folks," she shouted.

The crowd didn't need any coaxing. The shouts and cheers were much louder this time around. Norma Rose ended up with a second glass from one of the girls still scrambling about with trays.

"This time, we're gonna toast Wayne," Twyla shouted. "He's feeling a bit down, knowing you were disappointed that Brock isn't here."

The room rumbled with agreement. Wayne stood up beside Twyla, at her urging, and tipped his hat.

"To Wayne!" Twyla shouted.

Her toast was repeated several times as people tossed down another glass. In honor of Wayne, Norma Rose held her breath and swallowed the contents of her second glass. It was easier this time, and the warmth in her belly was almost satisfying.

"Now, then," Twyla said, smacking her glass down by the other one. "We're gonna do one more thing."

The crowd cheered.

"I knew you'd like it!" Her laughter was contagious. The entire room filled with *yee-haws*, and she waited until it died down before she said, "We're gonna have a dance-off!"

The room had already been transformed, but now merriment bounced off the walls as people applauded.

"Grab a partner," Twyla encouraged. "Dac Lester is over there by the bar. You all know Dac doesn't dance, don't you?"

Once again cheers abounded.

"He's gonna be the timekeeper. One hour of solid dancing. You leave the floor, and you're done. The last couple on the floor will win a full bottle of Minnesota's finest!" Twyla pointed to Dac again, who now held a bottle of corn whiskey over his head.

"What about the woman?" someone asked. "A bottle is fine for a man."

The crowd laughed, and Norma Rose stretched on her toes, trying to see who'd asked the question. It was a female voice, but she didn't recognize it.

Twyla looked lost for a moment, and turned her gaze to Norma Rose. Unsure what her sister was asking, for there was a definite question in her gaze, Norma Rose nodded, thinking she must be asking permission to give away a bottle of wine.

"How about a snow globe?" Twyla asked.

Norma Rose flinched, and a growl rumbled in her throat. It shouldn't matter. She shouldn't want the stupid thing. Wouldn't want anything to remind her of Ty when all was said and done.

Twyla was still looking at her, seeking permission. Despite how jagged and shallow her breathing had become, Norma Rose pulled up a smile and nodded again.

"All right, folks, the prizes are a bottle for the last man and a snow globe for the last woman still on the dance floor one hour from now!" Twyla shouted. The floor was already filling up, yet she added, "Come on, there's still room!"

Norma Rose was teetering between anger and astonishment. Her sister had livened up the place, but was also giving away her snow globe. A trivial carnival prize that held no significant value, or meaning—or so she wished. The truth was, she liked that snow globe and didn't want to give it away.

Two solid hands gripped her waist, and shoved her forward, toward the dance floor. Her heels slid onward although she tried to stop them, and the quickening of her heart—though she hadn't turned around and the owner of those hands hadn't spoken—told her exactly who held her.

She would not dance with him. Would not.

He didn't give her a chance to protest once they

reached the dance floor. With both hands still grasping her waist, Ty spun her around and, holding her much too close for comfort, started to glide her across the floor.

Fuming, she pressed her hands at his shoulders, trying to put some space between them. Enough to make an escape. His hold was firm, and the cocky grin on his face wilted her persistence.

"Yee-haw," someone shouted. "Even Norma Rose is on the dance floor."

"And she's all mine, fellas," Ty said, "so watch out."

Laughter echoed around the room and Norma Rose pushed on his shoulders again, though not overly hard—she didn't want people to notice. "I am not yours," she hissed.

Ty merely grinned.

She returned one as false as his.

"Twyla, did you slip your sister a Mickey?" someone else asked.

"Of course not," Twyla answered.

Norma Rose twisted to find her sister, but Ty glided them deeper into the crowd, forcing her more tightly against him.

"This was all Norma Rose's idea," Twyla said,

somehow appearing next to her. "To get this night drumming."

"Did your daddy skip town?" Twyla's partner asked, who just happened to be Jimmy Sonny. "Or do you girls have him locked up somewhere?"

"No, and no," Twyla answered, steering Jimmy in the opposite direction.

Whatever else she'd said was lost in the noise.

Ty's hold eased up a bit, but before Norma Rose could take advantage of it, he grasped her hands. "You do know how to do the bunny hop, don't you?"

"The bunny hop?" she repeated, rather appalled. The dance was said to mimic rabbits mating. She'd seen it performed, and had practiced the moves in her bedroom alone, as she did with all the other popular dance moves. Once in a while, she'd accept an offer to dance, but very rarely. Her sisters were always looking over the railing, and she hadn't wanted one of them to make a scene. Which is what would have happened if they'd caught her on the dance floor. They were all on the floor now, and couldn't make a scene. Or could they? Twyla certainly had got the crowd keyed up.

"Yes, the bunny hop," Ty said, with a full open-mouthed smile. "Follow me. I'll show you."

"I will not follow you and you will not show me anything," Norma Rose insisted. Yet, considering half the room had noticed her and was watching, she didn't hold true to her protest. Instead, she followed him. And mimicked him. She kicked out one foot and hopped three times on the other before sliding toward him until their stomachs touched, which jolted the air right out of her lungs.

"That's my girl," he said as they broke away, to kick the opposite leg and hop three more times before gliding into one another again.

"I'm not your girl," she said, trying not to enjoy how close he held her.

"Then pretend you are," he said into her ear. "You're good at pretending."

Whoops and hollers echoed above the music, and she didn't even try to answer him. She was good at pretending, as good as him.

The drinks Twyla had encouraged Wayne to swig had helped his playing, or the toast had, because he was now pounding out a tempo the dancers loved.

When they slid together again, Ty's arm wrapped around her, locking her stomach and hips against his, and Norma Rose put on her best smile, laughing along with the rest of the dancers. Ty's eyes flashed a challenge as he turned his face sideways. She was up to any challenge he wanted to send her way, and did the same. With the side of his cheek pressed against hers, he led them forward, past other dancers to the edge of the floor, where he twirled her around and started back in the other direction, his cheek to hers.

It was exhilarating, being part of the crowd rather than watching from the sidelines, and Norma Rose let the excitement in, gave it free rein to continue working its magic.

In the center of the floor, Ty released her, but took her hand as they kicked, hopped and glided back toward one another. By now, Norma Rose had found the rhythm in every step and discovered newfound freedom in performing each one.

The two glasses of hooch she'd had must have gone to her head. Why else would she be participating instead of protesting? Then again, not participating would suggest she was against the crowd having fun, which she wasn't. However, she shouldn't be dancing with Ty.

They crisscrossed the dance floor, arriving at each corner cheek-to-cheek, and stopping in the middle to kick, hop and glide into one another, only to sweep back over to another corner, again cheek to cheek.

Her heart raced, her feet felt as light as feathers and the euphoria floating inside her was incomparable to anything she'd ever known. It was like she was a bird, released from its gilded cage to soar at will. And she was soaring.

Wayne barely paused between songs, and as others started tapping their heels, and shuffling their feet back and forth while dancing side by side, arms stretched over each other's shoulders, Norma Rose watched eagerly.

She'd seen people doing the Charleston, but had yet to try it—outside of her bedroom.

"Later," Ty said next to her ear as they once again glided to each other. "We have to pace ourselves if we want to win."

A splattering of reality hit Norma Rose like drops of cold rain. "I am not dancing a full hour with you," she said, while their cheeks were pressed together. She plastered another smile on her face as they passed other dancers.

"Yes, you are," he said.

"No, I'm not."

They'd reached the edge of the dance floor and his brief pause made her wish she hadn't protested.

He swung her around and headed back in the other direction.

"Oh, yes, you are," he said before they reached the center of the floor. "I didn't win that snow globe for you to give it away."

"How do you know it's the same one?" she asked, kicking one leg.

He waited until they'd hopped and glided together before saying, "I saw the way your sister looked at you, asking permission."

"This was all very impromptu," she admitted. "People were leaving."

"I saw that," he said, gliding her toward another corner.

Her cheek was hot, throbbing and more sensitive than ever. Between dancing and talking, she was breathless, and other parts of her had grown highly responsive, and throbbing, and hot. She truly didn't know breasts did such things.

Pulling her mind off her body, she asked, "From where? You weren't in the ballroom or dining room."

"Looking for me, were you?"

"No."

"Yes, you were," he insisted. "I saw you watching out the window when I took my truck around to my cabin."

They were once again in the center of the room, kicking and hopping, doing it all without thinking. Which gave room for other thoughts to return. "I know who you are," she said.

He lifted a single eyebrow. "Ty Bradshaw, private eye."

"More like Ty Bradshaw, a snitch." Her breathlessness as she pressed her cheek against his took the sting out of her words.

He laughed. "Is that worse than being a fed, or better?"

Dancing made it difficult for her anger to renew itself, and Norma Rose couldn't find an answer. She wanted to feel anger strong enough that she could chew on it, taste it, but instead, she felt the rumble of Ty's laugh again and the heat of his body. The smell of his cologne was getting to her, too, as was the touch of his hands. With each dance movement, he touched her someplace—her back, her waist, her shoulders, the palms of her hands—and every touch had her craving more.

"When are you government people going to realize it's tax money, our tax money, that pays your salary?" she asked, hoping to dredge up a bit of the loathing she'd earlier experienced.

"I do realize that," he said. "I thought of it the entire time I was overseas."

The song switched again, and this time it was a slow one, giving the dancers an opportunity to catch their breath. A few couples collapsed on chairs around the tables next to the floor, worn out from the exhausting moves of the Charleston.

Ty curled an arm around her waist and folded the fingers of his other hand around her palm, holding her arm in the air as their steps naturally flowed into a slow, easy two-step.

"The entire time I was in the army, I remembered my payment came from taxes paid by people who were pouring their own blood, sweat and tears into their private businesses back home. That's what kept me going—knowing I was protecting them."

He'd changed his clothes from earlier in the day. Now he wore a gray shirt that shimmered in the pale lights overhead, and Norma Rose had a hard time pulling her gaze off his shoulder to meet his eyes. Several local men had served in the war, including Uncle Dave, and she knew firsthand that they didn't like talking about what they'd seen, what they'd experienced. But there was more to it than that. More to why she was afraid to look him in the eye. She might get pulled in again. Start thinking of him as someone other than just a federal agent. Like the man who'd helped her look for her sister all afternoon. The one who'd won her a snow globe and bought her cotton candy.

"Don't frown, Norma Rose," he said softly.

She sucked in air, glanced up and instantly felt herself sinking. His brown eyes were so dark that the ceiling lights reflected in them like stars she could wish upon in the sky.

Little crinkles appeared near Ty's eyes as he added, "We're winning."

A few more people had found seats, but she answered, "There's still a lot of couples dancing."

"But we have a chance at winning," he said. "We just gotta keep pacing ourselves." He increased the pressure of his arm around her back. "Nice and slow until the end, when we wow them with the Charleston."

"Wow them?"

He grinned broader.

"What if I don't know how to dance the Charleston?"

"I'll teach you."

Her feet barely moved, as he eased her back and forth through the dance steps, but her insides were flying hard and fast, and so was her mind. Once again she attempted to remind herself he was a snitch. A government agent wanting to arrest her father, make her family penniless again, yet she couldn't believe it. How could she, of all people, *feel* this way about a man like that? For she was feeling things. Sensations and emotions she'd never imagined were a part of her. Her eyes started to smart and she had to close them.

Ty had won. At least that's what he told himself. Norma Rose was crumbling in his hands. Why then, did a hollow, sinking numbness spread across his chest?

The musician who'd almost put the entire crowd to sleep earlier transitioned into another song. An upbeat ragtime song that had the crowd cheering again.

Norma Rose lifted her chin, giving him that haughty and overly coy smile, and the numbness faded inside Ty, giving room for other things to arise. He hadn't danced in ages, not with a woman this pretty, nor could he remember the last time he'd had fun like this.

He lifted Norma Rose's hand higher in the air

and, using his other hand, twirled her around in a perfect pirouette. The audience, those watching closely and placing bets on winners, applauded.

She was more graceful than a swan. Had been from the moment he'd ushered her onto the floor. He hadn't planned on that—dragging her into the center of the room, dancing. The crowd was toasting Brock Ness and his radio deal when he'd arrived in the dining room. It had been seeing her reaction to giving away the snow globe that had put a knot in his stomach.

It was hers, and he'd see it remained in her possession. Pacing themselves, so they weren't exhausted for the last ten minutes of the dance-off, was how it would happen. He was used to waiting for the showdown, but Norma Rose was more like a mother hen, rushing in and using up all her energy in the first few moments. Teaching her restraint, in other ways besides dancing, was an enjoyable thought, too.

He was leading her through the long flowing steps of the fox-trot, a dance that could be altered to fit any tempo and rhythm. She was a fast learner, adapting to the easy, smooth steps even as he spun around for them to dance shoulder-to-shoulder instead of chest-to-chest.

The hardest thing about forcing one's mind to

occupy other thoughts was making the body follow suit, and in this case, his was being a hearty opponent. It had been ever since that first bunny hop, when her breasts had collided with his chest, sending his pulse racing so forcefully, he thought it might split his skin.

Her enjoyment did things to him, too. Those magnificent blue eyes glittered like diamonds and her smile was the first totally natural one he'd seen her make. There was no falseness behind it. Nothing hidden, fake, or shy.

He spun her beneath their clasped hands again, waiting until she'd made a full circle before pulling her close to sweep her across the floor. The heat of her palm, planted firmly on his shoulder, could have been the bottom of a logger's branding iron burning a stamp into the ends of logs in the north woods. He'd worked in one of those logging camps in upstate New York prior to the war, and wondered, for just a moment, where he'd be today if he'd gone back to it after returning home. Not here. That was a given. Not dancing with a beautiful woman.

Despite his efforts to last to the end, Ty was growing tired by the time there were only five couples left on the dance floor. The crowd, most of them having gained their second wind from sitting at the tables and downing a few more cocktails, surrounded the dance floor, cheering and shouting names.

Led by her sisters, people shouted their names. Norma Rose's cheeks were bright red, and Ty understood it didn't come from the dancing. Competitive to the core, her determination now matched his.

"Less than five minutes left," Dac Lester shouted. "One dance!"

The crowd cheered.

"What if there's more than one couple still standing?" a breathless woman asked, sagging against her partner as Wayne ended a slow song.

"There won't be," Norma Rose declared. The crowd roared and her glittering eyes sparked with energy. She stepped out of Ty's arms, but held one hand tightly. Lowering her voice, so only he'd hear, she said, "Time to teach me the Charleston."

"I think you already know it," Ty replied, pulling her into the center of the floor.

"I do," she answered proudly. "So, I'll teach you."

"I'm all yours," Ty said, striking a pose.

She laughed, and set her feet even with his.

Wayne struck the first keys with all the skill of

a master musician, and the dancer in both of them went to work. Heels clicking and soles shuffling, they edged toward each other and retreated as if playing a game of cat and mouse.

The crowd cheered, filling the entire room with noise that almost drowned out the music. Not that they needed it. He and Norma Rose were too tuned in to one another to need much of an outside encouragement.

Norma Rose knew the steps of the Charleston better than those living in the city that had created the dance and Ty kicked his last bit of vigor into full force. He didn't like losing, not even a silly dance-off. However, for the first time in about as long as he could remember, he wasn't thinking about himself. What he wanted. His focus was on her. She'd stretched her neck to allow this dance-off, giving her sisters some rope, and he was going to make sure she wasn't the one who got hanged in the end.

He'd seen enough of that already, the way she'd been responsible for her sisters, right down to the mistakes they'd made, which truly had nothing to do with her.

Nightingale wasn't blind, or brainless, as he'd just proven back in Dave's cabin, and how the man didn't see what he was doing to Norma Rose was beyond Ty.

She clapped and laughed as he tapped his way around her, and he did the same when she took her turn, bowing after she'd made it all the way around him and sashaying her backside with a toe-curling little twist before grabbing his hands. It was almost as if they were in competition now, trying to outdance each other.

With exclamations that drew everyone's attention, two other couples collided into one another and hit the floor, gasping for air as they tried to untangle legs and arms. All four barely managed to crawl to the edge of the dance floor without being trampled by one of the last couples still dancing.

"Just us and two others," he said, hooking her shoulder for a duo tap.

"I know," she answered, stretching her arm along his and over his shoulder to grasp the back of his neck, holding on tight as their steps matched perfectly.

She didn't sound as breathless as he felt, and he sucked in air until his lungs were full in order to keep up.

"There goes another," she said, as a couple danced right off the floor, crashing into a table and taking several bystanders down to the floor with them.

The last couple, besides them, was on the far side of the floor, and Ty wrapped his fingers around Norma Rose's palm. "Tap to the edge," he said.

Clicking her heels loudly, she added, "And back."

The crowd cheered them on. Ty laughed at how that increased Norma Rose's speed even more. In the center of the room, while she tapped around him, he crouched and knocked his knees together while flaying his hands in a crisscross pattern over his knees, in time with the music.

Head thrown back, Norma Rose laughed aloud. When she faced him again, she crouched down, knocking her knees and crisscrossing her arms in time with him.

The other couple followed suit, and knowing he needed a move to put their dance above the rest, Ty stood and tapped his way around Norma Rose while she stood. Then he grasped her waist. Hoisting her into the air, he tapped another circle. She held onto his shoulders, keeping her body in a straight line that allowed them both to maintain their balance. He hoped they looked as good as he felt, for it did feel marvelous, holding her up like that.

In response, the other couple attempted to copy them, but as the man hoisted his partner, their timing was off and they both went over backward. The ceiling above rumbled as the crowd erupted.

As Ty set her down, Norma Rose exclaimed, "We won! We won!"

Wayne still pounded on the keys, so Ty grabbed her hands to dance her into the center of the now empty dance floor. "Time's not up," he said. "Besides, we have to give them the grand finale."

"Which is?" she asked, tapping her heels and shuffling a fast four-step.

"I'm going to throw you around my back."

She shook her head, but asked, "You are?"

"Yes, I am," Ty answered. Without missing a beat or step, he hooked one arm around her waist and lifted her up, flipping her horizontal with the floor. "Just pretend you're an airplane." She stretched her arms out, no doubt having seen the move. "Ready?" he asked, still tapping to the music.

"Ready," she responded.

With a quick twist of his hips, he flung her sideways around his back.

In the split second that he didn't have a hold on her, the crowd went silent. Time seemed to stop, too, except for the pounding of his heart echoing in his ears. He wouldn't let her down. Wouldn't fail her.

His catch was as smooth as the rest of their dancing had been. He savored the relief deep down and flipped her upright to land on her feet.

Without missing a beat, she tapped backward and then forward again. "That was perfect," she said, catching one of his hands for another graceful pirouette.

"Time!" Dac Lester shouted. "Time's up!"

She finished her twirl and Ty once again grabbed her waist, tossing her straight up into the air. Norma Rose grabbed his shoulders, and as she started her descent, he caught her by the hips, stopping her before her feet touched the floor.

Holding her there, her head slightly above his, his heart stopped beating. Her eyes were so full of stars he could hardly see any of their wonderful blue, and her lips held a smile that would have made the Mona Lisa jealous.

The crowd roared and cheered, and Ty, unable to resist, gave in to the one desire he'd tried to bury since he'd first laid eyes on her.

He kissed her.

Chapter Twelve

Norma Rose clung to Ty's shoulders, lost in a different world, one that was far more vibrant and effervescent than anything she'd ever known. He tasted as good as he smelled, and she tilted her head, so nothing was in the way of their lips connecting.

If the roaring in her ears would stop, she'd have nothing to distract her from completely, fully, enjoying the connection. If whoever was shouting her name—

Wrenching her lips off his, Norma Rose blinked, several times, trying to make sense of the wild vibrations still racing through her body while trying to recall where she was.

Someone was saying her name, and she was… she was kissing Ty.

Oh, Lord.

"You won!"

Twyla's voice was now recognizable, so was the gleam in Ty's eyes.

Norma Rose's entire being experienced a flood of disappointment. They'd won. Which meant the dance was over. She swallowed and, gathering a few more bits of reality, pushed at his shoulders. "Put me down."

"I have," he said.

She wiggled her toes, testing if the floor was indeed beneath her shoes.

It was.

Sliding her hands off his shoulders, she pressed her feet harder onto the floor and locked her knees, afraid that without his hold, she'd collapse. Norma Rose begged and pleaded, silently, for that not to happen.

It didn't.

Perhaps because Ty still had hold of her waist, and twisted her, pulling her against his side. She shouldn't allow that. If she trusted her legs, she might not have. Between the dancing and his kiss, she didn't trust any part of her body right now.

Her thinking wasn't overly lucid yet, either.

"You won!" Twyla repeated.

Norma Rose's vision cleared, enough to see the crowd that had descended upon them. Twyla and

Josie were in the lead. One holding a bottle of whiskey, the other her snow globe, and both looked happier than she'd seen them in years. She wasn't sure who handed what to whom, but she ended up with the snow globe and Ty had the whiskey bottle.

"Your winners, ladies and gentlemen," Twyla said, stepping aside to wave a sweeping hand at both of them. "Nightingale's own Ty Bradshaw and my sister Norma Rose!"

For the first time in her life, finding a smile to plant on her face was beyond her, until Ty grabbed her hand and forced her into a bow.

Head down, he hissed, "Smile."

She did, partly because he sounded as flustered as her. They lifted their heads simultaneously, smiling at the exuberant crowd.

People moved in with congratulations, hugging her and patting Ty on the back.

"I haven't had this much fun in ages," Scooter Wilson said. "You gotta have dance-offs more often."

She nodded, but Ty spoke. "I don't know that I can handle more than one a year," he said. "That was a heck of a lot of work."

Laughter filled the room again.

"We'll step aside now," he continued, taking

Norma Rose's elbow to guide her forward. "And let others take a turn at dancing." He waved at Wayne. "That's one electric piano player."

Wayne made a show of bowing before he sat back down to play another tune that had people moving back onto the dance floor.

"Here," Josie said, handing over a glass. "It's just water. You look like you could use it."

"Thanks," Norma Rose said, glad her voice did still work. She drank the water, all of it; she was thirstier than she'd ever been.

She sat down in a chair that magically appeared. Maybe she had walked to it. Her legs were too shaky to know for sure and the bottoms of her feet stung so badly they were almost numb.

"I had no idea you could dance like that," Twyla said.

"Me, neither," Ty, who was sitting with his arm across the back of her chair, said.

Norma Rose tore her gaze off his arm to say, "Me, neither."

The occupants of the table—Josie and Scooter, Twyla and Jimmy, Dac, her and Ty—all laughed. Norma Rose took another look around the table, and at those filling the chairs. This was all new and she felt completely out of her element, yet comfortable at the same time. So many new things. Crazy things.

The craziest of all was how she trusted Ty. Even to throw her around like that. The idea of not trusting him had never crossed her mind. Not that she'd had a lot of time to think about it. She'd been completely caught up in the moment.

She couldn't believe it. This wasn't her, Norma Rose. This was some imposter, sitting here, listening to her sisters and Scooter and Jimmy and Dac, and even Ty, talk about the dancing. How word would spread and soon everyone would want to attend one of the resort's dance competitions. How it would be the talk of the town tomorrow. How she and Ty had won. How he'd thrown her in the air and—

The sweat on her forehead and the back of her neck turned ice-cold and whatever snapped inside her hurt. Norma Rose jumped to her feet. "Excuse me," she said, spinning away from the table.

"Norma Rose—"

She moved faster, edging farther away from Ty. He still caught her by the arm. "What's wrong?"

"Why don't you tell me, *Agent* Bradshaw?"

Sighing, he walked beside her, all the way through the arched ballroom doorway and into the resort's entranceway before he asked, "So, we're back to that again?"

Yes, we're back to that again, she wanted to shout. She didn't because she should never have forgotten it in the first place. Who he was. It was the only defense she had.

With no real place to go, she marched into her office, fully prepared to slam the door in his face. If he'd been weaker, and slower, and if her reflexes had been faster.

As it was, he was the one to close the door, shutting them both in her office, and he was the one who set the snow globe on her desk.

He grasped her shoulders and spun her around. She was prepared to hate him, but all the fight seeped out of her as she caught the way he looked at her. His eyes still shimmered, but his look went deeper than that and seared her in a most vulnerable spot.

"Something's happening here, Norma Rose," he said quietly. "I don't know what it is. I don't know how to explain it. I don't even know if I understand it." He shook his head slowly. "But I'll be damned if I can fight it."

She had no answer, for she knew exactly what he was talking about. If he was feeling anything remotely close to what she was, it was as confusing as hell.

His lips descended toward hers with all the exquisiteness of a snowflake falling from a still and quiet sky. As mesmerizing as the ones in the little glass globe. She had time to stop him, to protest, but not the willpower.

The first swipe of his lips was as dazzling as it had been on the dance floor, and her eyelids fluttered shut as all sorts of wild and outlandish sensations erupted all over again. Instantly transported into the universe she knew nothing about, but wanting to catch a glimpse of it again, Norma Rose wrapped her arms around Ty's neck and held on as the ride began.

His kiss turned demanding, and Norma Rose accepted the way it called to her very soul. Warm and probing, his tongue parted her lips. She welcomed the entrance into her mouth, thrilled by the feeling and caught up in the vibrations the action sent clear to her toes.

Even as the kiss continued, as her heart raced and her pulse thumped against her skin, as his hands roamed up her back, making her arch deeper against him, thrilled her in ways she couldn't fathom, one tiny part of her brain remained detached. She shouldn't be doing this. Shouldn't want this.

But a part of her, more powerful than that speck of common sense, argued passionately. She wanted more than this. She wanted the excitement. The adventure that being at his side had given her today and tonight. She wanted—

To become a doxy? that overly intuitive and obstinate piece of her brain asked. *Give this man the power to rule her? Lose everything because of primitive urges that dropped women who gave into them to the very bottom of society?*

Shut up! the other part of her shouted, but it was too late. Her conscience was making more sense. However, Norma Rose wasn't the one to break away from the kiss. Ty did that.

Air burned as she breathed in, and flamed again as it went out. Her chest heaved and her throat ached, yet she lifted her gaze, refusing to collapse in a heap of frustrated fury.

He was breathing heavily, too, and staring at her as if he was just as mixed up and torn as her. Without a word, he gave a single nod of his head and turned.

Ty left, closing the door with nothing more than a soft click, which resounded so many times in her ears he might as well have slammed it hard enough to rattle the roof.

What she'd recognized in his eyes, a reflection of her own, remained behind, and that's what made her lose all coordination. Using her desk as a crutch, Norma Rose dragged herself around the corner and fell onto her chair.

Regret. Pure undiluted regret. It was easy to recognize and hard to forget. After eight years she still knew exactly what it looked like. How it burned inside a person with the intensity of a wildfire and left nothing but charred remains.

Forrest Reynolds had looked at her like that. Regrettably.

Norma Rose shook her head, trying to rattle away the image. She hadn't seen Forrest close enough to see what was in his eyes for years. Only once since his father had found them in Forrest's car after his graduation party. On the day Uncle Dave was teaching her how to drive, she'd met Forrest on the road and had driven straight into the ditch, crashing into the tree and breaking Dave's arm.

Forrest had had regret in his eyes that day, too. It hadn't cut her as deeply that day and it hadn't hurt nearly as badly as she hurt right now. Ty's regret had gouged directly into her heart. Other things were different tonight, too. No one had found them. No one had dragged her all the way to the farmhouse and told her father to keep his gold-digging little doxies at home.

Galen Reynolds had done all that. And more. By the time he was done shouting from the rooftops the entire community thought she and Forrest had been having full-blown sex in the backseat of his car. Some still thought that. Claimed that's why Forrest had left town shortly thereafter, returning only a few times until he'd taken over the Plantation, when his father ran off to California with his latest doxy. A performer who did more than sing songs at their nightclub.

Karen Reynolds had gone with her cheating husband to California. Despite all the animosity she had toward Galen Reynolds, Norma Rose never experienced those feelings toward Karen. Perhaps it was because the woman attempted to dispute Galen's lies. Karen had been the one to come to the resort, which at that time had been little more than the farmhouse and pavilion, and apologize to Norma Rose and her father, but as her father had pointed out, the damage had already been done.

Norma Rose had taken one thing away from that visit. How Karen Reynolds had kept her head up, regardless of all the rumors about Galen and his doxies. That had stuck in her mind, the way the woman had been able to create a shield around herself that no one could penetrate. Norma Rose had used that, copied the woman's detached facade over the following months after Forrest left and Galen kept telling the gossipmongers that it was her fault. She'd perfected her own shield and used it continuously.

Until tonight, when it shattered, as if made of crystal instead of stone.

A knock sounded on the door, and Norma Rose closed her eyes, wishing whoever it was would just go away. Maybe she wished they'd just storm in, as usual. Maybe that would re-erect her shield. It was doubtful. She was so empty, so tired, she barely had the wherewithal to open her eyes.

She lifted her lids and let out a heavy sigh before saying, "Come in."

Josie peeked around the edge of the door. "Are you all right?"

"Of course I'm all right," Norma Rose lied, sitting up to shuffle a few papers about.

"What are you doing?"

Thankfully that little part of her mind which never let its guard down, the part she was growing to hate, had never failed her. "Looking for mu-sicians to hire for Big Al's anniversary party and Palooka George's birthday bash," she said.

Josie entered the room and closed the door. "I truly don't know how you do this every night, Norma Rose. Seeing to all the guests, making sure they have a good time, and all the while concen-trating on future parties." Standing near the edge of the desk, Josie ran a fingertip over the top of the snow globe. "Aren't you exhausted? You and Ty were unbelievable." Sighing, she added, "Oh, the things that must happen after I go to bed at night."

Ignoring the chill that had the hair on her arms tingling, Norma Rose asked, "What do you mean?"

"You," Josie said with more than a hint of dis-belief. "I've only seen you dance maybe twice in my life, yet you almost wore out the floor tonight. How often do you do that?"

"Never," Norma Rose admitted, once again too drained to lift a pen.

"Never?"

She shook her head.

Josie giggled. "Now that, I believe."

Knowing she'd never find the answer alone, Norma Rose asked, "What have I done, Josie?"

Frowning, her sister took a seat on the edge of

the desk, much like Ty had that morning. Norma Rose chomped her back teeth together. Why did this man consume her like he did? Every thought somehow led straight to him.

"You haven't done anything, Norma Rose, other than give the guests what they came for, a night of fun."

"Twyla and you did that," she said. "I'd never have thought of a dance-off."

"I wouldn't have, either," Josie said. "That was one-hundred-percent Twyla. Probably something she'd seen at one of the speakeasies she's gone to with Mitsy."

"What?" The word was out before she could stop it, but Norma Rose lifted a hand, halting her sister from answering. "Don't," she said. "I don't think I can take much more of learning what has happened behind my back."

"It was only twice that I know of," Josie answered. "And Bronco hauled her home before things got out of hand."

"How do you know?" Norma Rose asked, now needing to know. "Father never mentioned it to me, and he certainly would have."

"Because Bronco never mentioned it to Father," Josie explained. "It was his job to make sure something like that didn't happen. He didn't want Father to know Twyla had ditched him, especially not twice in a row. After all, if he can't keep track of two girls, how's he going to keep track of bootleggers?"

Norma Rose closed her eyes as a new wave of exhaustion washed over her. Why was she surprised to hear that? Everything else was crumbling, and there was no reason to believe all she'd thought real and true wouldn't turn into dust, too.

A thud had her lifting her eyelids. Josie had hopped off the desk and was holding out a hand.

"Come on," her sister said, taking Norma Rose's hand when she didn't offer it. "Time for you to go to bed."

"I have work to do, and the resort is still full of people."

"Twyla and I can handle it," Josie said. "You deserve a good night's rest."

Norma Rose made no attempt to move, or protest. She truly didn't have the energy, and the thought of reentering the ballroom was terrifying. People—those who remembered the scandal with Forrest all those years ago, and there were plenty of them—would be calling her a doxy all over again.

"We can handle it, Norma Rose," Josie was saying, as she tugged harder. "We should have done something long ago, demanded that Father quit trying to treat us like ten-year-olds."

Giving in, Norma Rose stood. She hadn't realized how hot and sticky her gloves were until Josie's touch made her feel things outside of her twisted emotions. "Why didn't you?" Norma Rose asked.

"Because," Josie said secretively, "living a clandestine life can be rather exciting."

"Clandestine?"

Though everyone always proclaimed Ginger was the prettiest of the Nightingale girls, and Twyla the most flamboyant, Josie, known as the quiet, sensible one, looked downright stunning. Not because of her stylish white outfit or perfectly applied makeup, but because of the mysterious gleam in her eyes and the tranquil yet knowing smile on her lips.

"Life is full of secrets, Norma Rose," Josie whispered. "Wonderful secrets that are all the more special when they are kept hidden."

Norma Rose's mouth went completely dry. There was so much behind this sister, more even than Ginger and Twyla had kept hidden, yet intuition told her no one would learn Josie's secrets, not if she didn't want them to.

"This way," Josie said, tugging Norma Rose toward the door. "We'll go up the back way. You have nothing to worry about; Twyla and I won't let anyone burn the place down while you're sleeping. It'll all still be here come morning."

Morning came early to the birds, frogs and other critters out to catch anything moving on the dew-covered leaves. For Ty, who'd tossed and turned all night, sunrise had taken forever. He'd left his cabin some time ago, but had found no answers walking the grounds of the resort, no resolve for the doubts and reservations piling up like trash in the darkest, deepest slums of the city he'd once called home.

He'd never lived in those slums, but he'd walked the streets there, knew—at least in part—how they'd come to be, and that was at the very root of the problems he'd been slowly unearthing all night.

Norma Rose was deep down inside him, too, and he was having a hard time figuring out why or how she'd gotten there. Slums could appear anywhere, and for the first time ever, he was considering his part in creating one. What could happen to this entire community if he took Nightingale's down with Bodine.

The resort was quiet, ghostly, and there was not a single piece of evidence of the gaiety that had kept the place hopping until just a few hours ago. Ty quietly made his way through the entrance hall and past Norma Rose's office to knock on Roger Nightingale's door.

Entering, Ty closed the door behind him just as the phone on the corner of Roger's desk rang.

"Hello," Roger answered, motioning for Ty to take a seat. "Brock, is that you?" he asked into the receiver. "Has something happened?"

Ty didn't take a seat, in case the man gestured him out within the next few moments, but did make note of the relief that appeared on Roger's face, meaning nothing must have happened to his youngest daughter.

"Not yet," Roger said. "We've got a lot going on here right now. Not to mention Palooka George's birthday party next weekend."

Roger lifted a brow as he glanced up. Ty didn't bother correcting him that Al's party was next weekend and Palooka George's the weekend after.

Roger guffawed at something Brock must have said. "She'd ditch them. I know that girl." After a pause he stated, "They'd all end up in California. The only one I could send would be Norma Rose and I need her here. With you gone, she's having to dig up a decent musician for the parties."

Roger scribbled something on a piece of paper before speaking again. "No one I'd trust with one of my girls." Roger's tone turned more understanding. "I know she's put you in the squeeze, Brock, but I'm calling you out on this one, boy. I need you to take care of Ginger. I don't have the time to deal with her right now."

Ty gave himself a moment before he released the pressure on his back teeth. Not dealing with his daughters could put the man in more trouble than any of the gangsters he associated with.

"Look," Roger said, once again gesturing for Ty to take a seat, "I have to go, but I'll call you in a day or so."

Ty sat as the man hung up and waited as Nightingale took a deep breath. The two of them had come to an agreement last night, but that had been before several other incidents had taken place.

"Ginger must be giving Brock a hard time," Roger said with a hint of a smile. "He wants me to send someone to get her."

"Are you going to?" Ty asked, ready to offer to take Norma Rose if that's who Nightingale chose to send.

"No," Roger said. "She made her choice, now she needs to see if it's what she really wants."

"Ginger?" Ty asked and then shook his head when Roger nodded. "Isn't she a little young for that type of lesson?"

"No," Roger said. "None of my girls are that young anymore. They're women, and a man who tries to control a woman usually finds himself in a tight spot." Leaning back in his seat, he said, "That's why I've let Norma Rose deal with most of their shenanigans. She's a lot like their mother was, doesn't let things fluster her." A thoughtful, distant look covered Roger's face for a moment. "She learned the hard way years ago."

The knot inside Ty's chest pulled a little tighter. He wanted to know just what lesson Norma Rose had learned the hard way.

Roger nodded toward the paper he'd written on earlier. "Brock said she should try Slim Johnson for the parties. Norma Rose isn't going to like that."

"Why? Isn't he any good?"

"He's a good musician and singer," Roger said,

"but he has a contract with the Plantation. She'd have to get Forrest Reynolds's permission to hire him."

"And there's bad blood between the Plantation and the resort," Ty said, thinking aloud.

"Oh, there's bad blood all right," Roger answered. "But it's between Norma Rose and Forrest. Galen, Forrest's father, saw to that years ago, which is why I had him run out of town. Galen claims otherwise, that he left for health reasons. Let him think that, and let those that think he ran off with one of his mistresses believe what they would. Galen's big mouth hurt Norma Rose, and though I've never told her, he's paying for that now. I took my time in getting revenge." Roger rubbed a chin that was still red from shaving. "He's in jail in California, on his way to prison. I didn't want to see his wife, Karen, hurt. She'd been good friends with my wife years ago. Karen had a blind eye where Galen was concerned, in most things. Or maybe she just didn't want to believe it, until she had to. Either way, she's divorcing him now."

Ty was even more interested to know what had happened, but his mind didn't have time to think too deeply. Roger's chair creaked as he leaned forward.

Elbows on his desk and fingertips tapping together, Roger leveled a solid stare on Ty that could have burned holes. "I never forget someone who's done me, or mine, wrong. And I always win in the end."

If he'd needed any urging, that would have been it, but Ty had made his mind up before he'd entered the man's office. He wasn't turning soft, but a soft spot had formed inside him. Norma Rose had put it there. He couldn't stop what he'd come here to do—Bodine had to go down—but he was willing to find a way for that to happen, if there was one, that maybe wouldn't ruin her life.

Nightingale had to be in on it, which also meant he had to tell Roger he'd deceived him. Ty stood and crossed the room to glance out the window that, like Norma Rose's, overlooked the front parking lot. "You play with some heavy hitters," he said, turning to lean his backside against the windowsill.

"I do," Roger agreed. "Does that scare you?"

"No," he answered. "No man scares me." Only one particular woman had ever uprooted that. Keeping that thought silent, he said, "But I am aware of what they are capable of doing. I've seen it firsthand. The extortion. The carnage. The murders."

Roger shook his head. "There are mobsters and there are thugs. The mobs, the ones I do business with, though some of their players are underhanded, don't go around killing innocent people. They're simply out to make money, which isn't a bad thing."

"No, it's not," Ty agreed. "Not when it's done legally."

Roger guffawed. "Legally." He shook his head. "Not even legal businesses do it legally. Our fine government sees to that. Why do you think Rockefeller, Carnegie and Morgan bought the presidency in 1896? And it's still happening today." Roger's expression turned hard. "I'm not saying every man should become a bootlegger, or a gangster, but let me tell you something, when a man has a mouth to feed besides his own, he'll do damn near anything to put food on the table. I know. I did it. I worked eighteen hours a day at the brewery and brought home seven hundred and fifty dollars a year. A year. And let me tell you about extortion. The government was already extorting a good portion of my salary, but that wasn't enough, they took the entire job away from me."

Ty couldn't say Roger was bitter, but he was serious and frank in his belief. It reminded him of his own father, how he'd struggled to have enough left over after taxes to buy the supplies to bake the bread he sold.

"When a man sees his children, his wife, the people he loves more than himself, going to bed hungry, he'll do anything, legal or illegal, to put food in their bellies, clothes on their backs, a roof over their heads. If he doesn't," Roger said with a loathing Ty had rarely heard, "he's not a real man."

Nightingale was silent for a moment, and out of respect, Ty held his own tongue.

"When there are no jobs," Roger continued, "men have to get creative and that's what happened around here. Unlike in the city, there are no soup kitchens in rural areas. Right now a cow is worth less than a jug of whiskey." With an indulgent gaze, he added, "It doesn't take a college degree to figure out which costs less to produce."

Ty wasn't exactly sure how the conversation had turned around. By the time Roger was done, Bodine would have come and gone and Ty still wouldn't have told Nightingale he was a federal agent.

Chapter Thirteen

"Stilling brew is just a small piece of the pie, Ty," Roger said. "Just like every other business, even legal ones, bootleggers need a way to get their product to market, to the big cities and beyond. That is where the mob comes in. It's an underground world as intricate as the one aboveground, and in some cases, just as cutthroat."

Ty rubbed the back of his neck, where tension was making it burn and ache. "Last night," he said, "when I told you I wasn't the man for you—"

"I thought I convinced you, you are," Roger interrupted.

Shaking his head, Ty crossed the room, but didn't sit down. Instead he stood in front of Roger's desk. "There's more to it than that. I am a federal agent."

Roger Nightingale was too smooth to reveal how

that news affected him. Slowly, he leaned back in his chair and crossed his beefy arms.

"I'm not a prohib agent," Ty said, "here to break up stills or arrest bootleggers. I'm not a revenue man, either, after tax money."

"Then what are you, and what are you after?"

"I'm a federal private investigator, here to see a specific gangster is arrested," Ty answered. "One I believe is behind Dave's poisoning, among other things. Ray Bodine."

Roger shook his head and cracked a bogus smile. "You're barking up a fallen tree, boy. Bodine's dead. Has been for a few years."

"No, he's not," Ty answered. "His brothers are in the pen, but Bodine didn't die at that shootout. The coffin paraded down the streets in New York, the one newspapers across the nation published pictures of, held sandbags."

"How do you know?"

"I opened it."

Roger didn't attempt to hide his surprise at that. "Hell," he said, eyes wide. "You're him."

Ty knew Roger didn't mean Bodine, so he asked, "The snitch Withers reported?" He was ready to clear up that falsehood, too.

"No," Roger said. "The bounty hunter. The night

282 The Bootlegger's Daughter

stalker. The mole. The phantom. Some claim you don't exist, but there's not a man with a bounty on his head that's not looking over his shoulder, wondering if he's your next target."

Ty didn't respond. There was no need. His reputation had preceded him. He'd acquired many nicknames over the years. As long as no one ever saw his face, he didn't care what they called him.

"You're a man with no past. Never leave footprints of where you've been, apart from the deaths or arrests of gangsters. But you don't do those yourself. You call in the locals. They get the credit for it, claiming only that they'd received an anonymous tip." Roger ran a hand through his hair, which looked to be growing whiter by the minute. "My background checks, they're all false?"

"No," Ty answered. "I am just who they say. Tyler Bradshaw, born and raised by Irish immigrants in New York City, although my father was English. I served in the army, attended law school afterward while serving on the New York police force, and then became a private investigator."

"Are you really only twenty-eight?" Roger asked. "That's a lot for a man so young to accomplish."

"I am," Ty answered. "I never stayed in one spot too long."

"Just long enough to make a footprint," Roger said.

Nightingale was nervous, and Ty couldn't say that pleased him. "I stayed in one spot long enough." The flashbacks were too strong to ignore. "Might still be in New York if Bodine hadn't wiped out an entire block of the neighborhood where I'd grown up. Where my parents had lived since moving to America."

"And now you're here," Roger said, wiping at the sweat beading on his temples.

"And now I'm here," Ty repeated. "And only three people know that," he pointed out. "The two of us and my boss, who rarely leaves his office in Washington."

"Why?" Roger asked. "Why are you telling me this?"

Ty took a seat and drummed his fingertips on the chair's armrest. He was on virgin soil. Not once in five years had he taken someone into his confidence, and proceeding was like taking the first step on a narrow log laid out as a bridge over a fast-moving river. "Because," Ty started, "Bodine will arrive at the resort this week. He's rented your farmhouse under the name of Ralph Brandon. His henchmen have been in St. Paul for a couple of weeks, scouting out an in to the Minnesota Thirteen trade."

"He's really not dead?"

"He's really not dead," Ty assured him. "And I do believe he's behind Dave's poisoning."

Roger sat quietly, lips pinched, most likely running scenarios through his head. With a heavy sigh, he nodded. "You bring Bodine down here, at the resort, and I'm ruined."

Ty couldn't deny that, nor could he offer an alternative. Despite his desire to shield Norma Rose, to somehow preserve the resort she cherished, his goal hadn't changed.

"I told you last night this resort doesn't just feed my family," Roger said. "The business we do here feeds this entire area, and beyond."

Ty understood the resort didn't just employ a lot of people, but that the popularity of the place helped other local businesses thrive. He didn't want to put a stop to any of that. Not even the bootlegging. That wasn't his job. The making and transporting of illegal alcohol was too big and vast to ever be stopped completely, and within his inside circle, no one wanted it to end. They focused on catching the real villains of the world. "Bodine wants in, Roger," Ty said. "In on the money being made by Minnesota Thirteen and he knows you're the key."

Roger's distress was made clear by the heavy sigh he let out. "I told you the mobsters I deal with are not in the business of killing innocent people. They aren't interested in owning entire cities. They're just out to put cash in their pockets."

"Up to now," Ty argued. "But it's getting bigger, and Bodine wants in. He wants that money in his pocket and he doesn't care who's in his path."

Roger stood and walked to the window, his shoulders slumped. "I'm ruined either way, aren't I?"

Ty couldn't lie, therefore chose to remain silent.

Norma Rose stayed in bed later than usual. Sleep hadn't eluded her, as she'd feared. The dream she'd been having had been too good to leave. Now, awake, lying in her bed, staring at the ceiling, she couldn't recall exactly what it had been about, other than it had been wonderful. It left her feeling warm and tranquil and something else she couldn't quite put her finger on.

Drawing in a deep breath, she let it out slowly,

relishing even that—just breathing—as a smile remained on her lips.

Her lips quivered and the smile slipped. What did she have to be this happy about? Memories overrode the mingling aftermath of the unknown dream. The dance-off. Ty. Sheriff Withers.

Norma Rose groaned. A deep and hollow sound that echoed off the walls.

Definitely nothing to be happy about.

Completely foreign to the way she normally reacted to anything that needed to be done, she pulled the covers over her head and seriously considered staying in bed all day.

The knock on her door wasn't what changed her mind. She'd never spent the entire day in bed and wouldn't today, no matter what she might have to face. Pulling the covers off her head and tucking them beneath her arms, Norma Rose said, "Come in."

Twyla, dressed in a yellow-and-black outfit that made her look like a beautiful sunflower in full bloom, bounded into the room. "Good morning, sleepyhead." Plopping onto the bed and kicking her heels to make the bed bounce, Twyla added, "Still tired from last night? You were magnificent."

Norma Rose bit her tongue just in time. She'd

been about to say last night shouldn't have happened, at least her dancing, that is, but if she said
that, she'd have to mean it, or at least pretend and
that she did not want to do. For reasons she still
had to discern. "Thank you," she said instead. "For
all you did last night."

"You're welcome," Twyla said prudently as she
stood and smoothed her skirt over her thighs. "You
can thank me for what I do today, later."

Throwing back the covers to climb out of the bed,
Norma Rose swung her legs around and planted
her feet on the floor. "What are you doing today?"

"Stay seated," Twyla said, holding up both hands,
"until after I speak."

Norma Rose's stomach fell, from past experience.

"Okay?" Twyla asked.

Considering she was rather frozen from fear,
Norma Rose agreed. "Okay."

Twyla planted her feet as if she was prepared to
defend herself, and her shoulders rose with a very
deep breath. Norma Rose's stomach hiccupped.
Last night had been a bad idea. Whether it had
worked or not, she'd pay for it today. Only the good
Lord knew how.

On the end of her exhale, Twyla began to speak

swiftly. "Father spoke to Brock this morning. Don't worry, Ginger's fine. I think Father is actually relieved she's not here. At least that's how it seemed. Anyway, Brock suggested we hire Slim Johnson for Al's party and Palooka George's birthday, and considering you and Forrest haven't spoken since that incident a million years ago, which really doesn't matter now that you have Ty, I told father I'd go talk to Forrest, to see if he'll let Slim out of his contract long enough to play for us." She huffed out a breath and flinched, as if waiting for the sky to fall. "What do you think?"

With her head spinning, Norma Rose was only able to ask, "What do I think?"

Twyla nodded.

Blinking or shaking her head didn't clear Norma Rose's mind. The entire world had gone crazy, that's what she thought. She didn't say that, nor did she agree with Twyla's suggestion. It was her job to get musicians, and she would, regardless of who that meant she had to talk to, and—she clenched her teeth to combat the little voice screaming in the back of her mind—she didn't *have* Ty. That single point of her sister's breathless announcement had struck hard.

Needing a few moments to put things into perspective, Norma Rose slipped on the robe lying across the foot of her bed and crossed the room to her closet, where she blindly chose a dress hanging among many. From the dresser she chose under-clothes, fully aware of Twyla watching her every move, waiting for an answer.

"I'm going down the hall," Norma Rose finally said, once her hands were full. "I'll meet you in my office when I'm done."

Twyla agreed with a delayed and baffled nod, and Norma Rose left the room, completely confused. Once shut in the bathroom, a single glance in the mirror told her a bath was in order. She'd gone to bed with hair damp from sweating on the dance floor last night and she now looked as if she'd been electrocuted.

After soaking in the tub, she sprinkled powder on her legs to ease the work of putting on the tight silk stockings, which she clipped to her thighs with garters, and then used a good amount of styling cream to secure the waves she created in her side-parted hair. She added cosmetics, liner and mascara, powder and lipstick, as well as two round dots of blush on her cheeks. Satisfied the makeup made her look more confident than she felt, she stepped into her silk tap pants and eased her cami top over her head, cautious of her face and hair. Turning to the dress she'd hung on the back of the door, she paused. Why had she chosen that one? It was purple, lavender really, with several layers of fringes on the skirt and thin straps over the shoulders. Much more suitable for evening wear and nothing like the conservative black dresses she was known for wearing.

The purple dress had leaped off the page of a catalog last winter, when snow had covered the ground. The only reason she'd ordered it was because it reminded her of the warm days of summer. Once it had arrived, knowing she'd never wear it, she'd almost given it to Ginger.

The hallway that contained the family's bedrooms was closed off from the guest rooms by a solid door, but she still didn't roam the area half-dressed and insisted her sisters never did, either. She glanced at the robe lying in a heap on the floor, but in the end, chose the dress.

Entering her bedroom, the full-length mirror caught her image as she closed the door. Norma Rose took a moment to examine the reflection. The same single question that had arisen while she'd been putting on her makeup entered her mind.

Would Ty think she was pretty? Did he think so already?

Disgusted, she turned away. With everything else going on, that was the one thing she thought about. The earth must have tilted on its axis, tossing the entire world cattywampus. There was no other explanation. Not for her thoughts and not for last night.

Norma Rose didn't change her dress. Instead she slipped on a pair of white shoes and gloves, and added a headband with a silver butterfly to flutter over one ear. The world had most certainly shifted. She wasn't even worried about facing Forrest. The time had come.

The resort was quiet, as it usually was on Sundays. Mondays were like that, too, and she normally enjoyed the time to catch up and prepare for the week ahead, but today she was primed to take on the world and set everything back in its rightful order. She couldn't say if the bath had revived her or if it had been the purple dress. Either way, the first place she stopped was her father's office.

He waved her in as he hung up the phone receiver. "Aw, Rosie girl," he said, plastering a smile as false as those she so regularly used on his face. "I'm glad to see you've recruited your sisters to help out more around here. That's how it should be, this is a family business."

He looked disheveled, a rare occurrence. Though faint, the air held a scent that sent her heart racing. Ty had been in this room. Just a short time ago.

"Dale Emmerson will be out here this evening," her father was saying by the time her ears started functioning again, "with some papers for you and your sisters to sign. I'll have a proxy for you to sign on Ginger's behalf."

An alarm, louder than any fire bell, went off inside her head. "What sort of papers?"

"I'm putting the resort and the other land I own in you girls' names," he said, pushing away from his desk.

He wasn't wearing a suit coat and sweat circles darkened his white shirt under his arms and between the suspenders on his back as he walked toward the window.

"Why?" she asked.

"Because it's time," he said. "Past time."

"What's happened?" Her mouth had gone dry. "Did some runners get caught last night?"

"No."

The bottom fell completely out of her stomach. "You've uncovered the snitch, haven't you?"

"Not the one Withers is worried about." Her father's sigh filled the room and hung heavy in the air. "I hate to do this, Rosie—involve you—but I need your help."

"I've been involved since the beginning, Father. The resort—"

"I'm not talking about the resort," he said, eyeing her directly. "I want you to leave that to Twyla and Josie for the next few days."

She braced against the shiver rippling her spine.

"I need you to help Ty, whatever he needs, no questions." His steady gaze was serious and grave. "The less you know, the better."

"Wha—"

He held up a hand. "No questions, Rosie." Crossing the room, he said, "I've done a lot of thinking and it's the only way. We could lose everything, Rosie. Everything. I'm setting things up so you girls will be fine, but a lot has to happen in order for it to work." He'd arrived at his chair and landed in it as if the world was crashing down around him.

"You can't say that and expect me not to have questions," she said.

"I don't expect you not to have questions, I expect you not to ask them. When it's all over, you'll understand why." He waved toward the window that overlooked the front parking lot. "Ty's waiting for you out front."

Ty was leaning against his truck like the world was his, cattywampus or not. His black suit didn't host a wrinkle, and his black suede shoes didn't hold a speck of dust.

Norma Rose closed the front door behind her, but stopped on the porch, eyes locked with his. "Questions, my ass," she whispered to herself, clutching the keys in her hand. This man was the root of all her problems, and would not be the one to bring down her father. Or her.

Chin up, she started forward, letting him know just who he was up against. Who would win.

Ty was more aware of Norma Rose than he was of himself as she stomped down the steps as haughty and overconfident as ever. He smiled—inside, where she couldn't see it—but he felt it nonetheless with each step she took. He'd never wanted a woman the way he did her. Now that he'd accepted it for what it was, it consumed him.

She didn't slow as she approached the truck, merely walked right past him, nose in the air. "I'll drive."

"You don't even know where we're going," he said.

"I'm sure you'll tell me," she answered, rounding the back of his Model T to march across the parking lot, toward the large garage.

"Do you have your keys?" He couldn't believe it was only yesterday he'd witnessed her sequester them all.

She flashed a set in one hand, though he was much more aware of how the fringes on her purple skirt flapped across her backside. It didn't matter who drove. Actually, not using his vehicle, as common as it was, wasn't a bad idea. He doubted Roger would let out their secret—the man would surely lose everything then—but involving the resort owner and his daughter heightened the importance of no one learning his real line of work.

Ty had weighed up the options, and in the end decided that if there was any hope of not bringing the resort down with Bodine, it lay in having enough information to arrest the gangster when he stepped off the train, which didn't leave a lot of time.

He waited until she'd backed the car out of the garage before climbing in the passenger seat. It felt odd, not being behind the wheel. He didn't like giving control to anyone and expected Norma Rose felt the same, which is why she insisted on driving. Accepting that for what it was, he closed the door, but kept one hand on the doorknob, ready to dive out if needed. He'd been told Dave broke his arm teaching her how to drive.

"Where to?"

"St. Paul," he answered. "We're going to find out who poisoned your uncle."

"How?"

"By retracing every step he took if necessary."

"Why don't you just ask Dave?"

"I have—he doesn't remember a lot."

"Perhaps—"

"Just drive, Norma Rose." He'd been aware of her before, but sitting next to her had parts of him imagining things that could never be. Rolling down the window helped defuse the scent of her perfume, but in truth, that didn't help much.

She focused on the road, and drove with skill, easing his nerves greatly—at least about her driving—by the time they entered the outskirts of St. Paul. Ty had also forced his mind to concentrate on solving who'd poisoned Dave's drink. "How well do you know the chief of police?"

"Ted Williams?" she asked, easing over a set of railroad tracks.

He didn't bother nodding, or looking her way; she knew who he meant.

"Well enough, I suspect," she said.

Ty let a breath out slowly before he turned her way. "I know your father told you I need complete cooperation from you, and I expect it."

"He did," she said. "But I have my own expectations." She turned the wheel, steering the car down a rough road lined with thick trees. "Like the truth."

"We need to head into the city," he said. "This isn't the way."

"An hour won't make any difference," she said, attempting to steer around potholes that jostled the Cadillac so hard his teeth rattled.

"An hour?" he asked.

"Or less," she said. "That will depend on you."

Curious and enticed by the way she attempted to sound mysterious and dangerous, he asked, "How so?"

She looked at him for the first time since walking out of the resort. A cold, calculating stare that did little more than warm his chest. Her eyes were too blue, her skin too perfect and her lips too kissable—a fact he'd never forget—to pull off the stare like she wanted to. But she tried. He'd give her that.

She'd slowed the car to a crawl and still stared at him as she braked to a complete stop and then made a show of cutting the engine. If she'd been a man, her father perhaps, Ty might have been growing nervous by now. He'd heard of this spot. The isolation, the trees and rock wall a short distance ahead, screamed this was the end of the line. Right now, Ty was thinking of the privacy it all provided, and what he could do with that—had things been different.

Removing the key, she opened the driver's door and stepped out. Ty chose to mollify her and climbed out as well, and followed her up the road to the rock wall, which was actually an overhang. The twin cities, St. Paul and Minneapolis—farther to the west—were visible, laid out in a bird's-eye view. The railroad tracks, streets, buildings, various lakes and the river, with numerous bridges stretching across dark water as the mighty Mississippi curled its way through the hills and valleys, neighborhoods and plats of industrial areas where smoke clouded the otherwise blue sky.

"Suicide hill," Ty said when she turned another cold stare his way.

She was good, barely lifting a brow at her surprise that he knew exactly where they were.

He gestured to the edge, and the swamp several hundred yards below. "More than one man has been said to take his own life by jumping off this ledge." When she lifted her chin, he added, "Despite the bullet holes in his chest."

Chapter Fourteen

Ty said no more, it was her turn. She'd brought him here to alarm him and was trying to not let her disappointment show. The trouble with that was he knew her too well. Perhaps because she was so much like him. A man used to hiding things saw them easily in others.

"And more than one of those men was a federal agent," she finally said.

He reached over and flicked the butterfly on her headband before tugging on her ear. "Norma Rose, I'm touched you're so worried about me."

"Worr— I'm not worried about you," she snapped, shoving aside his hand.

"Then why did you bring me here, if not to warn me?"

With lips pinched tight, she breathed through her nose and, he had to admit, her glare was a bit intimidating, just not to him.

"I'm warning you," she growled, "about what will happen if you don't tell me the truth. The whole truth. And don't give me that private-eye spiel again."

Ty opened his mouth, to spout off a comeback about her not being strong enough to push him over the edge, but stopped before the words escaped. She was going to find out, sooner or later, and he'd rather she heard it from him, yet the opportunity to utilize his answers as leverage was something he couldn't let go to waste.

"Fair enough," he said, turning around to make his way back toward the trees.

"What? Where are you going?"

"The sun's hot," he said.

She followed, but kept her distance, staying a good arm's length or more away from where he stopped. Crossing her arms, she asked, "Is your real name even Ty Bradshaw?"

"Yes," he said. "Tyler Bradshaw." When she opened her mouth, he held up his hand. "I'll tell you everything. The truth. But only if you tell me the truth, too."

She frowned. "I've never lied to you."

Ty didn't confirm or deny that, but instead asked, "What's the history between you and Forrest Reynolds?"

* * *

Norma Rose caught herself too late, after she'd flinched visibly, which Ty noticed. "That is none of your business," she stated, taking a step back to put more space between them. This had been a bad idea, bringing him here in the hope of scaring him. A man like Ty didn't scare easily, and unfortunately, she did. That wasn't something she liked admitting, nor did she want to, but his nearness made it impossible to deny. The pull inside her was worse today than it had been last night, even with all she knew, and that was not a good thing.

"I think it is," Ty said.

"What?"

"I think the history between you and Forrest is related to all that's happening."

For a moment she feared he'd read her mind. It wouldn't surprise her. He seemed to be living inside her. His presence had her heart beating faster and her palms sweating, and she felt a crazy, fanatic desire to kiss him again. "Forrest took over the Plantation last year when his father left town," she said.

"And?"

She wasn't afraid of Ty, but it felt like she'd lost, or was losing, and she didn't like that. Not at all.

Norma Rose turned around, not seeing the trees covering the hill and lining the roadway, but stared in that direction. She couldn't lose. Answers were what she needed, and Ty was the one to give them to her. If she had to give up a few herself, so be it. Forrest Reynolds had become the least of her concerns.

"Galen Reynolds inherited the Plantation from his wife's family. It had been successful before the turn of the century, when the White Bear Lake area was full of resorts. It started out as a yacht club with sailboat races that brought crowds of people into the area. My mother and Karen Reynolds were close friends. We kids grew up playing with each other." That was a long time ago, but even as young children she'd understood the Reynoldses had money while her family hadn't. She wasn't about to mention that, so added, "The flu, when it hit, took Karen's youngest son, August, two weeks after my brother Adam. They were babies really, only five years old. My mother died a month later."

"I'm sorry."

She hadn't turned around and didn't now. The sympathy in his simple statement was too strong and left a part of her feeling raw all over again.

Almost as raw as way back then, when Forrest's father had first begun to vocalize his hatred toward her family. As the bitterness of that seeped forward, she let it out. "Galen Reynolds claimed my mother got what she deserved, that she'd given the flu to August."

"The flu was everywhere. His son could have gotten it anywhere."

"I know." Enough of this. Now wasn't the time to rekindle the hatred she harbored for Galen Reynolds. The man could no longer hurt her. Spinning around, she walked past Ty, who'd stepped too close for comfort. "Forrest and I remained friends, and we dated while in high school, until his father put a stop to it," she said, as if there was no more to it than that.

Ty walked past her, all the way to the passenger side of the car, where he opened the door.

When her expectant gaze didn't produce a response from him, she said, "It's your turn to tell me the truth."

He laughed, which goaded her.

"I'll tell you the truth, when you tell me the truth," he said, climbing in. After shutting the door, he leaned over to glance at her out the driver's window. "Let's go. I want to visit the last drug-store Dave remembers being at."

"I did tell you the truth," she insisted.

He sat up and stared out the windshield, which meant she had to lean down to look in the window. "I'm serious. I want to know who you are," she demanded.

"I'm Ty Bradshaw from New York," he said off-handedly, "who needs to discover who poisoned your uncle before it's too late. Now either get in, or give me the keys. I really don't care which."

Norma Rose wrenched opened the door, mainly in reaction to his reference to time running out. Her father had hinted at that, too. Shoving the key in the ignition, she said, "I will find out who you really are and expose you for a rat."

With a single slicing gaze before he turned toward the windshield again, he said, "And I will find out what really happened between you and Forrest."

It took some maneuvering back and forth before she got the Cadillac turned around, but then she hit the gas. The car bounced and banged as the tires fell in between potholes.

"It takes a good driver to hit every hole in the road," Ty said.

She'd have liked to tell him to shut up, but was too busy holding onto the wheel.

"Slow down," he said, "before you break an axel."

With no intention of listening to him—ever—she pressed her foot harder on the gas pedal. Ty's hand grasped her leg. His fingers and thumb dug into the sides of her knee, making a nerve flex and shudder. With the grip of iron that she wasn't strong enough to fight, he pulled on her leg, forcing her foot off the gas. Trying to keep the car on the road while fighting the sensations zipping up her leg, Norma Rose hit the brake with her other foot.

Before letting go, Ty growled, "Slow down or I'm driving."

"It's my car," she snapped.

"I don't give a damn whose car it is. I'm not going to be stuck out here because you're throwing a fit."

"A fit? I'm not throwing a fit."

"Don't you care what happens to your father? To your beloved resort?" he asked.

Norma Rose opened her mouth, but didn't trust herself to speak. She did care. Why else would she be here, with him?

"The *truth* is, Norma Rose, that I'm not the enemy, and if you want to save Nightingale's from being raided, by either the feds or the mob, you'll stop acting like a spoiled brat and help me."

Her fury rose to an entirely new level. However, used to hiding things, she held it in as she drove, slowly, down the road. By the time she turned back onto the highway her rage had melded into determination for the deepest revenge possible. Without a word, she drove directly to Charlie McLaughlin's drugstore and parked along the street out front. She was out the driver's side before Ty could make it around to open the door for her, and she marched forward onto the sidewalk. Her nerves zinged beneath her skin, a mixture of fire and ice, yet she planted the often-used smile upon her face as they entered the store, him holding the door for her.

"Well, Norma Rose Nightingale, imagine seeing you here."

She couldn't take much more. Truly she couldn't. "Hello, Janet," Norma Rose said to the girl behind the lunch counter, whose eyes, thickly coated with kohl and mascara, had settled on Ty. "Imagine seeing you here."

"I work here," Janet Smith replied, curling her red lips into a smile and batting her lashes unabashedly at Ty. "I live in the new set of apartments just right around the block."

Hostility hung in the air so heavily between Norma Rose and the soda girl, Ty almost quivered. But then he chose, as usual, to take advantage of the opportunity. Curling a hand around Norma Rose's elbow, he guided her onto one of the squat stools along the counter. She flinched—inwardly, he sensed more than felt it—but made no show of pulling out of his hold. Once they were both seated, he asked, "What's your lunch special?"

"Grilled cheese and tomato soup," the girl named Janet responded.

"How's that sound?" Ty asked Norma Rose, purposefully ignoring the other girl's invitation to take full notice of her rather voluptuous curves.

He imagined Norma Rose wanted to tell him exactly how she thought that sounded, but she didn't, as he knew she wouldn't. Instead she smiled up at him. "Fine."

"We'll take two specials," he told the girl. "And two milk shakes." Glancing toward Norma Rose, he asked, "Chocolate?"

She nodded.

"Two chocolate milk shakes."

"I don't recall seeing you around," Janet said, once again giving him an open invitation with her eyes.

"I'm a friend of Norma Rose's." Sensing Norma Rose might soon snap, he added, "Could we get those shakes before the meal?"

The girl spun around and the drumbeat of her heels faded as she disappeared through a set of swinging doors at the end of the counter. Norma Rose said nothing while peeling off her gloves and discreetly examining her hands. They were no longer blue, and he wondered how hard she'd had to scrub them. After setting her gloves on her lap, she plucked a few napkins from the holder on the counter and slid one his way.

"Thank you," he said.

She remained silent.

He grinned, inwardly. "Who is that?" He didn't bother nodding toward where the girl had disappeared.

"Janet Smith."

"I caught the first name," he said. "How do you know her?"

"She lives in White Bear Lake, or did. I wasn't aware she'd moved."

There was more to her animosity than her just

living in the same town, and assuming he knew why, he pushed. "Another one of Forrest Reynolds's girlfriends."

She shot him a disgusted look. "Not that I know of, but I haven't kept track."

"Haven't you?"

"No, I haven't." Flustered, and most likely knowing he wouldn't give up, she whispered, "If you must know, her brother was a local whiskey runner who got himself caught a few months ago because he drank more than he delivered."

Her eyes grew wide before she lowered her lids, telling him what he already knew. That she'd said more than she'd intended, and that Janet blamed the Nightingales for her brother's arrest.

"Interesting," he said. "What's his name?"

Opening her eyes, she peered past him, to where Janet was reappearing at the end of the counter. He leaned closer. "What's his name?"

"Jeb Smith, but everyone called him Smitty," she whispered.

The clanging and banging made by the soda girl was obviously intended to break apart what must look like a tête-à-tête. Ty glanced her way, letting her know it wasn't appreciated, which had the effect he'd figured it would. She made more noise by turning on the electric mixer to stir their shakes.

"And he worked for your father."

"I didn't—"

"We're beyond that, Norma Rose," he hissed through a smile. "He was running Minnesota Thirteen, wasn't he?"

She pinched her lips together and nodded.

"Thank you," he said close to her ear. He lingered there for a few seconds, inhaling deeply, while telling himself it was for Janet's benefit. A minute later, he knew it had worked. Norma Rose's cheeks were rosy and Janet's were red.

"How's your uncle Dave?" Janet asked, plunking down two tall glasses so hard the frothy contents bubbled over the edges.

"Fine," Norma Rose said, picking up a napkin.

"I heard he was arrested the other night," Janet persisted. "Ossified on the street corner."

"You heard wrong," Norma Rose said, without any prompting from Ty. "Dave's at the resort and doing just fine. How's Jeb?"

The other woman spun around, but her glare could have cut through ice. A man carrying two plates holding soup bowls and sandwiches had come from the back room and was heading their way.

"Well, Norma Rose," the man said. "Janet didn't tell me it was you here. I talk—"

"Norma Rose is showing me the city," Ty said, interrupting the man. "Ty Bradshaw," he added as the man set down the plates before them.

"Charlie McLaughlin," the man replied.

"I'm staying out at the resort," Ty said, knowing Janet's ears were pricked. "Since the day is quiet out there, Norma Rose and I decided to visit the city. Maybe take in a picture show."

Again, Norma Rose played along. "Ty wanted to try one of your infamous milk shakes."

"And see a picture show," Ty added again with a grin that grew as Norma Rose blushed.

Charlie laughed. "Ted Williams said he saw the one playing over at the Capital Theater last night, said he'd never laughed so hard. Janet, you went with him, didn't you?"

Janet, stunned and nervous, shook her head. "Me? With Chief Williams?" she said, attempting to cover up her secret. "Of course not."

Ty took in all the information. A soda girl whose brother was in jail was dating the chief of police, and going to a picture show at the most expensive theater, which was owned by the Hamm's Brewing company, a company that was supposedly out of business due to Prohibition.

Not wanting it to appear like he was prying, Ty turned to Norma Rose. "We might have to see that one."

She almost choked on her spoonful of soup and Ty grinned, imagining the fun of sitting in a dark theater with her. Ears alert, he let the conversation flow naturally as he and Norma Rose ate. It wasn't yet noon and the establishment was empty except for the four of them, and he learned more each time either Charlie or Janet opened their mouths.

Once their plates were empty, he paid the bill while Norma Rose slipped on her gloves. Taking her arm to assist her off the stool, he asked, "Shall we go see when the next movie starts at the Capital?"

She frowned slightly, but at his silent urging agreed with what the others might have taken as real enthusiasm, though he knew it was false. "Why not?"

He nodded toward Charlie. "The shakes were as good as she said they would be. Thanks."

"Stop in anytime," Charlie said. "A friend of Roger's is a friend of mine."

Feeling Janet's glare, Ty asked, "How about a friend of Norma Rose's?"

Charlie laughed. "Hers, too."

Ty chuckled as if that delighted him. It did, actually. Especially the way she squirmed inwardly. He could read her as well as he could read himself. Perhaps even better.

With one hand clasped around her elbow, he led her all the way to the passenger door of her car, which he opened for her. Before she had a chance to protest, he helped her into the car and shut the door.

He walked around to the driver's side and once settled behind the wheel, started the engine. In her haste to exit the car before him, she'd left the keys dangling in the ignition. He turned, prepared to point out the dangers of that, but didn't. Janet's nose was glued to the drugstore window, and as Norma Rose was already looking at him, he simply leaned over and pressed his lips against hers.

She stiffened and Ty waited for her to pull back. When she didn't, he moved away and smiled as she leaned forward, following him for a split second.

Sitting back against the seat, she huffed out a breath. "Why did you do that?"

He expected more. A full protest. But was glad

she didn't give one. "Because I wanted to," he said, making no mention of Janet watching from the window.

The half smile on her lips caused a grin he couldn't hide.

She tugged her skirt over her knees. "Don't you mean because Janet's still watching through the window."

He shifted the car and pulled away from the curb. "Didn't see her."

"Right."

Ty laughed.

"Enough foolishness," she said then. "When are we going to start looking for who poisoned Dave?"

He claimed they were searching, doing research he called it, but besides eating lunch at the drugstore, where he'd asked no questions about Dave whatsoever, they hadn't done anything besides drive around St. Paul.

They traced the route from Charlie's store to the Blind Bull and back again, the few blocks from the police station to the drugstore, and then the distance from the store to the Capital Theater. Where she had hoped he wouldn't stop. She had no desire to see a picture show with him. None. She repeated that several times in order to convince herself.

When he finally parked the car, she glanced around at the trolley cars and visitors. "What are we doing here?" she asked. "I know Dave didn't visit Como Park."

"Perhaps not," he said, pulling the keys from the ignition. "But we are."

Considering all the people about, Norma Rose waited for him to open her door and then accepted his arm to walk across the parking lot. Situated in the northern part of St. Paul, over three hundred acres of land along the shores of Lake Como had been dedicated as a city park. She hadn't been here in years, but had heard of the vast improvements made lately. Walking paths, flower gardens, ponds, fountains and pergolas, even a fenced-off area with wildlife for city dwellers to observe.

All her years of dreaming about things she wanted to do were manifesting in a mere two days. The amusement park, dancing, a lunch date, walking in the park. All silly things she could have done by herself any day, but hadn't because she hadn't wanted to do them alone, or even with one of her sisters. She'd wanted to do them like this. With someone.

Norma Rose attempted to tell herself that some-one should not be Ty, but she'd never been gull-ible, not even when it came to lying to herself. He was now holding her hand as they walked along a gravel pathway, and she couldn't find anything she'd like to change. Especially not him, and she wasn't overly sure why.

"I can't tell you who I am."

Her footsteps faltered and she stopped. "What?"

"I can't tell you who I am, who I really am."

She could swear there was regret in Ty's tone, as she questioned all the while if she was hearing things. "Why?"

"I can't tell you that, either."

"Because I didn't tell you everything about For-rest?" Although she'd had no intention of telling him earlier, now it seemed silly. Galen Reynolds was the one who'd turned the whole thing into a fiasco, and Forrest had never tried to stop him. That had eaten at her harder than Galen's lies. Back then. Now it really didn't matter.

Ty squeezed her hand and started walking again, tugging her along. "No."

"Then why?"

Ty kept walking and Norma Rose kept alongside him, around a pond with a pair of white swans swimming gracefully and past flower gardens full of yellow marigolds and purple and white pansies. There was a wooden park bench on the far side of the flowers, and Ty didn't stop until they happened upon it.

"You're a beautiful woman, Norma Rose, and a smart one. You could go anywhere in the world, start up a legitimate business and—"

"The resort is a legitimate business," she interrupted.

He shook his head, but she couldn't leave it at that. He had to understand.

"Yes, it is," she insisted, "and it will continue to be after Prohibition is repealed, which it will be, mark my word. There is no black-and-white in the world right now. No defined line between right and wrong. It's not that every American citizen wants to break the law, it's just…" She couldn't completely explain how things appeared in her eyes, but she had to. "It's just that people know if they follow every law on the books right now, they'll starve. It may not be that way everywhere. In Washington or other places, but it is here."

"You've been listening to your father too long," Ty said. "People won't starve."

"Do you know what it's like to eat soup three

times a day?" She shook her head. "No, it wasn't really even soup. It was nothing more than water a few potatoes had been boiled in. Well, I do. And I know what it's like to be on the receiving end of judgments and lies." Fury wasn't filling her stomach this time, neither was regret or shame. "This is America, Ty. The land of the free and the brave, and if we give in, what then? We give up all our forefathers fought for. Give up the promises and hopes of millions of people who crossed rough seas and desolate lands to build homes and communities. Why? Because a few lawmakers think they know best? It's not the people who are trying to make a living that are the bad ones. Making and drinking spirits has been a part of society since the beginning of time, all the laws in the world won't change that. People can't change that quickly."

"So the lawmakers are the bad ones," he said with a shake of his head.

She'd wrestled with these things for years, and had formed a few of her own opinions. "The laws they made, the ones they are attempting to enforce, won't work. Surely you see that. How Prohibition has increased crime more than it's decreased it. It's failed, and no one knows what to do about that. How to make it right. But," she added with a wave of her hand, "look around. The economy is booming. Schools are being built, as well as churches and parks. Not by the government, but by private people. Those who know this will end and are investing in the future. In businesses that will survive. In their communities. In the stock market. In their families."

Ty cursed. She was good. Damn good. "You should be a lawyer," he said, meaning it. "What are you going to do when your father goes down? When the resort is seized?"

She shook her head. "That's not going to happen."

"Yes," he said, his stomach in his throat, "it is."

Chapter Fifteen

He'd discovered a lot today, getting close to putting a bead on Bodine. Ty should have been elated. He usually was at this point, but in the past, he'd never worried about people getting hurt. "Let's go," he said.

Norma Rose shook her head. "Why'd you bring me here, Ty? To the park?"

Because for a few minutes he wanted to forget who he was, what he was here to do. He just wanted to be a man on an outing with a woman. A beautiful woman who'd gotten under his skin and kicked his heart back into motion as if he had a hand crank sticking out of his chest like an old car. He couldn't tell her any of that. But he did take a moment to appreciate her beauty.

Stepping closer, watching him as closely as he watched her, she repeated, "Why did you bring me here?"

Ty grasped her shoulders and this time he didn't give her the option of pulling back. He went in with guns loaded, kissing her until there wasn't an ounce of breath left in his lungs, or a section of her lips he hadn't tasted. Then he stopped, took in a gulp of air and went in for seconds, parting her lips with his tongue to explore the sweet, intoxicating caverns of her mouth.

When Ty came up for air, he needed more than a gulp to catch his breath. That's when he noticed another couple on the other side of the pond, watching them. He was in deep and it was either sink or swim. He'd never sunk before. That just wasn't an option.

Curling an arm around Norma Rose's shoulders, he said, "Let's go."

She didn't protest. Walking beside her, the silence weighed heavy. Whatever he'd expected to gain from kissing her was backfiring more than a six-cylinder engine hitting on only four cylinders. He now wanted her more than ever. Not just to kiss her, either, but to love her. In every sense of the word. Deep inside his heart, which had been dark and cold, a forgotten organ simply doing its job to keep him upright, until she'd come along. It now beat to a different drum, hammered at the thought of her and left him feeling alive for the first time since he'd seen the carnage of Bodine's attack on his parents.

His heart wasn't all she'd opened up. He was taking things into consideration, too. Things he never had before. Prohibition wasn't working, he'd known that for a long time, but he'd never looked at it from the other side. Through the eyes of those using it to feed their families.

They arrived at the car and he opened the passenger door. The smile she flashed him was tender and as delicate as the flimsy flowers filling the beds they'd wandered past. It could be crushed so easily and he didn't want her or her smile crushed.

"Are we going home?" she asked, once he'd pulled out of the parking lot, onto the roadway.

Home. That was something else he'd started to want. The knot in his throat threatened to strangle him and he barely managed a nod.

"Then turn left at the stop sign. There's a road going north that eventually angles over," she instructed. "It'll save us from going back downtown."

He followed the road and the signs directing them toward White Bear Lake. The scenery rolled past unseen. How had this all happened in such a

short time? Her. The changes inside him. It would
be nice to say he'd felt them coming, but he hadn't.
They'd hit him unexpectedly, like a club on the
back of the head in a dark alley.

She was watching him, her gaze burning the
side of his face, which he kept forward, eyes on
the road, hoping she didn't speak. There was nothing he could say.

They entered White Bear Lake. "Is there anything you need from town?" he asked, the tension
about to snap inside him.

"No," she answered quietly.

He couldn't take the chance of glancing her way
because there was something else he needed to
consider. If he was feeling this way, how was she
feeling? Norma Rose was no doxy. She didn't give
away her favors for free. Yet, she'd let him kiss her,
more than once, and that said a lot.

Actually, she hadn't just let him kiss her, she'd
been a full participant, and that said even more.

Ty's mind and insides grew more twisted as he
drove the final few miles and pulled her Cadillac
into the garage.

"You can leave the keys in it," she said, opening her door. "I'll be in my office if you need me."

When he glanced at her over the hood of the car

her lips quivered, as if holding the slight smile there hurt.

"Father said to help you with whatever you needed."

Ty nodded. He should thank her for her help today, but figured it would sound as hollow as he felt. Out of respect, which he held strongly for her, he walked her to the front door of the resort and then he headed for Dave's cabin to confirm his beliefs.

Norma Rose closed the resort's front door behind her and leaned her head upon the heavy wood. The heat of Ty's kiss still radiated inside her and proclaimed the one thing that was never supposed to happen had happened. But how? She couldn't have fallen in love. Not with Ty. Not this fast.

"I'm glad you're back," Twyla said, walking out of the ballroom. "I'm afraid I have bad news."

Pushing away from the door, Norma Rose planted her feet onto the floor in preparation. "What?"

"Forrest refuses to talk to me," Twyla said. "Says he'll only talk to you."

Norma Rose took a step, and then another, each one growing more purposeful until she was marching across the foyer and down the hall to her office.

"I'm sorry," Twyla said. "I tried. I really did."

"I'm sure you did," Norma Rose answered, collecting herself with each second that ticked by. "Thank you."

"For what?" Twyla said, following all the way into her office.

"For trying," Norma Rose answered. "Please close the door."

Twyla did, and Norma Rose picked up the phone. "Thelma," she said once the operator down the hall answered. "Please ring the Plantation, Forrest Reynolds."

"Right away, Norma Rose," Thelma answered. "Hold, please."

She barely had time to sit down before Forrest's voice carried through the wire and into the phone. "Forrest here."

Norma Rose waited a split second, just in case her body had a reaction she'd need to counteract. At one time she thought she'd been head over heels in love with Forrest, until he'd betrayed her, without saying a single word in her defense that night he'd left town so long ago. When nothing, not even lingering bitterness, appeared inside her, she said, "Forrest, it's Norma Rose."

"I've been expecting your call."

"Then you know why I'm calling."

"We should talk—"

"We are," she interrupted. A sigh built then and she let it out. "What happened between us, between our families, was a long time ago and it's past time it ended." Before she lost her nerve, she continued, "We were teenagers who got caught alone together, something that happens to millions of people, and something that should never have escalated into a family war."

"Your father sent my father to prison because of it," Forrest said.

He sounded older, harsher than when they used to talk and laugh, but he didn't sound angry. She wasn't angry, either. She was just being honest. "My father may have paved the road, but your father drove himself there." She paused briefly. "You know that, Forrest, as do I."

The line was so quiet, she wondered if they'd lost connection, until she heard a faint sigh.

"Are you going to give me Slim Johnson for the next two Saturdays or not?" she asked, having said her piece.

"On one condition," Forrest said.

Wanting to focus her time on other things, she was prepared to write a check for any amount he requested. "Which is?"

"That I'm invited to the parties," Forrest said. "Both of them."

"Done," she answered without a thought. "Ask Slim to call me."

"I will," Forrest said. "I look forward to seeing you."

"It'll be good to see you, too," she answered, again speaking without thinking. "Goodbye."

"I'm glad you called," Forrest said as she was about to pull the phone from her ear. "And for what it's worth, I tried to stop my father's allegations."

She didn't have time to worry about Galen Reynolds, or if Forrest had stood up for her or not. "Thank you," she said. "But your sentiment is a little late."

Norma Rose clicked off then.

"Bee's knees," Twyla whispered. "You are one hard dame."

Sighing, Norma Rose leaned back in her chair. "Am I?"

Eyes wide, yet grinning, Twyla nodded, her head bobbing so hard her dangling earrings jingled.

Norma Rose released the air attempting to suffocate her from the inside. It had been what she'd wanted, to be a hard dame. One who held the appearance that nothing and no one got to her. It had worked for a while, years really, but was it truly who she was, who she wanted to be? What had it really gotten her?

"What's going on today?" Twyla asked. "Father's been locked in his office all day."

In the past, Norma Rose would have told her sister it was none of her business, but it was Twyla's business, and Josie's, just as much as it was hers. The resort belonged to all of them. "I truly don't know," she admitted. "Not all of it, but I need your help. Josie's, too."

"I don't believe it," Roger repeated. "I pay that man well."

Ty's instincts had been right, but convincing Roger was difficult and proved where Norma Rose got her stubbornness. "Someone paid him more," Ty said. "That shouldn't surprise you. St. Paul hasn't had an honest police chief in years. Dave said Charlie made his milk shake, but Janet carried it into the back room and then she left out the back door, to deliver a prescription order. He remembers her offering him a ride when he stumbled outside."

"With prompting from you," Roger insisted.

"I never mentioned her name, or anyone else's— Dave did. I just listened as he talked," Ty reminded. Roger had been in the cabin during the questioning, and still refused to believe it. "Dave also remembers Williams being in the car."

"Ted picked him up."

"No," Ty said, "he told Norma Rose he got a call and sent an officer out to pick him up."

"He probably didn't want to concern her," Roger said.

"I drove the route." Ty normally didn't bother convincing people, but this time he was determined. "Ted could have easily dropped Dave off on the street corner, driven to the station and told another officer to go pick him up." Ty crossed the room, laid both hands on Roger's desk and leaned down to look the man in the eye. "It all adds up. Janet wants retribution for her brother's arrest, and agrees to go along with accosting Dave, knowing when he'd visit the drugstore. Neither of them knew of Dave's allergy to alcohol and panicked before they'd delivered him to Bodine's henchmen."

When Roger once again shook his head, frustration bubbled inside Ty. "Think about it. A girl who never had enough money to take the trolley to St. Paul, now lives in a brand-new apartment and drives a Chevy straight off the lot. A soda girl doesn't make that kind of money. Add that to the Blind Bull being raided on Friday night and opening again on Saturday night, under a new name.

That isn't anything new, but I've seen buildings after federal raids. That didn't happen at the Blind Bull. It was an internal takeover with a few local cops thrown in for good measure."

"So Bodine now owns the Blind Bull," Roger said. "Then go there and bust him, leave my resort out of it."

"It's not that simple," Ty said, although he was thankful the man now understood certain aspects. "Bodine's not there. He has front men, just like you. Dave's the one who carries a suitcase full of samples for potential buyers—not you."

Roger growled an expletive.

"The only place Bodine is going to appear," Ty went on, "is here at the resort, and your only hope of avoiding a takeover, or a raid, which is what I'm sure his henchmen are planning by putting out the word there's a snitch, is for us to stop him before he gets here."

"Us?" Roger asked. "You want me to turn snitch by working with you, a federal agent?"

"You already have," Ty pointed out. "You know my identity, but haven't put a bullet in my back."

Roger leaned back in his chair and rubbed his chin thoughtfully. "No, I haven't," he finally said. "Do you want to know why?"

Ty didn't nod, but simply met the man's stare eyeball to eyeball.

"Because I want to know what's in this for you," Roger said. "You could call in all the backup you need. Could have right from the start."

"I need Bodine, not his henchmen," Ty said. "The only way to draw him out is a meeting with you."

"Which could mean the ruin of everything," Roger said.

Growing frustrated again, Ty straightened and ran a hand through his hair. There was only one way to make Roger see how serious this truly was. "You want to keep those daughters of yours safe? You may want to send the rest of them to Chicago with Ginger."

"What are you talking about now?"

Ty's insides churned. "I know Bodine. He won't stop until he gets what he wants, and deep down, you know that, too. Now, I can make sure that doesn't happen, but you have to—"

"Why?"

Frustrated, Ty bit his lips together.

"What's in this for you?" Roger asked. "Besides Bodine. He's just another notch on your belt. The stories I've heard, you don't work with anyone, just—"

"Because when this is all over, I plan on asking your permission to marry Norma Rose." The second the words left his mouth, Ty wanted to call them back. It was too late, he knew that, and wondered if he looked as shocked as Roger did. The idea he might have fallen in love with Norma Rose had been brewing in the back of his mind since returning from town with her this afternoon, but marrying her hadn't.

"No," Roger said firmly.

"No?" Ty repeated. Now that he'd admitted it, the idea was growing on him. Marrying Norma Rose. He could imagine Nightingale might have apprehensions about his daughter marrying an agent— many men might. Slapping both hands on Roger's desk, he leaned down again. "I'm about to save your business, your empire, and keep you out of jail. I'm the only one that can do it, I might add."

Roger pushed out of his chair to stand and lean across his desk, where they stared at one another practically nose to nose. "Me, my business, is one thing. My daughter is another."

"So you'd rather go down?" Ty asked.

"I won't be blackmailed," Roger said. "And neither will Norma Rose."

Chapter Sixteen

Her father's lips were shut tighter than a clam. Other than having her and her sisters sign various documents, he'd barely uttered a word in the past five days. The tension surrounding him was so thick Norma Rose could almost see it, but no matter how hard she insisted he tell her what was going on, he refused.

Refused.

She was furious, fed up and sick. Literally sick to her stomach. Hadn't been able to eat and at night she cried. Something she hadn't done in years. But Ty had disappeared. Utterly disappeared. It was as if he'd never been at the resort. In her life. Even her memories were foggy. If not for the constant ache inside her, she'd almost believe he'd been nothing more than a phantom she'd conjured out of thin air.

Norma Rose scrubbed her face one more time, trying to wash away the evidence of another sleepless night. Glancing into the mirror over the sink, she concluded all she'd done was take off a layer of skin. All the cosmetics in the world wouldn't disguise the bags under her eyes or the hollowness of her cheekbones.

She had to try. Tonight was Big Al's party.

After applying makeup, which didn't help, she pulled on a dress. A black one that was far more fitting for a funeral than an anniversary party, but it fit her mood. She then went to her room, where she added black shoes and gloves and rather than a headband, she put on a black pill hat.

Twyla and Josie both encountered her in the hall-way, their brows raised, yet they made no comment, at least not about her outfit. They were both dressed in vibrant colors.

"The decorating is completed," Josie said. "You have to come see it. The ice sculpture is gorgeous."

"Ice sculpture?" Norma Rose asked, needing something to say.

"Yes," Josie said. "I told you about it. They are becoming a rave."

"It's in the shape of a swan," Twyla added. "Most impressive."

Nothing could impress her. Not even all the work her sisters had done. Something she truly needed to appreciate. If not for them, the resort may have dried up and blown away. She just didn't have the energy it needed. That had never happened before, but she didn't know how to get it back. It was already two in the afternoon and she was just now venturing downstairs.

Her sisters, however, had been up since the break of dawn. When she'd asked them to take over Big Al and Palooka George's parties they'd jumped in like they'd been running the place all along. At the time, she'd believed she'd be glued to Ty's side, not mourning his absence like an army widow. That's truly what she felt like—a widow. Having lost the one man she'd loved more than life itself.

A sigh burning her chest escaped and covered the sob that wanted to be released. She was afraid to think where Ty might be. The mystery behind Dave's poisoning had vanished with him. At least that's how it seemed, considering no one would talk about it.

"You should add a long string of pearls to your outfit," Twyla said. "It would liven you up a bit."

Norma Rose caught the glare Josie shot at their other sister while she hooked her arm. "She looks lovely just as she is," Josie said. "Black has always been Norma Rose's favorite color."

"Yes, it has been," Twyla said, hooking Norma Rose's other arm. "Wait until you see the ballroom. Forrest Reynolds will be green with envy."

Josie leaned forward to once again glare at Twyla, and Norma Rose knew she had to respond. Her sisters had been extremely understanding over the past few days. "I'm excited to see the ballroom," she said, digging deep to pull up a portion of her past resilience. "But I don't give a rat's ass if Forrest is impressed or not."

It was Josie who started giggling. When Twyla joined in, Norma Rose's lips started to quiver. It was either laugh with them or cry. She went with laugh.

"I knew you were still in there somewhere," Twyla said as their laughter died down. "I knew it would take more than a good-looking lawyer to take down my sister."

Josie, done laughing, groaned. "Twyla—"

"No," Norma Rose said, stopping Josie's reproof. She hadn't been taken down. Just the opposite. Ty had lifted her up. Made her feel things she'd never imagined. "Twyla's right. Ty is good-looking." Loving him, as she now knew she did, may have made her stumble, but it hadn't brought her down. And no one would control her love life this time. No one. Looking at her sisters, she said, "And just so you both know, he's mine."

Both her sisters lifted their brows and then nodded.

Norma Rose didn't have to conjure up a smile. It formed all on its own. "And no man will ever bring a Nightingale girl down."

"Never," Twyla said.

"Ever," Josie added.

Arms hooked, they descended the sweeping staircase as one unit—three sisters working together—into the ballroom that was decorated more beautifully than imaginable.

People started arriving before Norma Rose had a chance to see all of the finest details, but she knew they were in place, so she wore her best smile and greeted each person as if they were a guest of honor.

When Forrest arrived, she even greeted him, leaning forward for him to kiss her cheek. He was as handsome as ever, but that stirred nothing inside her. Then again, no one could get a rise out of a corpse. She still felt dead inside, but now she was going to do something about it.

An elegant dinner was served before the music started, and by then, tired of twirling her thumbs on the sidelines—for her sisters had seen to every detail and there truly was nothing for her to do—Norma Rose stepped outside onto the balcony, where the evening sky was darkening and faint stars were poking through. Big Al and his wife were dancing, holding one another as if it was their wedding night instead of years later. Once unable to imagine what it would be like to share life so intimately with one person, Norma Rose now knew that was exactly what she wanted. Moving away from the huge windows, she didn't stop at the staircase, but walked all the way down to stroll across the freshly manicured grass.

Slim Johnson was a good musician, and the smooth even notes of the love song he played floated softly on the breeze, mixing with the sound of a few frogs calling to their mates.

Her wandering took her past the large pines that separated the lawn from the road leading to the cabins. Uncle Dave was back to his prime self, inside with the other guests, drinking soda water.

He refused to talk about Ty, too.

There had to be someone that knew where he'd gone. No one could just vanish, and all she had to do was figure out who that might be. Besides her father. He knew.

It would shock him, as it had her, but neither the resort nor her father would stop her from loving Ty. Ty probably wouldn't believe it, either, not at first, but she'd convince him. She'd already had to convince herself, which, in spite of all she'd believed in the past, had been relatively easy.

There was no sound or movement from the trees, but instinct flipped a switch inside her. Awareness had her heart and her breath quickening as she moved closer to peer into the shadows.

"Hello, Norma Rose."

Disappointment hit her like a sledgehammer. "Hello, Chief Williams," she replied. "What are you doing hiding in the trees?" She meant to sound casual, but an inkling of dread tickled her spine. The chief was on the guest list, as he was at most parties, yet she hadn't seen him arrive, and even if she'd missed him walking in, she'd expect him to be at the bar, consuming as much alcohol as the others.

"Just taking a stroll," he said. "Like you."

A rustle in the trees stung her already heightened sense of hearing. "I was just looking for Bronco," she lied.

"Bronco's out front." Ted took a hold of her arm as he spoke.

"Let go of me," she demanded, with no results. Her struggles were nothing against his strength, and once he'd pulled her into the trees someone else grabbed both of her arms from behind. Norma Rose opened her mouth to scream, but Ted clamped a hand over it. His other hand held the back of her head and one of his legs hooked around hers to stop her thrashing.

"Got those cuffs on?" he asked.

The music had just started when Ty arrived at the party, and he congratulated himself for purchasing a new suit in Chicago. The glitz and glamour of the shindig outdid the Ritz of New York parties, and he'd known Norma Rose would be dressed to the hilt. Black, as usual. She was a sight for sore eyes, standing next to the patio windows.

He was about to cross the room when Roger appeared at his side. It was just as well, get the business over first, then nothing would interrupt him and Norma Rose.

"Where's Ginger?" Roger asked as they left the ballroom.

"Safe." He'd thought about collecting Ginger, but as he'd told Roger before leaving, he wasn't about to put anyone in more danger. There was enough of that already. "I checked." He left it at that. Sooner or later Roger would discover what Ginger was doing in Chicago, and Ty wanted Bodine long gone by then.

Once in Roger's office, Ty handed over an envelope he'd negotiated hard to obtain while meeting with his superior in Chicago. "Your amnesty papers," he'd said. "Fully notarized. You help us catch the worst of the worst, and you, your properties, businesses and family will never be indicted."

"And my suppliers?" Roger asked.

The man didn't give an inch, but Ty already knew that. "I can't promise what happens outside of your property, but I will say you need to have a product people want to buy."

Roger rubbed his chin thoughtfully, reading between the lines of that answer before he asked, "When will it go down?"

Ty wished he had an answer. "I don't know for sure. I still haven't discovered when or how Bodine will arrive."

After putting the envelope, still sealed, in his desk drawer, Roger shook his head. "Norma Rose still isn't going to like this."

"I know," Ty answered. "I'm prepared for that."

"Are you?"

He shrugged, not exactly sure if he was prepared for anything when it came to Norma Rose. He'd put everything on the line for her and his gut told him it would work out. That's what he believed and would continue to do so.

"I saw her walk out the balcony doors when I was coming to meet you," Roger said. "Good luck."

Ty went out the front door; walking around the outside of the building would be faster than making his way through the crowd in the ballroom. He wasn't planning on asking her to marry him, not tonight. Not until this was over, but he had missed her. Lord, he'd missed her.

Night had fallen, but the moon was out, as were the stars, and they lit his way. He rounded the building and took the stairs leading up to the balcony three at time. It was empty, and he walked the length of it, looking through the windows for a glimpse of Norma Rose. He ran down the other set of steps and surveyed the lawn. The freshly cut grass held faint impressions. Footsteps. He followed them all the way to the tree line, where his stomach fell to his heels.

Lying beneath the pines was a single black glove.

A car started in the distance, and Ty bolted for the parking lot, shoving the glove in his pocket as he ran. Bronco was near the front door, just as he'd been earlier, and Ty shouted, "Norma Rose was just kidnapped!"

Bronco arrived at his truck as Ty opened the front door. "Take my car," he said, handing over a set of keys. "This truck will never catch whoever it is. Tuck and I will follow in his."

"They took the back road," Ty said, already running toward the other man's car. A brand-new Duesenberg that had a one-hundred-horsepower engine and was said to reach a hundred miles an hour. Ty hoped so. His heart had never beaten so frantically and he had never, not even in the trenches of war, experienced this terror.

The engine leaped to life with the growl of a lion, power rumbling through the entire car. Ty steered it toward the road that lead past Dave's cabin, as well as several others. When he came to the thin row of bushes that separated the road alongside the cabins from the hidden trail, he blasted through the greenery, giving no thought to the car's black paint. He had to crank the wheel around a tree or two before he bounded onto gravel again, where he hit the gas harder.

Used only for secret deliveries, the road was well used, but also well hidden. The moonlight barely filtered through the trees overhead, yet Ty refused to turn on the lights. When the other car realized they were being followed, he'd be on their back bumper. The road was only a couple of miles long, ending at the back of the train depot, where another hidden road entered as well, one that ran parallel to the main highway before heading west into central Minnesota, where the most popular shine in America was made. His superior had claimed the demand for Minnesota Thirteen was coming in strong from European countries, which meant every gangster was going to be looking for a piece of the pie, and the reason the government had given in to Ty's demand of amnesty for Nightingale.

He'd never have imagined a woman could make him see things differently, but she had and now he had to prove he was right to his worst critic. Himself.

First he had to find Norma Rose. Whoever had taken her was leaving a cloud of dust behind them. The train whistle was blowing as Ty arrived at the depot. The bouncing light on the engine was approaching fast and Ty briefly calculated if he could make it across the tracks before the train barreled past.

Tossing caution aside, he didn't let off the gas.

The light filled the interior of the car, the blast rattled his ears and he couldn't quite say if the car jostled so hard from the tracks, or if the front guard of the train slightly caught his back bumper. Either way, he cleared the tracks and wrenched the wheel in time to make the tight corner onto the second hidden road.

Then he allowed himself to breathe, ears ringing from the horn blast, or maybe the cursing he was sure the conductor was now doing. Eyes on the road ahead, Ty noted the absence of dust and braked to whirl the entire car around. At the highway he glanced both ways. The only vehicle on the road was heading south, so that's the way he went. It had to be the car Norma Rose was in. He became more convinced when it turned east on an unmarked road. The other car clicked on its lights then, most likely convinced it hadn't been followed. Ty also recognized that it was a St. Paul police car.

Why hadn't he warned her about Williams? The man had failed in kidnapping Dave, so had chosen the next best thing. The better thing. Roger would do anything to get his daughter back. So would Ty.

He eased off the gas to get his mind in order. His gun was in his truck and Bronco was nowhere to be seen in the rearview mirror. No doubt he'd been stopped by the train. Williams turned again, and Ty followed, but hung back. The next turn the other car made appeared to be a driveway. Ty took the Duesenberg through the shallow ditch on the driver's side of the road and squeezed the car between two pine trees, where he parked. He climbed out and hurried up to what indeed proved to be a driveway.

A ramshackle house, leaning to one side with shutters hanging off the windows, glowed in the headlights as the squad car rolled to a stop. Williams climbed out, dragging Norma Rose beside him while a third person, who Ty presumed from her figure to be Janet Smith, got out of the passenger side and hurried ahead to open the door of the house.

Cursing for leaving his gun behind, Ty scrambled through the bushes growing along the driveway and then around to the side of the house. There were no broken or open windows and he couldn't hear a thing, until the front door opened.

Staying out of the headlight beams, Ty eased to the edge of the house.

"She'll be fine until morning," Janet was saying. "You need to get back to the party before you're missed."

"You know where to park the squad car after dropping me off?" Williams asked.

"Yes. I'll also make the call, let the big man know the bird is in the cage. You just make sure you put that ransom note someplace where it won't be found until morning," Janet said. "I was afraid we were being followed there for a little bit."

"No one was following us," Williams said. "I had one eye on the rearview mirror the whole time. There were no lights behind us except that train. Which was perfect timing. That's why we took this little girl. No one would think to follow a squad car. And I know the perfect place for the ransom note. With Norma Rose out here, no one will go into her office until morning."

"When they can't find her," Janet said with a laugh. "We can't fail this time."

They climbed in the car, and their laughter hung louder in the air than the car's engine as Williams backed up and headed down the driveway.

Ty ran around the back of the house, just in case Williams noticed his car and came back. Throwing open the back door, he hissed, "Norma Rose!"

There was no answer, just thumping. Ty rushed toward the sound, stubbing his toes and tripping over furniture along the way. She was in the center of the main room, tied in a chair like an actress left by a villain in a silent movie.

"Are you all right?" he asked, while pulling the rag tied across her mouth over her head. "Hurt anywhere?"

"Yes and no," she said. "Ted and Janet grabbed me at the resort."

"I know. I followed." He searched for the knots in the rope wrapped around her.

"Where were you?"

"In Chicago until a short time ago," he answered, finally finding a knot.

"My feet are tied, too, and there's a set of nippers on my wrists," she said. "What were you doing in Chicago?"

"Damn it," Ty whispered, now searching for a knot on her ankles. "It's darker than sin in here. I was working."

"Open the front door," she suggested. "Let the moonlight in. This is Janet and Jeb's old house. Where they lived before he was arrested."

Ty found the knot, untied it and then he kissed her. Just a quick kiss, as she was still handcuffed, however, it soon turned into several short, sweet kisses when her lips met his with smooth perfection.

"Come on," he said against her mouth. "Let's get out of here."

She stood, with his help. "The door's straight ahead."

"Are you all right?" he asked again. "Not hurt anywhere?"

"I'll be fine once you get these nippers off my wrists."

Ty found the door and opened it, amazed by how much light the moon provided. She was even more beautiful than he remembered. He pulled out his pocketknife and picked the lock.

Rubbing her wrists while he pocketed his knife and the cuffs, she asked, "Did you find the snitch?"

"I'll tell you on the way," he said.

"No." She planted her feet stubbornly on the not-so-stable front porch. "Tell me now." When he didn't answer right away, she insisted, "I deserve to know. I was just kidnapped."

He'd already told her father—already told himself—that she was the woman he loved and would love from this day forward, but he'd yet to tell her. He couldn't. Not until a few other things were taken care of. "There is no snitch," he said. "Williams was trying to keep any suspicion off himself. He and Janet are the ones who attempted to kidnap Dave, trying to drug him with rotten shine so he'd pass out and make it easy on them. When he became ill instead, they panicked."

Even with the threat of Williams returning, Ty's mind was wandering. He wanted to kiss her, hold her. Tell her how beautiful she was with the moonlight glistening in her hair, off her skin.

"So they kidnapped me this time." Frowning, she asked, "Why?"

"There's a mobster by the name of Ray Bodine. He wants a piece of your father's action," Ty explained. He felt relief at that explanation. It was time he told her. "Kidnapping a family member is his way of getting it—rather than asking for ransom money, he'll ask for a partnership."

"This Bodine, he's the man you've been after since you arrived, isn't he? The reason you came to Minnesota?"

Done withholding the truth from her any longer, he nodded. "Yes." He took her hand. "Let's get you back to the resort. My car is in the trees by the road."

She shook her head. "If I go back, the only people to get arrested would be Ted and Janet, but—"

"No."

"Yes."

"No."

"Yes."

Ty growled. There was no way in hell he'd put her in that kind of danger.

"It'll work," she said. "You know it will."

He did. That was the problem. Looking into those magnificent blue eyes of hers, something fluttered inside him. This was Norma Rose, and her intensity, her drive and take-charge attitude were only a few of the things he loved about her.

"It'll work, Ty, they'll never suspect, never see it coming."

Hiding a grin and a good portion of his excitement—for this could work in more ways than one—he said, "On one condition."

"What's that?"

"That I stay with you."

She lifted a brow, glanced at the open doorway and then back at him. Her smile rattled his insides like nothing ever had before.

"Deal," she said.

Chapter Seventeen

Norma Rose paced the floor, questioning if she was doing the right thing. She'd always known she'd do anything for the resort, for her father, but that wasn't the reason she was doing this. Ty was, and from now on, he'd be her only reason for doing almost anything. Oh, and for herself, of course. Most definitely.

When she'd first heard his voice, calling to her, she'd thought she'd been dreaming, and then, not begging him to kiss her, really kiss her, long and hard, had taken all the will she'd ever dredged up. She'd done it, though, because that had to be the first step in convincing him she was serious. This old ramshackle house wasn't the ideal location to tell him what she felt for him was love, but it would serve the purpose.

She'd opened the windows, but not the curtains, so no one would notice the candle she'd lit. It was old and shabby, but at least the cabin was clean. The chair still sat in the center of the room, with the ropes wrapped and loosely tied so she could slip them on if Ted or Janet returned.

Far off, she heard a car, and the fluttering inside her said it was Ty. They'd have tonight, alone, together, and she planned on taking advantage of that.

The whistle, one that sounded like a whip-poor-will, made her smile, and she whistled back, although hers wasn't nearly as good as Ty's.

"Did you find Bronco?" she asked, meeting him at the door.

"Yes. They were on the main highway, searching side roads."

Her heart was thumping wildly and she tried to control it by concentrating on the conversation. "They?"

"Your father was with him."

"You convinced him, didn't you, that this will work?"

"I did." He closed the door. "But it wasn't easy." Taking both of her hands, he stepped closer. "About as hard as it had been to convince him to let me marry you."

Her heart completely stopped, and then started

up again, but it spit and sputtered like a pump going dry. "Marry you?"

"Yes. Marry me."

He was grinning, and she struggled to hold back her own. Convincing him wasn't going to be as difficult as she'd imagined, then again, since meeting him, nothing had been difficult. Especially the loving-him part. However, she couldn't just give in that easily. Where would the fun be in that? Biting her bottom lip, she shook her head. "I never said I'd marry you."

"That's because I haven't asked you yet."

His smile was so brazen, yet secretive, she wasn't sure if he was teasing or not. That brought forth the one thought she hadn't been able to rationalize. "Federal agents do not marry bootleggers' daughters."

"Aw-w-w," he said, drawing out the word. "So you do admit your father's a bootlegger."

He'd caught her on that one, and she grinned. "And you're a federal agent."

"Yes, I am."

"I knew it all along," she whispered.

"Yes, you did." He leaned closer. "Now, kiss me. I know you want to."

"How do you know that?"

He laughed. "Because we think alike, and I want to kiss you more than I've ever wanted anything in forever and a day."

"Anything?" she asked, her breath mingling with his.

"Anything."

Her heart swelled, filling her with tremendous warmth. She looped her arms around his neck and stepped closer. "We do think alike, don't we?"

"Yes," he answered, cupping her hips and tugging her closer yet. "We do."

She stretched on her toes, initiating the kiss, a first for her. Ty seemed to enjoy it so much, she went back for seconds. And thirds.

Norma Rose was fully aware of what was going to happen next, and she wanted it with all the passion she'd poured into the resort over the past few years. When kisses left them too breathless to continue, she buried her face in his neck, inhaling the wonderful scent of him as they held onto one another.

"I missed you," he said softly, sincerely.

"I missed you, too." Tears stung her eyes. For no matter how wonderful he made her feel, how glorious he made life, a bootlegger's daughter and a federal agent would not be a match made in heaven.

But she could have this one night. This one beautiful night she'd dreamed of since the night of the dance-off.

She took his hand and led him through the kitchen, into the bedroom, where she'd left the candle burning and had pulled back the covers of the bed.

He looked at her tentatively. "What's this?"

Nervous, especially considering all that was at stake, her smile shook. "A bed."

"I see that." He shrugged. "I expect you are tired, after being kidnapped and all."

Her stomach fell, then she caught the slight grin on his lips. Stepping forward, she cupped the back of his neck. "You aren't disappearing on me again. So don't try."

"I don't want to," he whispered before kissing her slowly, sweetly and completely.

Norma Rose's last fear dissolved. There'd be nothing scary about this. Ty would see to that. He'd instilled a unique trust inside her from the very beginning. Perhaps that's why, and how, she'd fallen in love with him so swiftly.

When the kiss ended, Norma Rose stepped out of her shoes, a signal he couldn't miss. With a smile that could have stolen her heart if he hadn't already done so, he kicked off his shoes and pulled her onto the bed as if it was the most natural thing in the world for her to lie down beside him.

It was.

They lay there, facing each other, not speaking, just looking at each other in the dim flickering candlelight. Her heart was pounding and her body tingled with anticipation, yet a sense of calmness filled her, too.

When he did lift a hand, it was to trail a finger along the side of her face. "You're sure about this?"

"Very."

"I told your father I'd keep you safe."

"And you will." She curled her hand around his wrist and leaned closer. "Ted and Janet won't be back until morning," she added, in case he was worried about that.

"We can't be positive of that."

"I am," she answered, brushing her lips against his. "Ted was going—"

He interrupted her explanation with several soft kisses before his hand cupped the back of her head and the pressure of his lips increased. Norma Rose closed her eyes, cherishing the kiss. Physical, arousing sensations spread through her system, and a purring sound rumbled in her throat.

Ty chuckled softly and she opened her eyes. She wouldn't beg, but heavens above she wanted him. His smile was so seductive, so real, she grinned in return.

His hand slid over her shoulder and down her side, resting briefly on her hip. "I've dreamed of you," he said, kissing the tip of her nose and then her eyelids.

"I've dreamed of you, too," she admitted.

"When?"

She couldn't remember not dreaming about him. His hand had slipped onto her thigh and was now working its way under her skirt, over the garter holding up her stockings. Another little growl vibrated against the back of her throat.

"When did you dream of me, Norma Rose?"

Sucking in air, for his hand had passed over the garter and was caressing the bare skin of her upper thigh, then exhaling at the wondrous sensations that were just shy of crippling, she whispered, "Every night." It was true, she had dreamed of him every night, and most likely would every night for the rest of her life.

Ty kissed her again, parting her lips with his tongue. Heady, uncontrollable needs grew stronger as his hand roamed higher up her thigh, under her silk tap pants.

Her breath was coming in snippets, and Norma Rose could no longer think, just feel. She scooted closer, wrapping her arms around his neck and arching against him, wanting every part of her touching him.

Ty turned her onto her back, leaning over her, kissing her, caressing her stomach beneath her dress. Following her own intuition, Norma Rose started to unbutton his shirt. She heard the soft, slow timbre of Ty's voice talking to her, telling her how beautiful she was, how soft her skin was, how kissable her lips were, but was too involved in experiencing his touch to answer.

Her dress was soon pushed up to her shoulders, as was her cami top, exposing her breasts to the warm night air and the wonderful caress of his hands. Norma Rose would never have believed her body could respond so to a man's touch, or how something could consume her so fully that there was no room for thoughts, but it was happening, and she was relishing the experience.

Ty kissed her breasts, making her gasp with pleasure. She ran her fingers through his hair, holding him against her as he suckled, sending phenomenal ripples throughout her system. Feverish heat swelled inside her, and focused particularly in one spot, a deep ache burned.

She'd always imagined sex was a male-dominated activity, but swiftly concluded that was not the case. At least not for her. She made sure of that, too, as she and Ty shed their clothes. There had been tugging and pulling and giggles from her, which he'd responded to with kisses, but once they were both naked, and lying side by side again, a completely new wave of excitement filled her. He was telling her again how beautiful she was, and this time she basked in his statements, feeling beautiful. How could she not when he looked at her like that? The flickering flame of the candle reflected in his eyes, and she'd never seen anything so spectacular.

Other parts of him were quite spectacular, too. His thick arms, his manly, sculpted chest and stomach, rather impressive thighs and a notably eye-catching part of him between his hips. Nibbling on her bottom lip, she tried not to stare, but found that impossible.

Ty let out a low chuckle.

Heat rushed to her cheeks, knowing he'd caught her staring, but still she laughed.

"Aw, Norma Rose," he whispered, kissing her lips gently. "I do love you."

If hearts could open and pour out love like a pitcher of milk, hers did at that moment. Her throat locked tight, too, and tears stung her eyes. Despite the way she felt, how she'd come to understand her love for him, she hadn't been completely prepared for his declaration.

"Let me show you," Ty whispered, once again kissing and caressing her lips, her neck, her breasts, her stomach.

When he parted her legs touching the very spot that burned uncontrollably, Norma Rose gasped and then sank into the mattress, overtaken with satisfaction, for that very spot had cried out for his attention above the rest.

The heat of his mouth between her legs nearly jolted her off the bed, but the unfathomable pleasure had nothing but her hips moving, arching into him. The commotion of that kiss sent her over some invisible edge. All her awareness was coming from inside her now. She gave in to it, a great unknown that was far more powerful than anything she'd ever experienced.

Ty continued to kiss her, leading her on a fascinating journey that escalated faster than she could comprehend. Her breathing was fast and labored, her body tingling from head to toe, and still a profound drawing need inside her, intense and commanding, kept climbing and climbing.

Just when she thought she couldn't take any more, an inner explosion let loose, shocking her and shaking her entire being with an amazing, wild force.

Ty squeezed her bottom and continued to kiss her as the intensity dissipated, leaving her body with a mesmerizing slowness. Planting his hands in the mattress on both sides of her, Ty kissed his way back up to her lips.

"What was that?" she whispered.

"Me loving you," he answered.

"I liked it."

"I did, too."

Sitting back, he picked something off the bed. Norma Rose had seen rubbers before, and wondered where it had come from, but not for long. The way he rolled it over himself caught her attention and that primal force inside her, which she'd thought had disappeared, was back.

Excited all over again, she whispered, "I have a feeling I'm going to like this, too."

"I hope so," Ty said.

Her body tensed unexpectedly as he guided himself toward her.

"Relax, sweetheart," he whispered. "Just relax."

She nodded, though held her breath as he found entrance.

"Breathe, Norma Rose," he said, leaning down to kiss her cheek. "Just breathe."

Forcing the air out of her lungs, she was in the middle of another inhale when he entered her completely. She couldn't say the snap that happened was painful, just surprising enough that she jerked slightly.

"It's over," Ty whispered.

"Over?" she questioned, having expected and wanting more.

"Just that," he said. "Now the fun begins."

Once again, he was right, and this time, the journey was more brilliant, more breathtaking and vibrant because he was with her the entire way. Every thrust brought them closer and his hard, muscled body gliding over hers was profoundly spectacular.

Now knowing what to expect, Norma Rose participated fully, enjoying every moment. When the intensity built brighter and hotter than before, she welcomed it, and the earth-shattering gratification that soon followed was grander than any gold-encrusted trophy.

Ty collapsed onto her briefly and she welcomed that, too, his hot, heavy body, fully connected to hers, as fully spent as she. After a moment, he rolled off her and pulled her close to his side, kissing her temple.

She ran her hand down his chest, over his ribs and stomach. There were a million things they could talk about, but Norma Rose didn't say a word. Not this time. At this moment, life was too perfect. She closed her eyes, holding that thought.

Ty had fought demons, many of them, over the past few years, and right now they were attempting to draw him into a battle. He'd missed her so much, wanted to be with her so badly, he hadn't fully assessed the situation. There were so many dangers to this plan, so many things he needed to tell her. But even knowing all that, right now, he just wanted to bask in her presence, in the love she'd opened up inside him.

Later, after her breathing turned low and even, Ty knew what he had to do. Loving someone meant protecting them, even if they didn't like it. Although he didn't want to, he slid off the bed and covered her with the blankets that had ended up balled up at the foot of the bed. Then he gathered his clothes, dressed and left the house, stopping briefly at the outhouse to dispose of the rubber. After checking on Norma Rose one more time, he made his way through the woods to the car hidden there.

He climbed in the front seat and leaned back, exhaling. Satisfaction still pumped through his blood, and despite everything, for the first time in his life he couldn't hide the smile on his face. Or the love in his heart. He was in love with Norma Rose. Fully and rather madly. His only hope now was that he could live with it. That she could live with who he was.

His light dozing was interrupted by the sound of a car, and he jerked to full awareness as the engine turned off. Whoever it was parked on the road and Ty left the Duesenberg, cautiously making his way through the woods in that direction.

Recognizing Bronco, Ty gave a low whistle to indicate his location, before he asked, "What's happened?"

Bronco approached, shaking his head. "You aren't going to like this, Ty. Roger has Ted Williams in his office."

"Blast. I should have known." Ty's gut knotted. "He's going to get someone killed."

"Norma Rose isn't going to like this, either," Bronco said.

"No, she's not," Ty agreed. This was a wrench he didn't need. It could ruin everything. "She's sleeping in the cabin. I'll go get her and meet you back at the resort."

"Need any help?"

Ty huffed out a chuckle. Bronco knew the Nightingale sisters, probably better than their father did. "No," Ty said. "She knows her father."

"All right," Bronco said warily. "I don't envy you."

They parted ways with Bronco heading back to the road and Ty toward the cabin. It had been hours since Williams had dropped off Norma Rose, and the man's absence was sure to be missed. Ty cursed again. Roger was playing with more fire than he realized. Bodine, or his henchmen, wouldn't react well to two botched kidnappings.

Although he hated to, Ty woke Norma Rose by gently shaking her shoulder. He'd lit the candle and her sleep-filled eyes were more gorgeous than ever. "Change of plan," he whispered, when she closed her lids after giving him a gentle smile. "Your father has Ted Williams in his office."

The blanket fell to her waist as she sat up. "What? I thought you convinced him—"

"I thought I did, too," Ty said, sitting down on the bed. "You know your father. He has to be in charge."

She looked at him and smiled. "And so do you."

Ty couldn't deny that. He took one of her hands and kissed the back of it. A few minutes wouldn't hurt, and he wanted her to know what was driving him. "When I returned from the war, I took a job with the New York police, mainly because they were hiring and I needed money to pay for law school. My folks ran a bakery, a small one, but they did all right, kept a few families fed." He shook his head, realizing how much that sounded like something she'd say. "New York is different to here. It's full of gangs, always has been. Some of the worst Old West outlaws got their start in New York. Ray Bodine had a cartel of thugs, thieves among other things. He started making businesses pay for his protection, claiming it would keep them from getting robbed. Another big-timer was trying to take over the neighborhood, with the same tactics, but Bodine wasn't about to let that happen, and to prove his point, he killed an entire city block of small business owners, including my parents."

Compassion shimmered in her eyes. "I'm so sorry."

Ty shook his head, but squeezed her hand. "I vowed to stop him, but knew I couldn't do that with the police force. It's as corrupt as half the gangs, just like most places. So I left the force and law school to become a private eye. I started unearthing gang leaders and then would call in the police to take them down. By the time Prohibition was in full force, I'd made a name for myself, but no one knew who I was. The one captain I worked with did, though, and he shared my name with the feds, who hired me to continue doing what I was doing. Incognito. A few years ago, I had a bead on Bodine, but he eluded us. To throw everyone off track, he faked his death and went underground, where his cartel grew bigger than ever."

"And now he's after my father's trade," she said.

"Other mobs have tried, but no one's infiltrated Minnesota Thirteen, and that makes Bodine want it even more," he said.

"What's going to happen now?" she asked.

Ty shrugged. "I don't know. We need to get back to the resort so I can figure that out."

"I'll get dressed," she said.

He felt as if more than Bodine was slipping away. She was, too, and that stung worse. He leaned forward and kissed her. "I don't know what's going to happen with us, either."

She leaned her forehead against his. "I don't, either. A bootlegger's daughter and a federal agent don't go hand in hand."

Having no reply to that, he briefly kissed her lips.

Sighing as their lips parted, she said, "I'd better get dressed."

Ty stood and gathered her clothes, handing each piece to her and watching as she put them on, wishing he'd taken more time to watch her remove them. Someday he would, when this was all over.

She'd just sat down to pull on her stockings when the sound of a car engine's filtered through the open windows. She heard it, too. "Bronco?"

Ty blew out the candle. Having no idea, but wanting to ease her fears, he said, "His car doesn't sound like that." He handed over her shoes and took her stockings, shoving them and her garters in his pockets. "We gotta go."

They'd barely made it out the back door when headlights lit up the yard. Ty pressed a finger to his lips and gestured for her to stay put. He peeked around the corner of the house. Anyone in the car would surely see them dashing for the woods.

"This has to be the place," a man said. "It's just as the girl described."

"Let's get this Nightingale dame and get out of here before that snoopy police chief shows up," a second one said.

"That idiot," the first one said, "thinking we'd let him run the show after he'd already botched things."

"He'll end up just like his little girlfriend," the other one said, laughing.

The voices grew closer and the front door banged open. Ty peered around the corner again. If it was just him, he'd make a run for it, but couldn't chance someone else being in the car and seeing Norma Rose. He tucked her closer to his side and pulled her down to a crouch as the beam of a flashlight shone through the window.

"There's no one here," one of them said.

"Probably hiding," the other answered. "Girlie, oh, girlie, come out, come out, wherever you are."

Norma Rose shivered and Ty gestured toward an old shed behind the house. She followed him through the dark, around the back of the shed. "I have to find a weapon," he whispered.

"Don't you have a gun?"

"I left it in my truck," he answered, kicking at the ground for anything of substance.

She let out a hiss before saying, "Here, it's a yard rake. I found a shovel, too."

He took the rake. "Give me the shovel, too."

She'd moved a few steps away. "No, I'll need it."

"No, you won't."

"Stop arguing," she insisted. "They just came out the back door."

A shovel wasn't much, but she would need something. With the rake in one hand, he said, "Stay here."

"No," she said, "You stay here."

Before Ty had a chance to react, or figure out what she was doing, Norma Rose shot around the building. "Yoo-hoo!" she shouted. "Over here." She turned around and while running past him, hissed, "Trip them with the rake."

Ty cursed, but kneeled down and stuck out the rake handle. The ground rumbled with footfalls, but he still caught a glimpse of Norma Rose rounding the far corner of the shed. The first thug went down, wrenching the hold Ty had on the rake.

The second one shouted, "Get up!" as he kept running, not noticing what had tripped his companion.

Ty leaped on the first one, yanking the man's hands behind his back. All he had were Norma Rose's stockings, so he used one to tie the man's hands while kneeling on the back of his head, keeping the thug's shouts muffled by the tall grass. Ty shoved the rake handle between the man's arms and back, so he couldn't roll over, and then found the man's holster and pulled out the gun.

He'd just jumped to his feet when a resounding thud and scream shattered the air. He ran around the building, heart thumping, and fueled with raw, burning fear. The other corner of the shed was bathed in the headlights of the car, and Ty raced forward to where Norma Rose stood over a prone body.

"I hope I didn't kill him," she said. "I didn't mean to hit him that hard."

Ty took the shovel from her hand and pulled her into his arms. "Don't ever do that again," he growled.

"Did you expect me to hide in the bushes?" Without waiting for his answer, she kissed his cheek.

"Please check to make sure I didn't kill him. You got the other one, didn't you?"

"Yes," Ty answered, unsure what else to say. There wasn't much. He kneeled down to check the other man and found a pulse. "You knocked him out cold."

"Good." She let out a loud sigh. "Now what?"

"Now we hope there's no one else in that car."

She spun toward the headlights. "I never thought of that."

"Obviously," he answered, tying this man's hands with her other stocking. If anyone was in the car, they'd have surely shown themselves before now, which did offer a pittance of relief.

"They would have already climbed out, wouldn't they?"

"Let's hope so." Ty stood. "This one will be fine for a minute. I have to get the other one."

Norma Rose started to tremble, but she held herself upright until Ty walked away, then she slumped against the wall and pressed a hand to her chest, where her heart was attempting to beat its way out. Too much had happened too quickly—being taken by Ted and Janet, Ty coming to her rescue, Ty taking her to bed, the thugs—she couldn't think this fast, let alone live it.

But she had lived it and survived. Thrived, during Ty's lovemaking. She pushed off the wall and glanced around the corner, toward the car. Ty was ushering a man around the long vehicle, and she watched as he unhitched the trunk and forced the man inside.

"The trunk?" she asked, when he started walked toward her.

"Yes, I don't know how long your stockings will hold up."

"My stockings?"

"That's what I tied their hands with." He then hoisted the man she'd hit with the shovel off the ground by the shoulders and started dragging him toward the car. "I'll need you to open the trunk this time."

"What are we going to do with them?" she asked.

"Take them to the resort," he answered. "You'll have to drive Bronco's car. I have it hidden in the woods."

Chapter Eighteen

Norma Rose was at the window in her office, watching the front lot. The same place she'd stood five long days ago when Ty had driven away. Her love for him had grown desperate. She knew where he'd gone this time—after Bodine—and rather than wallow in self-pity, she was praying to the heavens for his safe return. He was still an agent, she a bootlegger's daughter, and she had no idea where that might lead them, but she would never give up on him. On them.

None of the cars rolling into the parking lot were the Duesenberg Ty had driven away in that night, with the two thugs who'd been responsible for Janet Smith's death in the trunk. The sleek automobiles parking out front were early arrivals for Palooka George's party coming up in two days' time. Norma Rose wasn't worried about the party or the guests' accommodations. Her sisters had everything under control. Thank goodness, because to her, the party seemed frivolous.

In this very room, she'd discovered Ralph Brandon was Ray Bodine's alias. He hadn't arrived at the resort to claim the reservation he'd made for the farmhouse. She hadn't expected him to, not after what Ty and her father had said, but she was concerned. If Bodine recognized Ty, he'd be killed for sure. Mobsters, especially the cutthroat ones like Bodine, had communication lines that burned hotter and faster than phone lines, and Ty would be the subject, put on a list far and wide.

She'd told her father it was imperative no one learn Ty's real identity, but he still hadn't sent anyone after Ty, insisting that would implicate him and the resort. Fury had never lived so strongly in her, or remained there so long.

Her door opened and she turned from the window, pinching her lips as her father walked in. "Have you seen this?" he asked sternly.

Silently, for she'd barely said two words to him in days, she took the envelope and opened the flap to reveal a stack of bills. She handed it back and shook her head.

"It's from Brock," her father barked.

She had no emotion to waste on this. "He paid off his family's debt. You should be glad."

"He should have been taking care of Ginger rather than making money," her father bellowed.

"Ginger's fine. Palooka George told you that when he arrived." Gesturing at the envelope, she added, "Looks to me like Brock's done both." An inkling of jealousy stirred inside her, at what Ginger had managed to find. Norma Rose paused, realizing she, too, had found it. "I'm happy for them. Very happy, and you should be, too. You should be proud your daughter knew a good man when she saw one." Moving toward the door, she said, "Excuse me, I have work to do."

"If I'd sent anyone after Ty, it may have gotten him killed."

Her fingers, curled around the doorknob, squeezed harder and she swallowed. "Or saved his life."

"He'll survive, Rosie. He's the best there is."

"I know that, and I hope you're right," she said, opening the door. "Because I won't survive if he doesn't."

"Rosie—"

She left the building.

Taking the trail, she walked to the Northlander, the cabin she'd refused to rent even when her sisters claimed several guests wanted cabins rather than rooms upstairs. People could sleep on the floor for all she cared.

In the cabin, she sat down at the table. There was nothing here of Ty's, no mementoes or signs that he'd ever been here, but she pretended. So far as to believe she could smell his aftershave. Dropping her head on the table, she closed her eyes. There were no tears left inside her, just emptiness. She tried to fill the gap with fantasies of how things might have been, but that was no longer working. Not after five days.

Emptying her lungs, she lifted her head and her line of vision caught something in the window. A reflection of herself, ghostly and thin, like she was there but wasn't.

Frowning, she looked harder at the faint image. After all she'd been through, this was how she ended up? A weak and fading image of who she'd been. Her frown increased. When had that happened? Why? A flutter happened deep inside her, as if an almost forgotten part of her wanted to return.

Ty hadn't let her down, yet; in a sense, she was letting him down. Believing the worst, when in fact, he was the best there was. She could love him with all her heart, but that didn't mean she had to lose herself. Who she was.

Norma Rose pushed away from the table. He'd promised he'd be back, and she'd promised to be here. Her. Norma Rose Nightingale. And the Norma Rose Nightingale Ty knew would never have sat around moping until his return.

Her resolve stuck. She rose, marched to the door and pulled it open.

Ty had imagined this sight ever since driving away from the resort with those two thugs in the trunk. Dressed in black, as usual, with her hair slicked in waves and gloves on her hands, she was the vision of every waking moment and dream for the past five days. There was surprise in those magnificent blue eyes, but also determination, just as he'd expected. Norma Rose would never have sat around, sulking over his absence. Just one more thing he loved about her.

She lifted her chin a bit higher, even as her hands curled at her sides. The desire to kiss her was greater than ever, but he liked when she made the first move. Whether she admitted it or not, she liked to be in control as much as he did.

"I was just seeing to the cabin," she said. "Making sure it was presentable for the next guests."

"And is it?" he asked.

"I expect so." She turned then and her shoulders indicated the deep breath she took. "Have you ever heard of a phone?"

"A phone?"

"Yes, it's a little black device that can let people know you're okay. So they don't have to worry."

Smiling, he stepped into the cabin and closed the door. "I do believe I have, but I couldn't call you."

"Why not?"

There had been a dozen reasons, including how he'd refused to waste the time calling her when it could be spent driving back. None of that mattered any longer. "One of us had to make a choice, Norma Rose," he said, "and I didn't want that to be you."

She turned around. "A choice?"

He nodded.

Her understanding came swiftly and she lifted a perfectly shaped brow.

"I'd already made a choice, Ty."

Neither of them moved, as they stood there, facing each other like some kind of Old West gun-fight. His heart beat the seconds away as he forced his feet and mouth to remain still. Until a smile lifted the corners of her mouth.

She took a step forward and pressed her hands to his chest. "I chose you, Ty. Even before I was kidnapped. I'll leave the resort, become a federal agent's doxy and never look back. Never regret my decision."

He grasped her face and kissed her, long and hard, before he whispered, "I'm no longer a federal agent."

She hissed in a breath. "No. Did they see you, discover your identity?"

"No, no one knows I was behind it, but Bodine was arrested," Ty said, rubbing the softness of her cheeks. "The one you knocked out with the shovel was his son. He'd only been a kid, fifteen or so when Bodine faked his death, and over the years became his father's new righthand man. Yet, when push came to shove, he saved his own hide and gave away his father's hideout in Wisconsin."

"If they don't know who you are, why—"

"Because you told me Prohibition won't last much longer. I agree with you. Which means I'll soon be out of a job. I might as well switch professions now." He grinned. "How would you feel about being married to a lawyer?"

"A lawyer?"

He nodded. "I just have to take my bar exam. Or I could become a police chief now that Williams is in jail." Bumping his nose against hers, he added, "Or we could just live off my bank account for a few years. I've collected a lot of bounty money over the years."

She grinned, but shook her head. "I never said I'd marry you."

Ty took her hands to roll her gloves over her wrists and off her fingers. "Only because I haven't asked."

As she started unbuttoning his shirt, she stepped out of her shoes. "Are you going to?"

Walking backward, toward the bedroom, and pulling her forward by her waist, he asked, "Do you want me to?"

She parted his shirt and ran her hands over his chest. "I'll tell you in an hour or so."

He swept her into his arms and spun around, carrying her into the bedroom. "I thought you might say that." After a long, solid, and overly hot kiss, he lowered her onto the bed and kissed her once more before stepping back. "I'll be back in an hour."

* * *

Norma Rose laughed. As much as she loved him, she also loved the fact she'd met her match. She held one leg up in the air and unhooked her stocking from the garter on her thigh. "Don't make me find a shovel, Ty."

He let out an exaggerated groan. "You're never going to let me forget that, are you?"

"Probably not." Tossing the stocking at him, she lifted her other leg. "I, too, like to be in control once in a while"

He laughed. "You don't say?"

She unhooked that stocking from its garter and started to roll it down. "Surely you can find another way to convince me to say yes."

Stepping forward, he snagged the toe of her stocking, pulled it off and tossed it on the floor with the other. "Do you need convincing?"

She hooked him by the waistband of his pants, pulling him closer. "You tell me."

He told her all right, and convinced her, several times.

* * * * *